Zach Piper has escaped his father's cult only to find himself in a world he doesn't understand. Abused and neglected, he's grown up an outcast among outcasts. He has no business trusting anybody after what he's been through, but when Cameron Cronin takes him in and shows him a world he never knew, he willingly hands over his trust. In Cameron he finds honor and decency—someone who cares.

Cameron lives without love and he prefers it that way. He never wants to fall in love again. The last man he loved shattered Cameron's heart as surely as his trust. When he takes in much-younger Zach, who recently emerged from his own hell, he hears the familiar whisper of long-dead feelings. But he doesn't want to love. He cannot trust he won't be broken again if he does.

As time passes and the two men get to know each other, Cameron's feelings for Zach deepen whether he wants it or not. But just when Cameron decides to trust in Zach, and act on the love he knows is there, both of their pasts come storming back to threaten everything they've built. When their lives hang in the balance they must trust each other enough to get out alive.

TRUSTED

Until You, Book Three

Karrie Roman

A NineStar Press Publication

Published by NineStar Press
P.O. Box 91792,
Albuquerque, New Mexico, 87199 USA.
www.ninestarpress.com

Trusted

Printed in the USA
First Edition
October, 2018

Print ISBN: 978-1-949909-16-6

Also available in eBook, ISBN: 978-1-949909-08-1

Warning: This book contains sexually explicit content, which may only be suitable for mature readers, scenes of graphic violence, memories of past abuse, and rape.

For Angela, who understands…

Prologue

"ZACH, STAY THERE, honey."

"But, Momma—"

"It's okay. Momma's, okay."

Momma said she was okay and Momma didn't lie to him, but there was so much yelling and he was scared. How could she be okay with all that yelling? He wanted to scream, but Momma told him to stay real quiet. He wanted to go see what was happening, but Momma told him to stay in the stream and finish washing. It sounded like Momma needed help. But he was just a little boy and Father always told him he was no good at anything, so what could he do to help anyway?

But she was his momma and she was the only one who loved him.

That shouting was getting louder, but he couldn't hear Momma yelling back now; she was crying and making a funny noise. He was going to go help; he didn't care if Father said he was a useless little shit. She was his momma. He looked down so he'd put his hand on the right rock to hoist himself out of the water, but something was wrong. The clear water of the stream was all red—the brightest red he'd ever seen.

Zach screamed.

Zach wasn't sure if the scream in his nightmare carried over into the real world—he hoped not. He sat quietly for a moment, listening. He couldn't hear anyone coming toward his room. Sweat danced trails down his back and plastered his hair to his head. His body was working through the last of the tremors as his breathing slowly calmed back to normal.

This wasn't the first time he'd had this nightmare, and it wouldn't be the last. But it seemed worse this time, and Zach couldn't quite work out why. Perhaps it was the turmoil of the last few days.

Three days ago, Zach had fled his father's religious cult with two young girls, one a maybe fourteen-year-old who'd been about to be forced into marriage with his father. The three of them had almost literally crashed into two men, Ben and Ethan, who had been searching for Ethan's infant nieces. The little girls had been kidnapped by their father and taken to the cult. It had all been such a mess, made even worse by his father's plans for the mass suicide of the cult members.

But he was safe; the girls were safe; everyone was safe. Ben and Ethan and the FBI—they'd saved everybody.

Right now he was sleeping in the house of Ben's brother, Cameron. Cameron had also helped in their eventual rescue. Just thinking about Cameron woke up the butterflies in his belly, causing them to flutter around like crazy.

When he'd first encountered Ben out there in the wild, he'd thought him beautiful—and then he'd seen him kissing Ethan. Raised as he had been, secluded from the world in his father's cult, Zach had no idea men could be together in the same way the men had been with the women of the cult. He hadn't known such a thing was possible. Suddenly, the way Zach had always watched the men of the cult with such fascination and yearning had made sense. *He* finally made sense.

But all of that was nothing compared to how his body had reacted when he had seen Cameron for the first time. Beautiful hadn't seemed a good enough word to describe Cameron. Zach didn't even know of a word that could define the perfection he saw in Cameron Cronin. All he could think was how he wanted to press his lips to Cameron's just like he'd seen Ben do to Ethan.

For now, the remnants of the nightmare clung to him, refusing to leave him in peace, so he knew he'd never get back to sleep. In the past, there'd never been anyone to comfort him, no one for him to go to for a few whispered words or a gentle touch to ease him through the lingering terror, but tonight Cameron's face flashed in his mind, so he pushed the covers back to go in search of him. Everyone had been kind to him since his escape, but there was something about Cameron, something he didn't understand but knew it made him feel good—safe—anyway.

As soon as he left his room, he noticed lights toward the end of the long hallway and heard soft voices coming from the same direction. Zach walked quietly, unsure of his welcome.

Four men sat in the room at the end of the hall: Cameron, Ben, Ethan and the FBI agent who'd been in charge of the raid on his father's cult, Alec Banner. They were talking, and none of them seemed to notice his arrival.

"Cameron," he called softly. His voice was so quiet he wasn't even sure if Cameron would hear him from across the room, but he must have because he jumped up from his seat, immediately striding forward.

Zach's tummy churned in that good way as Cameron came toward him. Everything about him was so perfect. He was tall and broad, thick muscles cording his arms and legs. He was so handsome. His face looked hard, as if it had been chiseled from stone, all angles, but it was stunning to look at. He had a bit of stubble covering his jaw, and Zach yearned to scrub his fingers over it just to see if it scratched his skin like he thought it would. Cameron's pale-blue eyes never wavered as he watched Zach with concern.

"You okay, Zach?"

"Only a nightmare," he replied, nodding his head.

"Do you want to sit with us for a while?" Cameron asked and Zach looked over his shoulder at the other men, shifting his gaze to each of them.

"No, that's okay. I just...needed to know you were here." His words sounded pathetic to his own ear, but he saw only concern in Cameron's gaze.

Cameron reached out an arm as though he was going to touch him and then just as quickly pulled it back. "I'm right here, Zach. I'm not going anywhere...you're not alone anymore."

Zach nodded, suddenly embarrassed a dream had chased him out here to these men like a frightened child. He nodded and turned to walk back to his room.

When he got there, he pulled his blankets onto the floor, hoping the familiar hardness of the ground would help him sleep. Comfort wasn't something he was used to.

Cameron had told him he wasn't going anywhere. He'd also offered for Zach to stay here with him until he got himself sorted out. The rest of the cult members were staying together. They'd set up a campsite just outside of town until the FBI had interviewed them all, but Zach didn't want to go with them. He'd always been invisible to most members of the cult—an outcast even among outcasts.

Zach had accepted Cameron's offer because he'd need help learning how to live in this strange new world he'd been dumped in. He'd lived on the periphery growing up, knowing there was another world there but not really understanding it. Hushed and whispered conversations of the decadence and sinfulness of the world had often reached his ears. Awed stories about televisions and phones and other such evil inventions of mankind had often enthralled him. Regardless of the threads of knowledge he had, though, he really knew so little of this world he'd suddenly been thrust into since his escape. And with his father arrested and the cult disbanded, there was no going back behind the closed walls of their commune. He'd have to find his way in this world, and he'd have to find it alone—or perhaps not as alone as he'd thought, if Cameron was truthful with him.

Chapter One

CAMERON

"Come on in, Zach. Cameron, you can wait out here if you like." Alec Banner spoke with the kind of calm authority you'd expect from the FBI.

"Zach?" he asked because as far as he was concerned Zach was running this show and Cameron would follow his lead.

Zach looked at him, his eyes wide with nerves. "I'd rather you come in with me if you can."

It was settled. Cameron would be going in whether Banner liked it or not if that's what Zach wanted.

It had only been a week since the raid on Arnold Piper's cult, and the FBI was finally getting around to interviewing Piper's son, Zach. Cameron glanced at Alec, who gave a stiff nod and led them into the stark interview room. From the looks of the room, if Cameron didn't know better, he'd think Zach was the criminal here. The space was cold and imposing, designed to unnerve those who entered.

"Take a seat. We'll be taping the interview. Okay, Zach?"

Zach nodded and Alec got right to business, officially beginning the recording and asking his first of probably many questions.

"Zach, what is your relationship to Arnold Piper?"

"He's my father."

"And you're the eldest child?"

"I think so, yes."

"Think so?"

"I'm not positive my father has any children older than me because he kept me out of his life, but I do have younger brothers and sisters." Zach glanced at him nervously. Cameron knew Zach wasn't shy, but he also didn't enjoy talking about his father. Zach wore his shame, because of who his father was, like a badge of disgrace.

"And what is your understanding of your father's position in the Star of Life Commune?"

"Um...he's in charge. The leader. My father believes he is god's representative on earth."

"I see." Alec looked at his notes and tapped the page with his pen. "Could you briefly tell me about the day-to-day life of the cult? Who did what, etcetera?"

Zach flicked another glance toward him, and Cameron could tell he was a little lost by the broad question. Where *did* you begin with something like that? Alec was astute enough to pick up on Zach's confusion and rephrased his question.

"Start by telling me what your father's job was. What did he do each day?"

"Father preached a lot. He'd get everyone together and talk about god every day for hours. He'd tell us what god expected from us, what we needed to do to please him. He'd talk about the world outside our camp. Father would tell us the worst parts of it; twist it so we were afraid to leave his camp. He'd talk for hours on the evils of the cinema and technology and such. I don't even know if half the stuff he said was true. When he finished, we all had chores to do, but Father never worked. After he preached, he either went to meet with Mr. Watson and Mr. Lloyd and some of the other older men or he'd go off with one or more of his wives."

"How many wives did your father have?"

"Seven."

"Was that common for the men to have more than one wife?"

"Yes. But no man was allowed more than Father. The number of wives showed his importance. And for the women, it was supposed to be a great honor to marry Father or one of the other higher-up men."

Cameron shook his head at the arrogance of men like Arnold Piper. If he lived to be a thousand, he didn't think he'd ever understand the desire some people had to hold such power over others.

"And can you tell me the ages of your father's wives?"

"Not for sure. We don't know our ages, don't celebrate birthdays, but I'm sure his last wife couldn't have been more than fifteen when he married her two years ago because I remember her as a baby."

"What did the cult members call your father?"

"We all call him Father. Even his wives call him that."

Cameron watched as Alec shifted uncomfortably on his seat, his gaze quickly ghosting over the deformed fingers of Zach's left hand. Cameron suspected he wasn't going to like the question that came next.

"What about you, Zach? As the eldest son of 'Father,' how many wives did you have?"

"None." Zach's response was fast and sharp like a whip crack.

"None? We know younger men than you from the camp already had at least one wife, so I find it hard to believe your father didn't have you married off. As his eldest son, there must have been some prestige, some importance attached to it. Weren't you being groomed to take over one day? Perhaps you married little girls as well and simply don't want to confess. Don't want to get in trouble for it."

"Alec!" Cameron jumped to his feet as the name flew indignantly from between his lips. What the hell was this?

"Sit down, Cameron, or I'll have you escorted out."

"He's not the one in trouble here," Cameron retorted, leaning over Alec who remained seated, completely unimpressed with Cameron's attempt at intimidation.

"And I have to ask these questions to make sure. So, please. Sit down." Alec gestured to Cameron's seat with his eyes, but Cameron remained standing and continued glaring at the FBI agent.

"Does he need a lawyer?" Cameron asked through gritted teeth.

"It's his right." Came Alec's indifferent answer.

"It's okay, Cameron," Zach said as he pulled on Cameron's fingers. It was his gentle tug that finally had Cameron's ass back in his chair, though his anger remained potent; he wasn't fond of Banner's insinuations, and he sure as hell didn't like the hurt in Zach's eyes because of them.

"I had no wives because Father never believed I was good enough. I was a disgrace. He either pretended I didn't exist or took out his anger on me, but I wasn't important, and he'd never have let me have a bride." Zach kept his head down as he spoke, waves of shame seemed to roll from him.

Cameron glanced at Alec as he took in Zach's words, evaluating them for truth. He'd heard the vulnerability in Zach's voice, the pain, and had known instantly he was being honest, and his anger at Arnold Piper for what he'd done grew like a living thing.

"All right, let's move on," Alec conceded. "How did the Star of Life Commune come to be living in tents in the Shoshone National Forest?"

"Until just a while ago, we were living on farmlands. I'm not sure where. Father never shared those details with me.

There was a big farmhouse where Father and his wives and youngest children lived. Everyone else lived in cabins, and we had cows, chickens, horses and such. We grew our own food, did our chores, and went to Father's sermons. We weren't allowed television or anything too modern. We lived simply. I don't know what happened, but one day Father told us we needed to leave, so we packed up what we could into the buses and just left. Father said we'd camp until god provided us with a new home. It's happened a couple of other times I can remember."

"So this wasn't the first campsite since you left the farm?"

"No. We'd moved around a few times. Father said god was guiding him to our new home."

"And no one argued with your father about leaving the farm or moving campsites?"

Cameron kept his gaze on Zach as he took his time, considering his answer. The emotions playing across his face were a mixture of disgust, amusement, and anger.

"Nobody argued with Father over anything. Father told you who to marry and when. He told you who and what was good and who and what was bad. Arguing with Father was the same as arguing with god." Zach took a steadying breath and continued, "I remember this one man stood up to him once. Told Father he wasn't gonna let him marry his sister because she was too young. My father beat that man bloody for going against god. Kicked him out of the commune. Nobody ever saw him again, and Father married his sister the next day."

"What was her name?" Alec asked.

"Cathleen," Zach replied. "She's still married to Father, but she won't help you. She said it was the greatest honor of her life marrying Father—even after she'd watched him beat her brother."

Cameron's fists clenched, his nails digging into his palms. Zach's handsome face looked haunted, as though he'd never get over the fact that his father had been such a monster. Cameron itched to reach out and touch him, hold him, offer him some sort of support, tell him none of it was his fault—his shame. He dug his nails in farther.

It was dangerous for him to feel too much for anyone, let alone a man he was so drawn to. And he was drawn to Zach, not just physically—even though he was gorgeous—but something about Zach spoke to Cameron. His naiveté, his sweetness, or the way he looked at the world through almost childlike eyes? Or maybe it was his strength of character. Cameron couldn't pin down what called to him, but something did.

"Ben Cronin and Ethan Stone have made a statement that a week ago they came across you, Sophia Jacob, and Mary Jacob in the bush, approximately ten miles from Hawk's Rest. Can you explain why you were there?" Alec continued.

"Phia—Sophia—came to me because my father was going to marry her sister, Mary. She's only around fourteen or fifteen, we think, and she was scared. I offered to help them get away." Cameron noticed Zach shaking as he spoke, so he leaned over and gently squeezed his shoulder to remind him he was there, and he wasn't alone.

"Was that the only reason you fled?" Alec asked.

Zach looked at him and gave a tiny smile. "No. Father had always let it be known he had what he called the Jonestown Protocol. It meant that on the say-so from god—so really on Father's say-so—we were all to go to god." Zach finished abruptly.

"What exactly does that mean—go to god?"

"The parents were to give the children a 'special drink' that would put them to sleep and send them to the lord, and Father had pills for the adults. Anyone who didn't go through with it—well, Father had his soldiers who would take care of them with their guns."

"I see." Alec cleared his throat. "Go on."

"I'd overheard Father telling Mr. Watson, on the same day Phia came to me, it was time for Jonestown on the Friday. I'd planned to get out, anyway, to try to bring back some help."

Cameron didn't hear too much more after that. His mind was stuck looping around in the terror Zach must have endured knowing his own father was going to order the deaths of every person Zach had ever known—including his own sons.

What felt like hours later, Alec finally asked his last question—at least for now. Zach would be answering questions about his father for the rest of his life.

"Interview concluded at three twenty-nine p.m." Alec clicked off the recorder. "Thanks, Zach. You did well. I'm sorry if it got a little rough, but we have to make sure we get this guy."

When the three men stood, Cameron offered Alec his hand. "Thanks, Alec. Sorry about before."

"I understand, and believe me, I hate having to ask those things."

"Can he expect another interview soon?"

"With Maggie's testimony, and others from the cult, we've probably got enough for the indictment hearing, but once we get the indictment, the prosecutor will go through things far more thoroughly. We know where he's staying if we need him, anyway." Alec said.

"Good. Okay, we'll see you later then." Cameron wanted to get Zach out of there.

"Take care, Zach. See you, Cameron."

Cameron put his hand on the small of Zach's back and guided him out the door and down the hall. They reached the large room they'd been waiting in earlier, and Cameron recognized two young girls waiting in there. Phia and Mary were sitting with an older lady whose resemblance to them told Cameron she was probably their mother.

Zach moved quickly toward them and all three stood. Only Mary wore a smile. As Zach reached them, the older lady stepped forward and raised her arm, bringing her hand down, with a sharp crack, on Zach's cheek. Cameron lurched forward and grabbed Zach's shoulders as he flinched back.

"Don't you speak to us, Zachary Piper. You are a disgrace to our lord and your father." The woman spat.

"Mother—"

"No, Mary. Our Father Piper has been shot and may be going to prison because of this—" she gesticulated with her hand toward Zach as though she couldn't come up with a word bad enough to call him. "Many of our men are in jail because of him. You ruined everything, Zachary. Father should have gotten rid of you, too, when he—don't come near us again. You are unwanted by any of us, Zachary." The woman grabbed the girl's hands and yanked them back down on their seats and deliberately turned her head away. The older one, Phia, looked at her feet, but Mary looked at Zach, her expression grim.

Cameron had heard more than enough. He understood being blinded to somebody's faults, but the first steps to freedom involved facing the truth, and this woman needed to hear it.

"He saved your life, lady, these girls' lives—all of your lives. He stopped a pedophile from getting his hands on your fourteen-year-old daughter. You should be on your damn knees thanking him," Cameron hissed through gritted teeth. He didn't think he'd ever wanted to throttle someone before, and he couldn't say it was a pleasant feeling.

"It's okay, Cameron. Let's just go." Zach's voice was so soft as to be barely heard. Cameron followed him as he headed for the door, the hunch in his shoulders easily discernable and making it even harder for him to walk away from that woman without giving her more of his mind.

They reached his car without a word passing between them. Zach silently climbed in, his face turned toward the window.

"Zach, I'm so sorry. You didn't deserve what she said."

"I ruined their lives."

"You saved their lives, and one day they'll damn well understand that." Cameron was so angry he thought he may actually snap the steering wheel, which he currently held in an iron grip.

"Thanks for being there for me."

"I'm not going anywhere, Zach. I told you I'll be here whenever you need me."

Zach turned to him then and their gazes held. "I might need you a lot."

"It won't be a problem. I promise." He winked.

Zach scrutinized him for a while before finally smiling, the tension in his shoulders easing. "Still gonna teach me how to drive this thing?"

"Soon as you get your permit," he answered and revved the engine.

Chapter Two

ZACH

"So it'll be like what we watched on your TV but really big?" Zach asked, completely unable to contain his enthusiasm. Cameron was taking him to the movies. His first visit ever and he was wide-eyed with excitement.

"Yeah, and louder. Sometimes the seats actually vibrate with the sound." Cameron kept his eyes on the road as he drove. He hadn't said as much, but Zach knew Cameron was taking him today because his father's court hearing was only a few days away and because he was still reeling from the run-in with Mary and Phia's mother a few weeks ago.

What she'd said about him ruining everything and being a disgrace had hurt. All he'd wanted to do was keep them alive. He'd never stopped for a second to think maybe they had wanted to go to god. Even if he had, he'd have done the same thing because of the children. They at least deserved to have more of a life, a longer one.

"So we'll be seeing another Thor movie? The third one?"

"Yep. You've watched the first two at home so I thought it might be good to see the next one on the big screen. I hear it's the best—and the Hulk's in it."

"From *the Avengers*." Zach enjoyed television—well, movies anyway. He wasn't as sure about reality TV, as Cameron had called it. He didn't really get the purpose of it and couldn't for the life of him see anything real—or entertaining—about it.

"We'll get popcorn... Have you tried it before?" Cameron asked.

"No. I've had corn, though." Zach flushed. Sometimes he didn't know whether or not to be embarrassed about how little he knew or how few things he'd tried, but Cameron always told him it was what it was and not to worry. There was plenty of time for him to try stuff.

"Really not the same thing, but I'm sure you'll love it."

They pulled into the parking lot and Zach slid out of Cameron's truck. It was bigger than a lot of the cars he'd seen on the road, but its size suited Cameron.

Together they walked the short distance to Big Horn Cinema and Zach stood back while Cameron bought tickets for them. He'd had no idea how money worked until he got away from the cult, and he really needed to ask Cameron how he should go about getting some. Seemed you needed it for everything.

"Okay, let's get some snacks."

Zach followed Cameron over to an area of the lobby that smelled amazing. He could see some of the chocolate candy Cameron had given him that first day at his place, and his mouth watered. He loved the taste but tried not to be too greedy. He didn't have money to buy more.

"All right, so shall we get a jumbo popcorn to share and a couple of sodas?" Cameron asked.

Zach looked at the popcorn behind him. It was where the wonderful smell was coming from so Zach couldn't wait to try it. He nodded enthusiastically. "Yes, please. It smells really good. And could we... Could we share a candy bar?"

"I think we can manage one each." Cameron smiled.

Cameron handed over more money and then gathered their items before leading him into a large room filled with seats all facing toward a huge screen.

"Oh wow. It's enormous," Zach gasped. How did they make the picture fit on the screen? He remembered his father's rantings on the evil of cinemas. His father was so wrong about everything. Zach was betting he'd be wrong about this too. There was nothing evil here.

"Come on," Cameron called, and Zach followed him toward the rear. There were a handful of other people spread throughout the room, but Cameron led them to the middle of the empty back row.

As they took their seats, Cameron showed him the drink holder. They set the popcorn between them, and Zach popped a handful into his mouth. It was salty and soft but kind of chewy. He hadn't had anything like it before, but it was amazing.

"Good?" Cameron asked.

"Mm-hmm," Zach grunted around his mouthful. "Delicious," he said when he'd finally swallowed what was in his mouth.

He watched as Cameron took a handful and popped a few bits in his mouth. His jaw worked as he chewed, and Zach stared, fascinated, as his Adam's apple bobbed as he swallowed. It was really quite difficult to look away from Cameron sometimes.

"Explain to me about Father's court hearing again? What will happen?" Zach asked. He shouldn't have because he didn't want to ruin the mood by bringing the topic up, but he didn't understand what was going on. Sure Agent Banner had tried to explain, but it was all big words and meanings he didn't know. Cameron would explain in a way he understood.

"Well, I'm not big on the law, but my understanding is the prosecutor—that's the man who is going to fight to put your father in jail—has called a grand jury to get an indictment." Cameron kind of rolled his head and shrugged his shoulders. "It means a group of people will listen to evidence—including what you've told Alec regarding your father—and decide if he should be charged. That'll be happening in the next few days."

"And if he is charged?"

"Then he will go to trial where somebody will decide if he's guilty or not."

"But he is guilty." He'd told them all what happened. Cameron had explained marrying young girls was illegal, so his father was guilty. Why didn't he just go to jail?

"The legal process can be very long, Zach. Everybody is entitled to a fair trial. Your father will get a chance to defend himself."

How could he possibly defend what he'd done? How could it be excused? In the commune, Father decided if somebody had done something wrong, and you certainly weren't allowed to defend yourself. Knowing how bad the commune was, though, maybe the way things were done out here was better.

The lights were dimming, and Zach wasn't going to let thoughts of his father ruin his first theater experience, so he put Father and crimes and juries to the back of his mind and turned to the screen.

The giant screen lit up, revealing an advertisement Zach recognized from the TV. A few more played, and then the screen got even bigger as music began, and Zach knew from the credits that the movie was starting.

It was so loud and so large that the booms of explosions and the loud music rocked his entire body and sent shivers up his spine. He grabbed Cameron's hand, not because he was scared but because he wanted to share this with him in a physical touch. He didn't let him go for the entire movie.

And Cameron didn't seem to mind at all, only turning to him several times and smiling when Zach jumped or gripped tighter as he was carried away by the action on screen. Touch had never been a big part of his life—especially not gentle touch—but holding Cameron's hand was far better than he ever would have thought.

"ALL RISE," THE stern-faced bailiff called out into the quiet of the courtroom.

Everyone quickly ambled to their feet, apart from Zach's father. Arnold Piper had earlier declared the law of man did not apply to him. Therefore, these proceedings did not concern him. Only the law of god meant anything to him—though Zach noticed it was his father's own twisted interpretation of god's law he seemed to follow.

Even as the elderly judge entered the room and turned a baleful glare upon his father, Zach could see he remained seated. His father was completely unwilling to give any legitimacy or respect to this court.

"Mr. Piper, I see you remain unwilling to stand. That's okay, sir. We can just tack on another contempt of court charge for you," Judge Harrow boomed as he took his seat. The judge was a loud man, and even when he was speaking calmly, his voice thundered through the courtroom. Zach would hate to be around if the man chose to really let loose and shout at someone.

Once the judge was seated, the others in the courtroom took theirs. It was a large room, made to look small simply because of the number of people who had squashed themselves inside. Even more were waiting in the halls, trickling through the building and out the front doors. There was a sea of people; many of whom had come to gawk at the crazy cult members. Even more were here to see the Hollywood stars who had somehow become embroiled in this horrible scandal. They were all here to see if his father was going to be indicted for his crimes.

The stars, Ryan and Lucas, sat behind him alongside Ben and Ethan. Cameron was at his side, just as he had been for the last several weeks through this nightmare of his existence. Zach hadn't known what a Hollywood star was when he'd first met Ryan and Lucas. He hadn't even seen a television. Whispered stories from people who had come to join his father's cult and his father's fire and brimstone ranting had brought the outside world into the sanctuary of the commune but seeing things—experiencing them—had been unlike anything he could have imagined.

Zach often watched repeats of *the Witches' Hammer* over and over again, pausing on the faces of the men he actually knew in the flesh and desperately trying to make sense of how it was possible. For a while, he *had* thought of technology as some kind of magic, but he loved it all— especially the movies.

In any event, they were all here today—these men who surrounded him. The famous stars, Cameron, who hadn't abandoned him since he'd been practically dumped on his doorstep, and the two men who'd rescued him and the rest of the cult.

Ethan looked awful. Zach knew his sister, Maggie, was gravely ill. Ethan and Ben were guardians to her twin daughters during her illness, and it was obviously taking its toll—the man's pain was carved into his face. Zach was touched Ethan had taken time away from his sister to be here for him today. He'd never been cared for in his father's cult, but he had people who cared now.

"I'll make this quick so the media can get their headlines out on time. Mr. Piper, the grand jury has returned a true bill finding sufficient evidence to send you to trial for charges of rape of a minor, deprivation of liberty, and conspiracy to commit murder. Mr. Saunders, you've already put forward another bail request for your client and I am again denying it immediately."

"But your honor, my client has no previous convictions—"

"Let me save us all the time, Mr. Saunders. Your client has made it abundantly clear he has no regard for the law of this court. Given he is also used to a transient life, I find there is nothing to compel him to remain for trial if he were to be released on bail. Therefore, he will be remanded in custody until the trial date. That is all."

The gavel thudded on the bench, making Zach flinch at the harsh sound. Before he'd even comprehended what had just happened, Zach was following everyone else to their feet again as the judge left the room with the same fanfare and swiftness as he'd arrived.

"Are you okay?" Cameron quietly asked.

"I'm not sure what just happened," Zach admitted, turning to look at the man beside him. Cameron was watching him with the same compelling intensity that he often did. It did funny things to his insides when he caught Cameron looking at him like this.

Cameron was perhaps an inch or two taller than Zach, but despite having put on weight since escaping his father's cult, Zach still could have used a few pounds. Cameron was much broader and heavier.

"Your father is remanded to trial, so he'll be going back to jail now and will stay there until his trial, which will probably be a few months down the track."

"So he won't be getting out today? He can't get me?" He hated the vulnerability in his voice, but where his father was concerned his weakness was ingrained.

Cameron's warm fingers quickly touched his cheek before he pulled his hand back, as he always did, and then rested it on his shoulder. "No, Zach, he can't get you. I'd never let him hurt you, anyway, even if he did get out."

The funny little feeling fluttered in his insides again. He wanted to say something to Cameron. Something to assure him he was grateful for everything Cameron had done for him.

"Great news, Zach," Ben said as he approached from behind.

Zach turned to face him. Despite being Cameron's twin, they didn't look much alike at all. Ben was much shorter, but Zach knew he wasn't a man to be messed with. Behind the almost perpetual smile he wore, there was danger lurking in Ben. His partner, Ethan, only ever looked happy when he was looking at Ben.

"Yeah. At least we're all safe for a while longer."

"He won't be getting out, Zach. Too much evidence against him. Especially with a few of the members willing to testify," Ethan said. He liked Ethan, even with his sometimes terse demeanor. He'd caught him a couple of times this morning goofing around with his toddler nieces, and a man who loved kids and was willing to make a fool of himself to amuse them was okay in Zach's eyes. Especially after the childhood he'd endured with his coldhearted and cruel father.

"Let's go celebrate. My treat," Lucas enthused as they began making their way toward the exit. It had taken them a good twenty minutes to get into the building when they'd arrived earlier because of the media chaos surrounding all of them—Lucas and Ryan in particular. Ryan had had some kind of attack afterward, and he and Lucas had spent a good fifteen minutes in the restroom so he could recover.

From the noise coming through the closed doors, Zach suspected it was going to take just as long to get back out. He wondered if Ryan would have another attack while they were leaving.

"I'm taking Ryan through the underground parking garage. I called Harry earlier to get a car in there. We'll meet at Two Doors Down. I made a reservation earlier—just in case." Lucas said.

"Right. See you there," Cameron replied.

Lucas and Ryan turned right, heading for the stairs to the garage while the rest continued toward the front exit. As they'd done earlier, Ben, Ethan, and Cameron somehow managed to surround him so the press of the crowd was kept mostly away. There wasn't much they could do about the microphones and cameras shoved in his face but putting their bodies between him and the mob helped.

Cameron was at his back, his heat noticeable. Occasionally the scuffle of bodies pressed Cameron up against him, and god, his hard, firm body was so strong and stable along his length. Zach's body responded to the stimulation so he did everything possible to will it back under control. Nothing seemed to be working as whatever he was feeling for Cameron had its way with him.

He'd thought some men from the camp beautiful, and some had stirred feelings in him, but those emotions had been like pale moonlight in comparison to the bright sunshine he felt around Cameron.

It took them a good ten minutes of pushing and shoving their way through the crowd before they reached Cameron's car. Zach was thrust into the back seat and Ben slid in beside him, leaving the two bigger men to take the front seats. No one spoke as Cameron fought the traffic surrounding the courthouse and made his way to where they were meeting Ryan and Lucas.

The Hollywood stars were already there, seated at a table in the very back of the restaurant, by the time they arrived. Cameron ushered him into a seat beside Ryan and then took the one next to him. Ryan looked pale and his eyes were wide, but regardless of his discomfort, he offered Zach a smile.

"You okay, Zach?" he asked softly.

Zach nodded, unsure if he really was, but he was getting there. "Are you?" he asked in reply.

"Don't like crowds—at all. It's getting better but…ugh." Ryan gave a dramatic shudder and smiled at him.

"How're you settling in, Zach?" Lucas asked from the other side of Ryan. "Ben tells us Cameron has been teaching you all about this grand old world of ours."

"I'm getting used to everything. We rarely ever had modern appliances, so lots of things have been a shock. It's been kind of like…I knew things but had just never experienced them. My father and some of the senior men talked about the outside world, so I knew about it, had been in cars, but to see it…experience it. I was overwhelmed at first."

"He's doing great," Cameron offered and gave him a warm smile.

"Are you planning on studying?" Ben asked.

"I'm going to try to get my GED, I hope. Cameron has spoken to me about it, and he's found a lady, an old teacher, to come and help me."

"He's very bright. He'll be able to do anything he wants."

Zach's cheeks warmed at Cameron's words and he knew there'd be a pink stain on them. He wasn't used to praise, but Cameron had told him he just needed to smile or say thank you whenever someone offered it to him. He smiled widely at Cameron now.

Over the past several weeks, the feelings he got around Cameron had only intensified. He hated being apart from him and loved every moment they spent together. Though he knew Cameron thought of him as innocent and naive, he'd never treated him like a fool. He'd opened his home to Zach, but as welcoming as he'd been, he hadn't opened his heart. And Zach had come to realize that's what he wanted from Cameron more than anything else. Now he just needed to find the courage to go after it.

"How's the business going?" Cameron turned and asked Ryan, no doubt perceiving Zach needed the attention off him for a moment. He always seemed to understand what Zach needed.

"We're almost ready to go. The Krispins are helping fund us. Ben is itching to get into it, and he's trying to convince Alec to join us now that he's wrapped up the case with Zach's father and the cult." Ryan's voice was riddled with pride as he spoke about the venture he was going into with Ben, Ethan, and now possibly FBI agent Alec Banner.

The four of them were opening a private investigation agency specializing in missing children. The experience with Ethan's nieces being kidnapped by their own father had prompted it.

"Yay, Agent Banner," Lucas snorted.

"You don't like Alec?" Zach asked, surprised. He'd always found Alec Banner to be a pleasant man.

Lucas smiled fondly at Ryan before answering. "Oh no, I like him just fine. I just don't like the way Ryan looks at him."

"Hey, he's a good-looking guy, and I seem to remember you couldn't take your eyes off your new costar for a while there," Ryan answered.

"You're jealous?" Zach asked Lucas. They weren't allowed to be jealous in the commune. Wanting what someone else had was a sin, except for Father, of course. But then he just took whatever it was he wanted.

"Doesn't hurt to make him a little jealous sometimes." Ryan winked. "Keeps him interested."

"Oh, that's rubbish, Ry. I'm always captivated by you."

"Oh god," Ben groaned and smacked his forehead.

So it was a good thing to make someone jealous? It made them pay attention. That was interesting.

"Got a name for the business yet?" Cameron asked no one in particular.

"We're leaning toward Chasing Hope..." Ethan looked to Cameron as he spoke.

Zach leaned forward a little in his seat as talk turned to the generalities of the new business and the types of cases they might take on—thoughts of jealousy momentarily forgotten.

After hearing Cameron talk about the business over the last few weeks, he longed to, maybe one day, join Chasing Hope in some capacity, though he hadn't found the courage yet to tell anyone of his dream. And he thought now how appropriate the name was. After all, that is what all these men at the table had done for him—helped him chase hope.

Chapter Three

CAMERON

"He seems to be doing well, Cam," Ben said around a mouthful of hot dog. It was perfect weather for a cookout in the backyard and for Cameron to spend some time with his brother and his family. They were also celebrating Zach's father's indictment. Ryan and Lucas had flown home this morning because Lucas was due on set. Cameron didn't know any other "big stars," but he couldn't imagine too many were as low key and unpretentious as those two.

"Yeah, he is." Cameron's gaze was fixed on Zach even as he spoke with Ben. "Everything has been an eye-opener for him, but he's taken it all in stride."

Zach was playing with Ethan's three-year-old nieces. It was some type of tag game Cameron didn't understand. He had zero experience with children—though neither did Ben until several weeks ago. Ben had taken to his father-type role with relish. Of course, Ben was just a big kid at heart anyway.

The little girl's mother was too sick for them to have been left behind with her while Ben and Ethan came out here to support Zach at the indictment verdict. Cameron knew it was killing Ben to see his boyfriend's pain at the imminent loss of his sister. He'd told Cameron it wouldn't be too much longer—Maggie was fading fast now, which was a blessing because she was suffering.

"He's still got heart-eyes for you, big brother. You know that, right?"

"I'm sure it's nothing," Cameron hedged. He was terrified to get into this conversation with Ben because he'd make him face the issue like he always did. Cameron didn't really like reality—it hadn't been too kind to him in the past.

"It could be something, Cam. Why couldn't it be? Because of Jimmy?" Ben spat the name out with pure hatred like he always did. Cameron couldn't even begin to imagine what might happen if Ben and Jimmy ever found themselves face-to-face again.

"I don't want it to be anything," Cameron mumbled because he knew Ben wouldn't like his answer.

"Cam, it's been—"

"It'll never be long enough, Ben. No amount of time could pass to make me want to risk my heart—my life—again."

Cameron's gaze followed Zach as he ran after the twins. Their chubby little legs were pumping hard while Zach was almost running on the spot so he wouldn't actually catch them. It was the chase they all enjoyed.

Zach was the first real test of Cameron's resolve to keep his heart locked away since Jimmy. In fact, he'd kept himself away from most people, the occasional random hookup out of town the only sex he'd had in years. And the only requirement then had been that his partner was willing; he didn't even need to be particularly attracted to them. But, he lusted after Zach—he was honest enough to admit it to himself. Regrettably, though, his fear was greater than his desire.

"Okay," Ben sulked. "I'll leave it alone for now." He shifted uncomfortably. Cameron knew how hard this was for him. He knew Ben wanted to fix it—fix him, but Cameron wanted to stay broken because if he was put back together then...then he might risk love and love could always break him again.

"How's Ethan doing?" Cameron changed tack, knowing Ben could talk about Ethan for hours. Ben idolized Ethan, and that would frighten Cameron if he couldn't see Ethan adored Ben right back.

"Remember Mom? The last few months of her cancer?"

Cameron nodded because he'd never forget the wasted scarecrow who had once been his vibrant, loving mother.

"Well Maggie's there. It's fucking pitiful. Heartbreaking. And I can see every time we visit her another little piece of Ethan's soul shrivels and dies. He won't let the girls see her now—and Maggie agrees. They don't want them to remember her like that." Ben's voice hitched at the end, evidence he wasn't immune from the pain of the situation.

"Jesus. What can I do?"

"None of us can do anything now; you know that. I fucking hate being helpless, Cam."

Ben was a man of action and always had been. Having to stand by and witness Ethan watching Maggie waste away slowly would be killing him.

"It's just so unfair, you know. Maggie's so young and she's got the girls—they're gonna lose their mom. Why is it never the bastards like Zach's dad who die young?" Ben ground out and almost instantly looked contrite. "Sorry, that wasn't very nice of me."

"Oh, fuck nice. We're all thinking it. What that man did to Zach—and I'm guessing there's a whole lot I don't know— fucking miserable prick." Cameron turned and found his brother watching him intently, an inscrutable look on his face. As Cameron stared back, the barest hint of a smile began twitching at his lips.

"Tell me again how you don't want Zach...?"

"Ben, come on."

"You come on. You like him, and you obviously care about him, so why—"

"No. No, I can't. I just... I mean, of course, I care about him; we all do, but that's it. I don't feel anything more." Cameron tasted the bitter bald-faced lie on his tongue and nearly choked.

"That's not it. You won't let yourself feel anything else," Ben finished off hurriedly as Zach approached them.

Zach's face was flushed with exercise, and his eyes were bright with joy. The girls were tearing around him, tugging on his legs or arms. Zach endured it with a sweetness so innate for a young man who'd known little aside from cruelty in his life.

"The pixies wear you out, Zach?" Ben asked as he came to stand at Cameron's side.

"They've got more energy in their little fingers than I've got in my whole body. How do you do it all the time?" Zach was puffing a little as he spoke.

"Ben can match them for energy," Ethan said as he snuck up behind them, his phone call home obviously over.

"How is she?" Ben grabbed Ethan's hand as he asked, the comfort of touch not lost on him.

Ethan grunted and nodded. "Same." Ben reached up and carded his fingers through Ethan's hair and pulled him down so their foreheads touched.

It was a tender gesture, a heartbreaking one for his lover, who was suffering so. A lump rose in Cameron's throat and regret grew in his heart. He'd had intimacy once—or at least thought he had. But he'd never have it again, and that was through his own choice.

Cameron observed, fascinated, as the two men rallied each other and turned to their daughters, their sad faces now lit up with smiles for the girls. "You girls ready for a swim?" Ethan asked, his voice cracking the slightest bit as he forced it into one of joy rather than grief.

Maya and Riley clapped and nodded and danced around as though they didn't have a care in the world. Of course, for children of their age, the world was literally that moment in time and place. Cameron thought it was probably lucky for them, given what they were facing.

Ben and Ethan took off with the girls to get them changed and ready for the pool. The weather, though warming, was still cool, but Cameron's pool was heated so the temperature would only be a problem when they were getting out.

"Are you going to join them?" he asked Zach who was standing quietly at his side.

"Soon, yeah. What about you?" Zach asked hopefully.

"I'll come in, yeah. I've never really been around kids—it's eye-opening."

"I've never been around kids like *that* before." Zach's gaze was on the door the little girls had just disappeared through, and he looked thoughtful.

"How do you mean?"

"The kids in the camp didn't run around and play; they weren't allowed to."

"Ethan mentioned about the twins being drugged when they were at the cult. I guess your father wanted them seen and not heard." Cameron hated that monster for what he'd done to Zach—and so many others.

"You know what? The longer I'm out here, away from the cult, the more I can see we were all just...mindless..."

"Zombies?" Cameron suggested. Zach's vocabulary was surprisingly good for someone who grew up as he had but sometimes he still had to search around for words.

"Yeah, we were zombies in there. Nobody ever showed much emotion or life. Except Father when he was screaming at us because we were sinners. There were never any big fights, except for ones my father was in, and then nobody fought back. People just...I'm not sure how to explain it. They had no life in them." Zach finished, and Cameron caught a glimpse of a haunted look that often transformed Zach's features.

"At least they're away from him now," Cameron said, but his words were hollow to his own ears. He knew, as Zach did, his father's reach was long, even from behind bars.

"At the indictment hearing, Alec said Father was still running things from prison. How can people continue to follow him, believe in him, once they know he wanted them all to die?"

Cameron understood why, and it sickened him.

"Some people are the sheep, needing something or someone to follow. They're lost and sometimes the thing they think they've found to save them is the thing that's going to hurt them most. Sometimes they find a wolf and by the time they figure it out, it's too late." Cameron stopped himself from saying more—he didn't want to expose himself to Zach, not like that, not yet.

Zach was watching him, wheels noticeably turning in his quick mind. "What if you're not a sheep or a wolf?"

Cameron didn't have a hard and fast answer for Zach's question. He'd known a wolf, and he'd been a sheep. What other kinds of animals were there? "Then you're human, I guess. Flawed and imperfect and prone to mistakes but hopefully doing the best you can."

"It was kind of like growing up in a cage at the cult. There were no bars or fences, but we were still locked away. I know everyone else has each other to help them but they…I couldn't have gone with them. Most of them hate me even more now, like Phia and her mom. I'd have been all alone if it wasn't for you, and I can't ever thank you enough." Zach was watching him, the hearts Ben had been talking about, beating away in his eyes.

The intensity of Zach's stare left him speechless and unable to look away. Words that shouldn't be spoken perched on the tip of his tongue ready to leap out into the world and set him up for more heartache and pain.

High pitched screams and giggles of delight broke the spell holding him and Zach in its thrall so they could hardly even blink for fear of losing sight of the other. They turned together and watched as Ethan dove into the pool, emerging immediately with arms raised to catch Maya and Riley as they prepared to join him. It was the happiest he'd seen Ethan since the whole mess with his sister began.

"Come on, let's get in," Zach urged and ran for the pool, jumping in fully clothed. It reminded Cameron of how Zach had tossed himself into this strange world with similar abandon. Cameron laughed at his exuberance—it was something he'd been missing for a long time.

He stripped off his shirt and joined them in the pool.

Chapter Four

ZACH

"Brake! Brake! That's it, now ease into the corner." Zach heard the panic in Cameron's voice and did his best not to smile.

Zach was twenty-one, soon to be twenty-two and was only now learning to drive. He hadn't been exactly certain of his birth date, but Agent Banner had found papers, when going through the files they had confiscated from his father's cult, confirming his date of birth. There was no official birth certificate and no mention of the mother's name, but the paper listed that Zach had been born on May twenty-fourth. It was the best they could do. Embarrassingly, Zach had cried when he'd learned his birthday.

He was certainly old enough to have had his license years ago, but as with so many of the things life offered a young man, Zach had missed out. Cult life had seen to that.

Cameron had helped him get his learner's permit two days ago, after the FBI had helped rush through official identification for him, and so somehow the task of teaching him to drive had also fallen to Cameron.

Cameron was introducing him to so much of the world.

"So anyway, Pamela said my math is almost beyond help, but she thinks she can do it because she is the best teacher ever. Even if she thought I was beyond help she'd still do it because she's lonely," Zach announced as he edged too quickly into another bend.

Out of the corner of his eye, he saw Cameron gripping the armrest, and his voice sounded strained as he said, "Slower around the corners, Zach. The brake is our friend." Zach quickly flashed him a smile and then returned his attention to the road. "So Mrs. Gandy is lonely, huh?" Cameron continued.

"Sure. Her husband of forty-four years died last year, and her only son lives in New York. He doesn't come home to visit often. She had a cat, but it hasn't been around for a while. That tells me it's probably dead. Cats do wander off and die."

Zach had grown up surrounded by people and yet had been terribly alone. He'd been shunned by the cult, but he'd somehow retained a love of people. The few people he'd met since he'd been staying with Cameron had been a fascination to him. He'd questioned them about anything and everything and had listened to their answers with unfeigned interest.

"What about friends?" Cameron asked.

Zach eyed the brake lights of the car ahead of them, wondering if he should start slowing yet—and at what point Cameron would start white-knuckling it again.

"She's got a few, but she says they might as well be dead. All they do is sit around and complain about aches and pains instead of being happy they're still here. That's stupid really. Who knows how long you've got? Why waste it complaining about stuff?" Zach eventually tapped on the brake, decelerating to sit at a safe distance behind the slow-moving car in front.

"It's what most of us do. We spend so much time worrying over what we don't have we can't enjoy what we do. Human nature, I guess."

Zach was quiet for a while as he continued along Big Horn Avenue. It was almost a straight shot now until they hit Bridger where they'd turn around. Driving there and back would give him another two hours' drive time and probably another ulcer for Cameron.

"No. I don't think it is human nature," Zach finally said. "You know those kids we watched in the documentary the other day? The refugees who just wanted to play soccer? They weren't sitting around complaining and *they* had reason to. I think they were so damn happy they got out of that place all they wanted was to play soccer."

Those little eight-year-old Syrian refugees had been delighted to get a soccer ball. Their simple joy should put others to shame. They had literally nothing else but the soccer ball, but it had been enough to bring them joy—for a short time anyway. They'd escaped a war zone and had more reason to complain than anyone, but they didn't. Zach had never known people lived that way until he came out of the cult. Some might say it's better not to know but not to Zach. He wanted to know everything.

"Maybe if you have too much then you can't see that you've got more than enough," Zach quietly finished.

Zach did know about having nothing. He'd come out of his father's cult with only the clothes on his back and even those had been in poor condition.

"True. They always say the more you have, the more you want."

"You know I grew up mostly in tents. Even at the farm Father never gave me a cabin. Father always said possessions were the devil's tools. None of us had our own clothes, there was a laundry room where clean clothes were stored, and when you needed to change your clothes, you went there and picked some that fit. Toys weren't allowed;

books were but only ones selected by father—and you can imagine those. Furniture was the bare minimum and a lot of it was camping gear so we could take it with us."

Zach hadn't spoken in-depth about his father since the interview with Alec. He was ashamed of his upbringing, deeply ashamed of his father, but mostly he regretted he'd done nothing to stop his father sooner. He was waiting for someone else to realize that, too—to see him for the coward he was.

"What did the kids play with?" Cameron asked.

"They played games, mostly. Father had them drugged whenever he needed to keep them quiet when they were real little. As I told you the other week, I'd never seen kids act like Maya and Riley. There was strict discipline, so once they got to a certain age, they'd been more or less trained to be quiet."

"Shit." The single word seemed to burst out of Cameron.

"Yeah, it was shit. Could have been worse, though, and we got out...alive. All of us." Zach had learned to enjoy swear words since his escape. Most he'd never heard of, but television was an excellent teacher.

"Check your speed, Zach," Cameron instructed as he noticed the speedometer edging up at the same time Zach did. Cameron had warned him this stretch of road was notorious for speed traps.

"I cannot believe I am driving. Sure, we had buses and a handful of cars at the camp, but I was never ever allowed anywhere near them. The only time I got in them was when it was time to move around to a new site."

"How often did you move?"

Zach huffed; a slight snarl curled his lips. "Not a great deal. I don't really have exact times; we had no calendars or anything, but from things such as Easter, which we did celebrate, I'd say we were at the farm for maybe ten years. It's harder to judge when I was younger. We'd be going about our lives, and one day out of nowhere father would decide Satan had found us, and off we'd go. I think he did it to keep the rest of us...muddled up. So we couldn't ever relax."

"It must have been difficult...growing up that way, living like that."

"It was hard work, but it was what we knew. I guess people can get used to anything."

"Sometimes even the most horrible things became normal when you live it long enough," Cameron said. From the quaver in Cameron's voice, Zach got the impression those words were personal. He locked them up in his mind to think about later. He couldn't help wondering what horrible thing Cameron had gotten used to at some time in his life.

The next hour and a half passed in far less profound conversation and with a fair bit more of Cameron's strangled instructions, sometimes practically screaming out of him. Zach had discovered he enjoyed driving and he liked to do it fast.

By the time they were on their way home, it was late and Cameron had promised Zach Chinese food. Zach's life had been so narrow but now it was opening up and he wanted to try everything. Chinese had taken his fancy this week. Cameron called ahead to order it shortly before they hit the outskirts of Cody so they were able to call in and pick it up on the way home. The last five minutes of their journey Zach spent admiring the delicious aromas creeping from the takeaway containers on Cameron's lap.

"I can't wait. This smells so good, Cam," Zach enthused as they set out the containers and he began digging into the food.

He knew Cameron was watching him as he heaped a small portion from each box onto his plate, sniffing each as he did so. "Ooh this one smells the best," he exclaimed.

"I bet you say that about them all." Cameron laughed.

"I know, but this one has got to be—oh no, no I was wrong. This one definitely smells the best."

Cameron laughed again; he sat back and watched as Zach demolished everything on his plate.

Takeout nights were rare, but they were easy—at least the cleanup was; it only took Zach a few minutes to toss the containers and put away any leftovers. Zach wanted to do as many chores around the house as he could. He was yet to come to terms with the concept of money, but he understood enough to know he wasn't providing any to Cameron for his keep. Cameron had explained that Lucas Evers, Hollywood star and friend, had set up a trust fund to cover Zach's expenses until he was able to provide for himself. But this didn't sit well with him, so he was going to work hard, and he planned to pay back everyone—one day.

Zach had always earned his keep; he'd always worked hard. Some of it had been fear that his father might throw him away if he didn't, but even without the idea of money in the commune, he'd understood he needed to work to earn his place there.

After dinner, they moved into the living room where Cameron poured his nightly whiskey and sat in his favorite chair. Zach grabbed a Coke and sat on the sofa beside him.

"So...you still haven't guessed," Zach said, hoping Cameron remembered what he was talking about.

Cameron smiled. "Okay, I'll keep trying. Um...Fireman? Or police? Librarian? Maybe a dentist?"

"Nope." Zach shook his head, a small smile playing across his lips. "Guess again."

Cameron huffed and leaned back in his seat. He brought his glass to his lips and Zach watched as he sipped at the dark honey-colored liquid. Zach knew, as soon as he swallowed, Cameron's tongue would poke out and lick at his lips, and that was his favorite part of watching Cameron with his nightly whiskey.

Sure enough, Cameron licked at his lips and lowered the glass to the arm of the chair. He looked away from Zach as though seriously pondering the question he'd been asked.

"Lumberjack? Accountant?" Cameron continued to guess.

"Accountant? Come on, Cam, guess properly. I just told you what Pam said about my math. I can't even do grade school level." Zach smiled to prove he wasn't upset, even though his inability to understand math was true.

His father had made sure Zach could read, but that was really as far as his education had gone. Math was a giant mystery to him; he knew a bit of geography and history from reading some basic textbooks left lying around for him to steal and read out of sight of his father. Science was not allowed in his father's cult. It was an abomination to god and not to be taught.

In the time since his escape, Pamela Gandy had come in and assessed where he was with his education. The idea was for him to get his GED, which would eventually allow him to go on to college. He was so far behind that it seemed unlikely, but he'd talked to Cameron a lot regarding his options, and after working with Pamela, Zach at last had an inkling of what may lie in his future. Of course, nothing would settle until his father was dealt with.

"Okay, lawyer then? Horse doctor—"

"Horse doctor?" Zach scoffed.

"Professional chocolate taster?"

"Is that a real job?" Zach sat forward and asked with enthusiasm. He loved chocolate.

Cameron laughed and took another sip of his whiskey. "It probably is, but I think there's something else for you. And I've used up all my guesses. So let me have it. What are you going to be when you grow up, Zach?"

"Well, I'm already grown up—" he flicked his hand at Cameron's leg, slapping it lightly. Joking though he may be, Zach didn't want Cameron to think of him as anything but a grown man. "And I was thinking I'd like to be a therapist. Work with kids and young people who've been through bad stuff...the ones who didn't get the good childhood we were all promised."

He'd also been seeing a therapist for the past few weeks who was helping him come to terms with not only his past but also the future he faced. In many ways, he was like a child in a man's body. His sheltered childhood was a handicap now he'd been cast out into the real world, but he was doing everything possible to overcome it. The man sitting beside him, looking extraordinarily handsome, as the shadows of the flames from the fire flickered across his face, was helping him every step of the way. When Zach faltered, Cameron grabbed him and propped him up. Zach had no idea where he'd be without him.

"You'd make a great therapist, Zach. You're smart, kind, easy to talk to, and you've got a good heart. I think that's a great choice. What did Pam say?"

Zach sat a little straighter in his seat. All his life he'd had negative words tossed at him as though he had no feelings, as though those words wouldn't hurt. Zach had done his best not to let them, but when you hear often enough that you're useless, you can't help letting it seep in and become a foundation for who you are. Dr. Warren said Zach was digging up his foundation, though, and Cameron, Pam, Dr. Warren, Ben, Ethan, and even Ryan and Lucas, had all grabbed a shovel and were digging with him. He suddenly chuckled aloud at his thoughts.

"What's so funny?"

"I was thinking about something Dr. Warren said about digging up foundations."

"Huh?"

"Never mind. Anyway Pam said it's doable. She said it'll take me a while to get my GED because I'm so far behind, but the fact I can read is a big help. She said I'm intelligent, though, so I can do it."

"Was there ever any doubt? You're very bright, Zach. I think you can do whatever the hell you want and therapist sounds great."

"Have you ever been to a therapist?" Zach asked though he suspected the answer was no. He knew Cameron had spoken with Dr. Warren, but that was regarding him.

Cameron seemed to have everything together, but then he was also very private. Zach had lived there for weeks now, and while he knew a lot about Cameron's life, he had the impression a huge chunk was missing, hidden behind a wall of Cameron's making. He couldn't imagine Cameron wanting to see someone—a stranger—to talk about personal things.

Cameron shifted uncomfortably on his chair and took another sip of whiskey. Zach allowed himself a brief moment to admire the way his throat worked to swallow the liquid and the little peek of tongue, but then he went back to studying Cameron's reaction to his question. And what he saw led him to believe that perhaps he'd read him wrong.

"Yeah. Yeah, I've been to a therapist. I struggled after we lost Mom so I went to see someone, and they helped, but when Dad died not long after, I didn't cope very well. I should have kept going, but instead... I needed help, but I didn't get the right kind. And then after—" Cameron suddenly jumped from his seat, went to his bar, and started pouring another whiskey. He rarely had more than one drink a night, but apparently tonight warranted a second. Zach ignored the tinge of guilt that this conversation was to blame because sometimes talking about problems helped.

"Anyway, after that I felt better," Cameron continued as he returned to his chair. Zach had the distinct impression there was a whole chunk of story missing, but it was Cameron's business, and he couldn't force him to share, as much as he might want that.

Sometimes he'd notice Cameron got a certain look in his eyes that told Zach it was time to change the topic to something lighter. He saw the look now.

Maybe one day he'd learn what put that look in Cam's eyes.

"So tell me more about this Easter bunny in all the stores right now..." he asked.

"You know what? I don't know where it came from. We could google it. But on Easter Saturday night the Easter bunny comes and leaves chocolate eggs for children. Sometimes the eggs are left at the foot of the bed, but my folks used to do an Easter egg hunt."

"What's that then?"

"Well, they'd hide eggs all through the house and yard. Then they'd leave a basket at the end of our beds so we'd run all over the place like crazy looking for the hidden eggs." Cameron laughed, his gaze far away as though he was lost in the memory. "Of course we always ended up in a fight because one of us usually found more eggs than the other. But then Mom would produce some eggs she claimed the Easter bunny left with her so she could make it fair. Then we'd spend the rest of the day eating chocolate until we were sick."

"Your parents sound like they were very nice people. No wonder you and Ben turned out so good. Easter was always about Jesus, for us. Father got particularly riled up over it, you know with the whole crucifixion. He made it terrifying. There was nothing joyful, even though I'd have thought the resurrection should be a joyful thing."

"Your father has a…warped view, Zach. I don't think it's anything to do with religion or god, though. I think he's just a very sick man."

"I know. God and Jesus are supposed to be all about love, but there was nothing of that with my father. I can't believe in what he did."

"No, I guess you can't. It's okay to believe in god, though, if you want. God is supposed to be a loving god."

"Do you believe?"

"No. We weren't brought up to believe, although our parents made sure we knew about religion—all religions—so we could decide for ourselves. I kind of envy people who do believe. It must be nice to have faith that there's something after this life, but no, my logical brain tells me there's no god."

Zach nodded as he considered Cameron's words. As far back as he could remember, Zach had trouble believing in god, and he wasn't sure why. Yes, he'd read the *Bible*, but even when he was young, he'd been able to see it really had nothing to do with what his father taught, and so he'd been unable to believe.

Coming out of his secluded life in the cult, he'd also had no idea there were other religions—or the trouble caused throughout the world because of that. According to his father, it was black-and-white: there were those who believed in his god—his way—and then there was everyone else who didn't. Those people, his father had said, would one day burn in hell.

"Dr. Warren said religion is a difficult subject, and you shouldn't discuss it with people you don't know because it can cause arguments."

"Sure can. But we know each other, Zach, so if you want to talk about it with me, I'm happy to."

Zach suspected it'd be a good long while until he'd sorted out his beliefs in his head, as messed up as they were, but as always, he appreciated Cameron was there for him if needed.

They sat quietly for a while, each lost in their thoughts. Zach's crept toward Cameron as they often did. His stomach fluttered and he got a little giddy around Cameron like he had the first time he'd seen him. It was a physical reaction he hadn't yet been able to control. But, more than the physical attraction he was happy around Cameron—calm and peaceful. Zach was fond of people but hadn't always liked being around them at the cult, but he loved being around Cameron.

"Cam?"

"Yeah."

"Is the Easter bunny gonna come here?" He smirked.

"You bet your ass he is." Cameron laughed, and just like that, the lightness he so loved about their time together was back.

Cameron settled in his chair, looking relaxed once more. Zach searched his mind for another topic—one that wouldn't lead back to Cameron's dead parents or his own miserable past. Cameron beat him to it.

"I was thinking about your birthday."

"What about it?" Zach asked. This was the first year Zach would be certain how old he was and the date of his actual birthday. It was also the first year he'd be allowed to celebrate it.

"I thought we might fly out to California—"

"No way. To the beach?"

"Yeah. Ben and Ethan are gonna meet us in LA, and you can swim in the ocean, walk on the sand. We might even get some surf lessons."

Zach was dying to see the ocean, catch a wave, and lie on the sand. But surely a trip to California would cost a lot of money, and he was already taking so much from Cameron. "That's a little bit expensive isn't it?"

"Not really. Zach, I'd be going out to visit Ben soon anyway, so the only extra expense is your flight, and it's my birthday gift to you. And you can't complain about gifts...so say thank you and start asking me the millions of questions I know you'll have about the plane trip, LA, the beach..."

"I won't ever be able to say thank you enough, Cam."

Cameron watched him for a while with an odd look, and Zach would have given anything to know what he was thinking. Sometimes he believed Cameron looked at him with the same longing he had for Cameron, but surely that couldn't be true. What did he have to offer Cameron?

"The only thanks I need is seeing you doing so well, Zach. That's it. Now ask away."

"Okay." Zach laughed and tried to sort through the hundreds of questions in his head.

Chapter Five

CAMERON

He'd taken Zach up in his helicopter many times and he'd loved it, but flying on a commercial plane was an entirely different experience. Cameron had made sure Zach had the window seat, and the young man's face had been pretty much glued to the little window since they boarded. Now, as the plane rumbled along the tarmac for takeoff, he noticed Zach straighten in his seat.

"Oh my...oh my god, Cam," Zach excitedly exclaimed as the front wheels lifted off, and the plane angled upward into the sky. Zach never turned away from the window, but his hand blindly fluttered around behind his back until it found Cameron's and he patted it several times. "We're up, we're up."

Zach had an almost childlike joy of life so rare in adults. Sadly, so many adults had that sense of delight and wonder beaten out of them by the harsh blows of life. Cameron dreaded the day Zach lost it too. But if Zach had managed to preserve his sweetness, despite the nightmare of his childhood, perhaps it wasn't inevitable that he'd lose the ability to experience—and show—such obvious happiness.

Cameron watched Zach as he continued peering out the window. He couldn't see Zach's face, but imagined his eyes were wide with awe, his mouth pulled up into a grin or perhaps a little circle of shock—he'd seen it a hundred times since Zach had moved in.

Spending time with Zach was unlike any relationship he'd ever had. It was always fun, inspiring, and sometimes sad—most times it was all three combined. The newness of this world was etched into Zach's face, often lighting up his features to enhance his natural charm.

"We're so high up. I can't make out anything, not like in the chopper." Zach spoke with his face pressed to the tiny window, but Cameron heard him.

"We'll get up to about thirty-four thousand feet. Much higher than the chopper," Cameron answered. He heard the ping come from the cockpit, advising the passengers they were now free to move around the cabin. "Hey, we can get out of our seats now and walk around. Do you wann—" Cameron didn't even get the question finished before Zach was up and out of his seat.

He'd paid the extra for an exit row, so Zach had no trouble getting past him and into the aisle. He made a beeline for the flight attendant who'd spoken to them before takeoff about their extra duties because they were in the exit row. Cameron knew poor Monica was either going to be grilled about her life or how this whole flying thing worked.

Cameron remained seated and just observed. Zach was innocent and naïve, but he was not a fool, and Cameron knew it was important for him to have independence. He'd met a few people in Cody as he began to venture out alone and it was a big step for Zach. Cameron could hang back and give him that, but he'd also be there if he fell.

Monica tossed her head back and laughed at something Zach said. Sometimes people looked at Zach as though he was an oddity, especially if they recognized him from news reports. Cameron was always ready to jump to Zach's defense if that happened. But this time Zach was chuckling, too, so she must be laughing with Zach and not at him. The relief of this was tempered with an unwanted spike of jealousy. Zach wasn't his—could never be his, and yet Cameron didn't like the way Monica tentatively reached out and touched Zach's arm as though she were testing the waters to see how she'd be received.

Cameron tried to convince himself it wasn't envy because that was just silly. He knew from Ben that Zach preferred men, so there was nothing to be jealous over, but the simple truth was he didn't like another person's hand being on Zach at all.

He watched as Zach wandered the aisle and used the toilet, only coming back to his seat once the beverage service commenced. The grin on his face was enormous and changed his entire appearance, making him even more handsome, if that was even possible.

Zach was a stunning-looking man. His sandy hair, vivid green eyes, and light smattering of freckles screamed typical boy-next-door, but Zach was anything but average. Zach had taken to his new world with the kind of wide-eyed wonder, courage, and dignity Cameron had rarely witnessed. Cameron had never known anybody quite like Zach, and every day was a fight not to fall for him—he dreaded the day he'd be too tired to fight anymore.

"They're going to bring us a drink. Monica said on some flights you can buy something to eat too. Including hot food, if you want it. Up here—in the sky—they can cook you food. There's a little kitchen-type thing up there behind the curtain. What are you gonna have to drink? Monica said you can have whatever you want, except milkshakes."

"Maybe they save the milkshakes for first class."

"What's that?"

"Well you pay a lot more money to sit in bigger seats and get better meals and service. They wouldn't have first class on this flight. It's more for longer flights traveling overseas."

Zach looked at him thoughtfully and then glanced around him. "Can't imagine why you'd want better than this. We're flying, and we can walk around while we're doing it, and we're gonna have a drink." Zach shook his head, clearly unable to believe it himself, before turning back to the window.

A few minutes later Monica, another flight attendant, and their cart pulled up. Cameron watched as Monica's gaze went directly to Zach, and the professional smile changed into something more. "Hi, Zach. What can I get you?"

"I'll have a Coke, please."

"And you, sir?"

"I'll take a Coke too. Thanks." Cameron replied.

Monica quickly served their drinks, smiling at Zach as she said, "This is the best Coke on the plane. I made sure. We can't have your first flight being anything but perfect." Cameron didn't see how one Coke could be better than another, but it was something for Monica to say while she continued flirting with Zach.

"Thank you," Zach replied.

"Well you come on back and see me again once you're finished, and I can tell you more about flying while I work."

Zach nodded, his attention already taken by his drink. "I will. Thank you, Monica."

Cameron almost laughed. He had nothing to worry about. Zach was no more interested in pretty young Monica than he was in delightful octogenarian Pam Gandy.

Well over three hours later—and a quick stop in Salt Lake City—they approached LA. Cameron was relieved because he'd picked the right side of the plane, and Zach would have a view of the ocean in just a few minutes.

"Keep watching. You'll see it any moment," he encouraged. If the size of LA itself scared Zach, he wasn't saying, though that could be shock. Cody, Wyoming, must have seemed like an enormous city to Zach, so he couldn't imagine what he'd be thinking of LA.

"There. There's the beach. It's exactly like you said with the sand and the waves and...oh god, it's enormous, Cam."

The plane was starting to turn into its approach, so Zach would see nothing but ocean now, the size of which had to be astounding to him.

"How's it look? Rough waves or flat?" Cameron asked.

"They look small, but everything does from up here. Lots of white, so that means it's rough, big waves?" he asked hesitantly.

"Yeah, big waves, big white."

"I can't believe we're here." Zach was quiet for a moment before continuing. "I'm real sorry Ben and Ethan couldn't meet us."

"Me too." His brother and his partner, Ethan, had planned to meet them at the beach, but Ethan's sister, Maggie, had taken a turn for the worse. In fact, Ben had told him she probably only had a few days left. Cameron had packed his good black suit in case they needed to fly up to a funeral from here.

By the time they landed, collected their bags, and fought their way through traffic to the hotel, it was late afternoon. The traffic had horrified Zach, and he'd already told Cameron he'd never be moving to a big city. Cameron suspected it was mostly because their speed had never gotten above fifty, and Zach liked to drive just a little faster than that.

"Do you wanna go for a walk to the ocean?" Cameron asked as soon as they'd dumped their bags in the hotel room.

It was light enough to go for a walk along the nearby beach. Cameron had made sure the hotel was close to the water; that was why they were here, after all.

"Yes." Zach unequivocally responded. He unzipped his bag and pulled out the flip-flops they'd bought at the airport. It was going to be fun to watch him walk in those for the first time, but Zach had been determined to have the correct beachwear.

"Try them out," Cameron encouraged. He had his own flip-flops on already, and though he didn't regularly wear them, he was quite relaxed in them.

Zach sat on the edge of the bed and slipped his comfortable sneakers off. The socks came next and Cameron smiled as Zach gave the flip-flops a sideways glance as if he expected some kind of trouble from them. He dropped them on the floor and then pushed each foot into its matching shoe. He curled his toes, testing out the feel of the shoe, and then he stood and took a few steps.

Cameron was surprised to hear a smattering of laughter coming from Zach as he walked a few laps of the room. "Weird," Zach muttered. As much as Cameron hated the way Zach had grown up, he loved watching him as he experienced something new.

"Do you think you'll be okay in them?"

Zach nodded vigorously. "Yeah, let's give it a go."

Their hotel was one block from the beach. Cameron could see Zach from the corner of his eye as they walked together. His gait wasn't quite as graceful as usual, but he was managing in the new footwear.

It didn't take long for them to get their first close up glimpse of the Pacific Ocean and what a glorious view it was. The sun was on its way to kiss the horizon, and the vivid purples and oranges of the sunset were stunning. Zach's head swung side to side and up and down as though he couldn't decide where to look.

"Wow." It seemed to be all Zach could get out as his gaze finally settled in the direction of the setting sun.

Both were so entranced with the gorgeous show nature was putting on for them, neither noticed they'd almost reached the sand. Cameron felt the difference of the soft sand to the hard concrete under his feet and stopped to reach down and remove his flip-flops. Walking on sand in flip-flops was a big no.

Zach came to a stop beside him and slid his feet out of the flip-flops. Cameron watched as he walked around a little, scrunching his toes and digging his feet into the sand. Then he bent and picked up his sandals and looked over his shoulder at Cameron.

"Come on." He smiled. "Let's go."

Zach didn't hesitate as he took long strides through the sand. Cameron followed close behind, smiling when Zach eventually get up to a little trot toward the shoreline.

When Cameron caught up, Zach was standing ankle deep in the ocean, the small waves gently lapping at his feet. Zach's arms hung loosely at his side, his head tipped back and his eyes closed.

"It's just like you said." Zach inhaled deeply and then turned his head to look at Cameron. "Smells amazing. It's so beautiful, Cam."

"Yes, it is," Cameron replied, not even looking at the scenery. Though Zach was unaware of it, Cameron didn't even try to lie to himself that he'd been talking about anything or anyone other than Zach. "Happy Birthday, Zach."

"Thank you. I still can't believe you did this for me."

"You deserve it."

"Not sure about that. All I know is I'm the luckiest man in the world," Zach simply stated.

Cameron tossed his flip-flops back on the beach, and easing out a little farther in the waves, he turned, offering his hand to Zach. He took it and walked out a little farther with him. The waves were rolling against their tummies and Zach was laughing wildly. It was contagious. Cameron was quickly laughing with a levity he hadn't experienced in years.

He sent a little splash Zach's way and then did his best to run back to shore. With surprising speed, Zach caught him around the waist. They both fell headlong into the waves, flailing and laughing. Cameron felt like a kid as he splashed and wrestled with Zach in the salty waters.

By the time they dragged themselves, laughing and fully clothed, from the water, they were breathing hard. Despite the exhaustion and ache in his body from messing around in the surf, the weight on Cameron's shoulders was lighter than it had been for a long, long time.

Not many people would have come through what Zach had without bitterness, but somehow he'd had managed it. His ability to enjoy living was one of the many things Cameron admired about him because he knew he'd failed to do the same. Zach was both innocent and yet incredibly wise. Perhaps wise wasn't the right word. Zach was very astute, but with a simplicity that allowed him to easily look through the bullshit and hit right at the heart of the matter.

Because he'd grown up without being surrounded by the crap, he never needed to wade through it to make sense of things. Cameron loved that about Zach. And loving anything about Zach scared the hell out of him.

Chapter Six

ZACH

Zach had wanted to wake early today, but the sun was well up when he woke. Swimming with Cameron in the ocean for the last three days must have exhausted him. He stretched lazily and gave up on the idea of watching the sunrise.

He was having the time of his life. He may not be sharing a bed with Cameron, but he was sharing a room. He felt so close to him, literally, since there was no wall between them as they slept less than six feet apart, nothing but air separating them.

Last night, after they sat up in their beds watching a movie on the television and eating a giant pizza they'd ordered from room service, Zach had lain in his bed watching Cameron as he'd drifted off to sleep. The longing to hold him had been almost unbearable. He found Cameron so strikingly beautiful that sometimes his heart actually ached at the sight, but the ache might also be because he couldn't have him.

He looked across at the other bed, expecting to see Cameron still curled on his side, a hand under his cheek as he slept, but the bed was empty. Zach sat upright and cast his gaze around the room. There was no sign of Cam. The drapes covering the door to the balcony were slightly parted, allowing a thin strip of sunlight into the room.

After quietly sliding out of bed, he padded to the bathroom and inched the door open, enough to see clearly into the room.

Zach should have backed out then, but he froze instead. The shower wasn't running, but the room was steamy. Not so thick that it clouded his view when Cameron stepped out of the shower gloriously naked, with only a towel in his hand, as he rubbed at his damp hair. Cameron froze as soon as he caught Zach watching.

Despite the way he'd lived growing up, Zach had never seen another naked man, and he was mesmerized. Cameron was incredibly broad across the shoulders. His chest and the midline of his firm stomach were covered in sandy hair that continued down to create a nest for his thick cock to rest in. Cameron's dick was both longer and thicker than Zach's, and as Zach's focus remained steadfast, it gave a little jerk. Behind the shaft, his large heavy balls rested against his thick thighs.

Beads of water cascaded over his skin, dancing paths over the ridges and valleys of his muscles. Zach's mouth was absolutely watering at the sight even though he had no idea what to do with any part of the man standing so serious before him.

"I've never seen another man's dick before," he blurted using the term he'd heard so often on TV. In the cult, words such as that weren't used, and certainly dicks weren't spoken about at all. His cheeks flooded with warmth and color immediately as Cameron remained still and silent before him.

Emboldened, Zach moved forward and tentatively traced his fingertip from the hollow of Cameron's throat, chasing a drop of water down his solid chest and rigid abs until it pooled in his belly button. He curled his finger in the little indent.

He noticed the simple touch was enough to harden Cameron's dick, and Zach licked his lips as he watched it grow. Even thinking the word dick seemed so...bold, so grown-up and delightfully sinful to him.

"Zach..." Cameron whispered.

"Please, just let me..." Let him what? Zach didn't know. He only knew he wasn't ready to pull his fingers away from Cameron's body. He wanted to touch him, experience what another man's—no Cameron's—body would feel like beneath his hands.

Cameron gave the slightest nod and closed his eyes. Zach returned his gaze to the mass of hard flesh before him.

Zach put both hands on Cameron's shoulders and lightly traced his fingertips all over the damp skin. Testing, teasing, feeling. Instinct took over and he circled Cameron's nipples, pinching them until they hardened. He couldn't believe he was doing this. He couldn't believe Cameron was allowing it.

Zach chanced another glance up at Cameron's face as he continued touching him and found pale-blue eyes watching him with a burning intensity. Cameron's jaw was clenched, and Zach wondered if he was trying not to enjoy the feel of Zach's hands on him. Or maybe he was enjoying it too much—too quickly.

Little whimpers and moans fell from Cameron's lips, encouraging Zach to continue, telling him Cameron was enjoying what he was doing.

Zach reached one hand up and threaded his fingers in Cameron's wet hair. His palm rested on Cameron's cheek and his thumb brushed the smooth skin there. Zach's heart thumped wildly in his chest when Cameron leaned into the touch.

He was so lost in touching Cameron that when one of Cameron's hands rested on his cheek, mirroring his own actions, he startled. Cameron immediately pulled his hand away.

"No, don't. It's okay," Zach tried to reassure him, but he knew he'd broken the spell.

"I'm sorry, Zach. I can't. This is..." Cameron let his words trail off. If Cameron said it was wrong, it would devastate him. How could Cameron think something that felt so right be wrong?

"Cameron..."

"I'm sorry."

From the other room, Zach heard Cameron's cell ringing and reluctantly let go of him. Without a word, Cameron stepped out of the bathroom.

Zach's shoulders sagged in defeat, furious with himself for ruining the moment. He'd wanted to touch Cameron and be touched by him since they'd met, and now that it happened, he'd flinched like a frightened child.

He dropped his pajama bottoms and hopped straight into the shower. He didn't like the idea of washing right away, as though the fact they'd just been touching each other was wrong and needed to be cleansed away. But it was over—for now.

Cameron would pick the encounter all apart, look at it from all angles and decide it was wrong for them to be together and he'd done the wrong thing by letting Zach touch him. Somehow, in some way, Cameron would believe Zach had been hurt by this and blame himself. But Zach allowed himself a small measure of hope because his touch had clearly affected Cameron.

The room was empty when he got out of the shower. The thick drapes were still pulled across the sliding door leaving the room dimly lit from the trim of sunlight around the edges. He pulled the curtain aside and his breath caught as he saw Cameron standing on the balcony with his back to him, looking out over the view. The morning sun was forming a halo of light around him with his light-colored hair seamlessly blending into it.

"That was Ben," Cameron said, his voice soft and sad sounding, as Zach pushed the door along the rail. "Maggie passed away overnight."

"Oh no. I'm so sorry." He'd only met Maggie one time, briefly, but she seemed a very nice person. He knew her brother Ethan better, and he liked him a lot. He'd always be grateful to Ethan and Ben for helping him escape the cult and going back to ensure Father couldn't hurt anyone else.

Ethan was a nice man, fiercely protective of his nieces and Ben, and Zach ached for the pain he must now be feeling.

"I've booked us a flight up to San Francisco tonight. I'm not sure what we can do to help, but I think we should be there. The funeral will be in three days, so I want to stay for that. You don't have to come if you don't want to…" Cameron trailed off.

Zach had observed Ben and Ethan be there for each other during the whole drama with the twin girls and his father's cult, and he wanted to be the one Cameron leaned on now. Cameron might not be his to protect and love and care about, but he was going to anyway.

"I'll go. I'd like to be there for you." At that, Cameron turned to look at him, his eyes sad and his lips turned into a frown. Without warning, he pulled Zach into his arms, dragging him in close and holding onto him.

"Thank you." Cameron's words fluttered into his hair. "I knew Maggie a little before all of this happened, but I didn't know her well. I'm not sure why I'm so sad, though. I think it's because she was young and her girls are too young to have lost their mom."

Cameron didn't give himself near enough credit for the enormous heart that Zach knew beat with such strength in his chest. "Maybe because you understand Ben will be hurting too," Zach suggested.

"Possibly," Cameron answered and released the hold he had on Zach, much to Zach's displeasure. They leaned against the railing, facing each other. "I guess it also brings back memories of losing my parents. I haven't been to a funeral since my dad's."

"I've never been to one," Zach replied, startled by the truth of his words. There was so much shame in what his father had done Zach wondered if he'd ever stop feeling it.

"What did happen when someone in the camp died?" Cameron frequently asked him about his previous life, and he was one of the few people Zach didn't feel ashamed in front of when he shared stories from his past.

"Nothing, actually. Father and the elder men buried them. No funeral or even words spoken. Everything moved on almost as if that person had never been." For an apparently religious group, it was a very unsatisfactory way to handle somebody's death, but then once they were dead they were of no more use to Father so...

"That's..."

"Awful?" Zach suggested. "You can say it. Most of the lifestyle my father created was awful. I'm not offended, just sad... And angry. At him, at the people who knew better but followed him anyway. At myself."

"None of it was your fault."

Zach had heard this over and over from Cameron, Ben, Dr. Warren, even Agent Banner, but Zach had been there, not them. How could they know if he was to blame or not? Some days it sure felt to him as though he should have done more.

"About before, Zach," Cameron said with a wince. "I'm sorry. It's my fault. I shouldn't have let that happen. It was a mistake and it won't happen again."

A mistake? Didn't Cameron enjoy Zach touching him? It sure looked like his dick had. "Didn't you... I thought you were enjoying it. I only flinched because you surprised me, not because I didn't want you to touch me. I want that, Cam. I want you to touch me so badly."

"I can't. We can't. You're too young, Zach, and I can't... I can't give you a relationship. I can't be what you need. I'm sorry. It won't happen again." Cameron turned and walked back into the hotel room and that apparently was that.

Zach wanted to scream at Cameron to say *he* was all Zach needed. Instead, he was left on the balcony thoroughly confused by what had gone wrong in so short a time.

Chapter Seven

CAMERON

Cypress Lawn Memorial Gardens was located a little way outside the city of San Francisco. It was a gorgeous, sunny day as Cameron stood in the grounds waiting for the service to commence. He wasn't sure if the perfect weather was a good thing or not. Surely beautiful, sunny days should be saved for happier times, not for days when a young mother was going to be put into the ground. Today should be dark and cold, the wind raging against the injustice of Maggie's death.

They'd seen Ethan and Ben twice since they landed in San Francisco a few days ago. Ben had looked tired, but Cameron had been shocked at Ethan's appearance. His eyes had been red-rimmed, his hair and beard messy and he'd obviously lost some weight. The burden of grief was written all over his body.

Cameron watched them now as they stood over by the chapel talking to the celebrant who'd be conducting the funeral. Ben had Ethan's hand tightly gripped in his own, and despite the considerable height difference, it looked as though it was Ben holding the much taller Ethan up.

The only thing about dying from something as cruel as cancer that wasn't absolutely horrific was Maggie had at least been given the time with Ethan to instruct him on exactly how she wanted her funeral carried out and her girls raised. Ben had told him she'd made countless videos for her girls and he had almost laughed when he described the novel-length instructions she'd left for them on how to raise the twins. Cameron was positive Ben and Ethan would need those instructions.

Cameron turned away from the pitiful sight Ethan's grief made and caught sight of their young nanny, Shelly, who sat with the girls under a tree, reading them a story.

Only a handful of mourners had arrived so far, but the service was due to begin shortly. Cameron cast a quick glance to Zach, who was standing silently beside him. Zach's attention was focused on the twins, which it tended to be whenever the little girls were around. Zach was as fascinated with them as they were with him.

"Do you think I'll ever see my brothers and sisters again?" Zach asked, the question catching Cameron off guard.

Arnold Piper had seven wives, so common sense told Cameron Zach would have siblings, plus they'd been mentioned in Zach's interviews with the FBI, but he hadn't really given much consideration to brothers and sisters.

"I'm not sure. Did you have much to do with them back at the camp?"

"No. They treated me the same as everyone. I was the oldest...at least I think I was. Maybe some of the younger ones might want to see me one day."

For the first time since he'd known him, Cameron caught a trace of bitterness in Zach's tone. Bitterness that his father may have cut him off from his family, turned them against him, and how could he not be bitter at that?

"We could always go and see them...ask them if they'd like to see you."

"You'd come with me?"

"I told you I'd be here for you, Zach."

"I know. I thought that maybe after…"

Cameron had dreaded this. He was furious with himself for what had happened with Zach in LA. He hated the situation. Not the touching—no, he'd loved that. In fact, he'd come hard in the shower—several times—just thinking about the feel of Zach's hands on him in the days since. The way Zach had tentatively touched his skin, so shy and yet bold all at once. The desire he'd seen in Zach's eyes, the way his breath had hitched with every touch…it had been one of the most intense experiences of his life.

But Cameron shouldn't have let it happen, even though he'd wanted it so badly. He definitely couldn't let it happen again.

"No. Not at all, Zach. I'm so sorry about that morning, but it doesn't change anything. I'll still be here for you."

Zach turned his green eyes on him, watching him with an intensity Cameron had rarely experienced. Cameron had never seen eyes that could look so innocent and yet so fierce at the same time.

"You're wrong, Cam. It changed everything," Zach murmured.

"Hey, Zach, Cameron. How're you doing?" Cameron hadn't even noticed Ryan sidle up beside them, so he gave an involuntary little start when he spoke.

"Hi, Ryan. I'm good, thank you." Zach answered.

Ryan looked as gorgeous as he always did. He'd had a brief but successful acting career before his fear of large crowds convinced him to pull the plug on it. His lover and former costar, Lucas, was still acting and his career was booming, especially after his Oscar win. They were a spectacular-looking couple who, unlike most stars, avoided the spotlight at all costs.

"Glad to hear it. Are you doing okay now you're out in the world?" Ryan smiled, but it was a half smile as though he was aware that big, joyful smiles at funerals were a no-no.

"I am. Cameron's showing me lots of new things."

"As long as he taught you how to use Google, you should be okay," Ryan replied.

Zach gave a half-hearted huff and said, "I'm getting better at it. We went to the beach right before we came here. I loved it."

"You should try the beaches back home in Australia. I may be biased, but they're the best in the world."

"You're from Australia? I didn't know that."

"Yep. You'll have to come with me and Lucas one day. He loves it there, but for now, home is here." Ryan looked away, toward where Lucas was talking with Alec Banner and he sighed a little. "Actually home is wherever he is," he amended, nodding his head toward Lucas.

"Anyway, enough sappiness. I'm really pleased to see you looking so good." Ryan dragged his gaze away from Lucas and turned to Cameron. "Cameron, you're looking good, too, just so you don't feel left out. You two must be good for each other. Ben told me you talk about Zach all the time. Zach this and Zach that. You're obviously very proud of him." Ryan rambled on, oblivious to the discomfort he was causing.

"Not much to be proud of," Zach answered, his cheeks pinking.

"Oh I think there is. Your life was spun upside down, Zach, and from what I hear, you've kept your feet on the ground."

"He's been amazing," Cameron said.

"Looks like it to me." Ryan replied before moving away to join Lucas, leaving Cameron alone again with Zach.

They stared uncomfortably at each other, neither knowing what to say. He wondered how long they'd have this awkwardness between them.

Cameron couldn't have been happier, when he noticed Ben waving him over, letting him know it was time to go in and take their seats.

There wasn't a large crowd in attendance, but the depth of the grief he sensed in the small group was equivalent to having two hundred mourners. Maggie and Ethan's parents weren't there, and he knew that was by Maggie's request.

Ben and Ethan sat in the front pew with Maya and Riley between them. They had stretched their arms behind the girls, their hands clasped. He and Zach sat behind them. Shelly was beside Ben so she'd be able to wrangle the girls in whenever they lost interest during the service.

Several times during the service Cameron leaned forward and placed his hand on Ben's shoulder giving it a small squeeze. Each time he did it Zach put his own hand on Cameron's thigh giving it a light squeeze, as if he was letting him know someone had his back too. Cameron was hurting to see his brother in pain, and god, it eased his mind to realize Zach was there for him.

It was almost unbearably sad in the little room, listening to people talk about Maggie. Ethan bravely told stories from their childhood and promised his sister he'd never let her daughters forget their mom. Cameron's eyes welled with tears then. He remembered his own mom and of course his thoughts necessarily drifted to his father. His parents were a package deal, as much in death as they had been in life. Always together. He wished he deserved to have that with someone.

Once they stepped back out into the glorious sunshine, things seemed far less morose. The twins danced around on the lawn, too young to fully comprehend what they'd lost. Ethan stood quietly watching them, his lips pulled into a grim line. Ben was at his side, as he'd been all day. Cameron ached with longing at the sight of the two men. He hadn't realized how much he wanted someone to walk beside him, share the burdens, hold him up when he fell. He thought he'd had that once, but he'd been so terribly wrong. Ever since Jimmy he'd been happy to remain alone, but as he watched Ethan lean on Ben, he realized how terribly wrong he'd been. He wasn't happy at all.

His gaze flicked across to Zach who was staring back at Cameron with an unreadable expression on his face. For a second, Cameron thought he was going to smile, but then his entire face seemed to shutter down, leaving nothing but the handsome shell of the man behind. What had Zach been thinking in that moment?

"Thank you, Zach."

Zach shook his head, clearly not knowing what Cameron was referring to. "For what?"

"For during the service...letting me know you were there. It helped." Cameron wanted to say more, but what could he say that wouldn't encourage Zach? He had to be more careful with how he behaved around the young man.

"You were hurting. It's hard to see someone you care about in pain," Zach offered.

There was an absolute truth to what Zach had said. Sometimes it was harder seeing someone you cared about in pain than being in pain yourself. And if you were the one who caused the pain...well, that was even worse. Cameron knew because Zach was in pain now, and he knew he'd caused it.

Cameron may have realized he was unhappy alone, but he was a long way from doing something to change it. Fear held him firm in its grip.

"HEY, DO YOU need a hand with that?" Zach called to him as soon as he stepped out of the car. They'd been home for a few weeks now and things were getting back to normal. The awkwardness between him and Zach from their encounter in LA was finally easing.

"Yeah, thanks."

Cameron passed a couple of the shopping bags to Zach. Until Zach had moved in a few months ago, Cameron had been a "run to the market as needed" and "eat a lot of takeout" type of guy. Now he went shopping once a week, religiously, to ensure the kitchen was well stocked for the home-cooked meals they ate almost exclusively.

The quiet and comfortable meals he shared with Zach at the end of each day had become so important to him—the moment he looked forward to most every day.

"Did you get the Hershey's?" Zach asked as he turned with his bags and headed for the house.

"Of course. Cookies and Cream, and plain."

"Both? You're too good to me," Zach cheerfully replied, with a hint of the flirtatiousness he'd begun to adopt.

Cameron had given him his first chocolate bar the day after he arrived. It had been one of Zach's many firsts Cameron had been witness to—and one of the good ones.

"I figured with the prep work for the hearing coming up, you deserved a treat."

Zach didn't make any kind of reply as they began putting away the groceries. They worked together in companionable silence as they often did.

"I'm okay, Cam," Zach suddenly broke into the silence.

Cameron put aside the boxes of cereal in his hands and turned to Zach, giving him his full attention.

"I know you are. I do. But I also understand it can't be easy to know your father will be going to trial for serious crimes and knowing you're the one whose testimony will likely put him away." Cameron had long since stopped dancing around the truth of Zach's father with him. It was what it was, and no amount of coddling Zach was going to make it any better. Zach didn't seem to need the coddling anyway.

"I kind of have to do it, Cam. I understand I do. What I don't get is why aren't all of the girls willing to testify? I mean, I get it when my father was first arrested because they were still, you know, under his spell or brainwashed or whatever you want to call it."

Cameron examined Zach intently as he spoke. He watched as the faraway look he often got clouded over his features. Cameron knew some of the memories, which sometimes stole the young man away, but he suspected there were many more nobody knew about that haunted him.

"They saw him as a god, and I saw him as a monster. I get that, but they've been away from him for a while now. Some of them have been talking to Doctor Warren too. They know what my father was doing was wrong—so why won't they all testify?"

Cameron wasn't always certain what to say to Zach about his past. He was in way over his head with such a difficult subject. When Zach first moved in, he'd spoken to Doctor Warren about how to help him adjust. He'd read books on cults and books by cult survivors, but he didn't really understand. How could he? It was a foreign world to him. And yet in a way he knew exactly what Arnold Piper's followers had been through—he'd been in a monster's thrall once before, and it, too, had been disguised as love.

"Many reasons, I guess," Cameron eventually answered. "Fear, devotion, shame. They grew up idolizing Arnold Piper. They never got to see things clearly, like you did." No matter how helpful Dr. Warren was, he couldn't be there every second to whisper the right words to say into Cameron's ear. The best he could hope for was that he was helping Zach.

Cameron bore the familiar itch in his bones to reach out and pull Zach to him, choosing instead to shove his hands in his pockets. He found it hard to explain why he needed to hold Zach sometimes, but he'd done it once or twice, especially when Zach's screams had woken him and he'd found Zach shaking and teary after a nightmare. He was happy to do it then if it helped, but the awful truth was he was still afraid to get too close.

It was Zach who came close to him this time, though, almost forcing his way into Cameron's arms. They were friends and Cameron should be able to offer him comfort when needed without freaking out. Cameron pulled his hands out and tentatively wrapped them around Zach.

"It's okay to hug me, Cameron," Zach said, voicing Cameron's thoughts. "It's not taking advantage or whatever else you might be thinking," Zach murmured.

Cameron pulled back immediately. "What?"

Zach stepped away from him and shrugged his shoulders. "I spoke to Doctor Warren about you. He said you might be thinking if anything happened between us again you'd be taking advantage of me but you're not...you wouldn't be."

"You spoke to Dr. Warren? About me? Why...? What?" Cameron shook his head, completely blindsided by the sudden turn in this conversation.

"I don't know much about relationships and emotions, but I know I like you. The problem is, Cameron, I'm not sure what to do with my feelings."

Cameron suddenly needed to sit. He hadn't expected this when he'd awoken this morning. Talking to Zach about his feelings for him had been the last direction he'd expected this day to go. If Zach didn't know what to do with how he felt, Cameron had even less of an idea.

"Just so I'm clear, Zach, what you're saying is...?"

"I want you... You must know I do." Zach stared at him unflinchingly, and Cameron knew he couldn't keep his secret from Zach much longer. Zach needed to understand why he could never be what he wanted.

"Um, growing up how I did," Zach continued in the face of Cameron's silence, "there was never any mention of being gay. It didn't exist in the commune. It was always men and women who got married and had babies. End of story. It was only when I saw Ben and Ethan together that I found out about being gay." Zach huffed and shook his head. "How pathetic is that?" he asked rhetorically.

The grocery bags stood on the kitchen countertop, long forgotten in the odd reality Cameron now found himself in. He fumbled behind him for one of the stools under the breakfast counter and half sat on it, unable to completely sink down and relax.

Somewhere in the back of his mind, he thought he should be worried about the ice cream, but what was melting ice cream when a twenty-two-year-old former cult member confessed they liked you. Liked you, liked you, not simply friend liked you. If only Ben were here to seek advice from on how to handle this...or let's face it, he'd have gone to

Ethan because he knew Ben would have been laughing his ass off at him.

"Anyway," Zach continued, interrupting Cameron's reverie. "I never found any of the women in the camp appealing. They were pretty, but I never looked at them the same way as I did with some of the men. You don't know what that's like. I thought I was some kind of freak, and I was the only man who felt that way in the world. I guess it was good my father never allowed me to marry. Maybe he knew. I don't know, maybe that's why he hated me so much."

"Zach, I…"

"Please, let me say this."

Cameron nodded but noticed how close Zach was to him now. He was a handsome man, made even more so by the weight he'd put on over the last few months. The neglected boy's body had filled out into a fit young man who was strong and powerful. A man who Cameron could easily fall for if he allowed himself.

"When I found out there was such a thing as homosexuality—you can't imagine the relief. It meant I wasn't some kind of aberration. I was normal. I was one of many. And when I saw you for the first time…wow that was something else. I might have actually stopped breathing. And then after that morning at the beach… I know you think it was a mistake, but for me, it wasn't. For me it was everything. Just touching you like that… I knew. I knew it was right and I wanted you."

Cameron should have expected this conversation because Zach was so courageous, so willing to tackle anything head-on. But Cameron was the opposite and he preferred living in denial. Too bad reality was dragging him kicking and screaming out of his safe little cave and into the real world. Or perhaps it'd be good to get this out in the open, over and done with.

"Zach, I don't know what to say. I'm flattered, obviously, but—"

"But you don't want me?" Zach peeked at him through the thick lashes of his lowered eyelids.

"Yes, I mean no. I mean... Oh, god. Um, I'm making a mess of this." It wasn't lost on Cameron that he was the one flustered like a schoolboy even though he was supposedly the worldly adult here. He couldn't seem to keep his composure in the face of the younger man's calm confidence. "What brought this on, Zach?"

Out of the millions of questions he had for Zach that was probably the least important and most innocuous, and yet he almost dreaded the answer.

"I've been thinking about it since that day at the beach. Longer, really. And now with the trial coming up and working on my GED, I know what I can expect from my life for the moment. I can start planning my life, and I want you in it, Cam."

"You know I'm going to be in it, Zach. I told you at the start I'd always be here for you."

"I want more," Zach whispered.

Cameron swallowed and hung his head. "I can't give you more."

For a time, Zach remained quiet, and when there was no response from him, Cameron raised his head to try to catch his gaze. He didn't have to try hard, though. Zach was standing across from him, his stare unflinchingly focused on Cameron now.

"Can't or won't?"

"Zach..."

"Be honest with me, Cameron. You said you'd always be honest with me. Be honest now. Do you like how I look?"

Oh, Jesus, Cameron would give his left arm to get out of this conversation, but he had promised Zach. He'd be honest with him now; he only hoped it really was the truth and not something he'd convinced himself was the truth.

"You're a very handsome man. Of course, I find you attractive."

"Do you like me?" Zach took a step closer as he asked the question.

"Yes, of course, I like you."

"As more than a friend?"

Zach was so close now his breath was ghosting over Cameron's face. There was still a hint of mint from his toothpaste but it mixed with the rich odor of his coffee.

"Zach, I like you as a friend, but there's things about me—my past—that you don't know and—"

Cameron's words were cut off by the press of Zach's soft lips to his own. For a moment, that's all it was as the shock of the kiss left Cameron frozen, and Zach's inexperience left him ignorant of what to do next.

The sensation of Zach's body pressing closer, his hand snaking around his neck, tangling in his hair snapped Cameron out of his motionless state. He wrapped Zach in his arms, pulling him even tighter against his body. He moved his mouth against Zach's, sliding and shifting them together. He licked at the seam and Zach gasped, his mouth opening automatically in response. Cameron eased his tongue inside and was met with the tentative movement of Zach's tongue tangling with his own. Their breathing quickened, and Cameron's pulse raced.

A shiver ripped through Zach's body, and a sigh fell from his mouth, bringing Cameron crashing back to reality. He released Zach and gently pushed at his shoulders, putting some much-needed distance between them.

"I'm sorry. I shouldn't have done that," he mumbled. He winced as Zach flinched at his words.

"I kissed you," Zach replied.

"No, this is my fault. I shouldn't have—"

"I'm not a child, Cameron," Zach shouted. "Innocent, maybe, but I'm not a child. I want this—you."

"I can't, Zach. It's not you. It's me."

"Oh, my god. I hear that on the television all the time. It's only an excuse when you don't want someone. You should have been honest and told me you didn't want me."

Cameron saw real anger flaring in Zach's eyes for the first time since they'd met, and he couldn't blame him. He'd totally fucked things up.

"No. It's not like that, Zach. There's so much going on and you're so young..."

Zach straightened and steeled his spine. "It's fine. I understand. You think I'm too young, too innocent. I get it." Zach turned his back and headed for the door. He stopped right before he walked out and glanced back over his shoulder at Cameron. "It doesn't change anything, Cam. It doesn't change how I feel about you and one day...one day you'll see. One day you'll let yourself want me back."

Cameron flopped back onto the stool, as soon as Zach left the room, and put his head in his hands. He went over the entire encounter, looking for where it had gone wrong, what he should have said or done instead. His mind kept snagging on the last thing Zach had said. "One day you'll let yourself want me back." Was that the truth? Was Zach astute enough to see that Cameron did want him but wouldn't allow himself to? *Did* Cameron want Zach? The simple answer was yes. The complicated answer was also yes.

Chapter Eight

ZACH

Zach's heart might beat right out of his chest it was thumping so hard. Thankfully, he'd managed to keep himself together long enough to get away from Cameron.

During his whole confession, he'd wanted nothing more than to run screaming. He'd been so nervous, so terrified, and by the end, plain humiliated. Doctor Warren had warned him how he might feel when he confronted Cameron, but Zach wanted—needed—to tell Cameron how he felt. He and the doctor had even role-played him talking about his feelings. Each time the doctor had varied his responses, including gently rejecting him, exactly as Cameron had done. But no amount of role-play could have prepared him for the intense pleasure he'd experienced when he'd kissed Cameron—and when Cameron had kissed him back.

Zach had watched a lot of television since his escape from the cult—despite Cameron's continual warnings that what he saw on television wasn't necessarily real life—and he'd been right. Zach had seen plenty of kisses in those shows: men and women, men and men, women and women. He knew tongues had been involved; he'd seen a peek of them during many of the kisses, but he'd had no idea people let their tongues dance together when they kissed—or how awesome it would feel.

"Zach?"

Zach stiffened at the sound of Cameron calling his name. He hadn't expected him to follow, and if he was honest, he was hoping Cameron wouldn't. He'd have preferred a bit of distance between them while he licked his wounds and while Cameron wrapped his head around his revelation.

Cameron's rejection had stung, even though it had been expected. It was important Cameron know how he felt, though, and if there were the slightest chance Cameron would feel the same way, then Zach was willing to take the risk. Doctor Warren had called him a stubborn son of a bitch when he refused his suggestion of waiting to share his feelings.

Zach was learning how life outside the cult worked, however, and he wasn't giving up on Cameron. Because he wanted it all: dating, marriage, kids, grandkids, growing old together. Everything.

"Hey," Cameron said as he finally caught up to him. "Zach, I'm sorry. I didn't handle that well. I do care about you...very much, but as friends."

Cameron looked so handsome...and very lost as he stood before Zach now. He might be eight years older, but right then he looked so much more innocent than Zach was, and as always, completely unaware of the impact he had on people, especially Zach. He didn't think Cameron had any idea how beautiful he was, but he'd noticed both men and women watching Cameron when they'd been out in public.

On the other hand, Zach knew he tended to fade into the background. His insignificance had been lifesaving when he'd been in his father's cult, but now—well the only one Zach really wanted to notice him was Cameron.

"It's okay, Cam. I'll be all right. I'm sorry if I made you uncomfortable. I just wanted…" He winced, not wanting to rehash it all. Both he and Cameron had probably had enough for one day. "Actually, is it okay if I had a bit of time to myself? Only for a little while."

Cameron nodded and looked away. "Of course, sure. Sorry. I should have given you some time. I was worried… You know what? I'm going to pop over to the hangar for a while. There's some maintenance for the chopper I need to check up on. I'll come home later tonight. Give you the day in peace."

Zach hadn't meant to chase him out of his own home, but a day to himself to recover and regroup might be a good thing. Besides, even though Cameron had pulled away from their kiss, it was all Zach could do to stop himself from searching out his full, warm lips again.

Space—for now—would be a good thing for both of them.

"Thank you, Cam." He almost added an apology for earlier, but Zach refused to apologize any further for his feelings.

Zach watched Cameron turn and walk away, admiring, as he always did, how close-fitting his jeans were around his butt and thick thighs. Cameron's ass was the best sight Zach had ever seen, and he'd become fixated on it over their months together. It didn't matter what was covering it—denim, cotton, fleece—that ass always looked perfect, especially the way it swayed as Cameron sauntered away from him.

Three hours after Cameron left, Zach was at a loss. He normally spent much of his time with Cameron or studying. He wanted to get a job, but Cameron insisted he get his GED first. It was his way to get into college. He also wanted to get his pilot's license one day and often hung out at the hangar. From the moment he'd set foot in Cameron's helicopter, he'd been fascinated. Cameron was already giving him lessons on his days off.

In his fantasies, Zach had visions of him and Cameron one day flying rescue choppers together. They'd save the day, be the dashing heroes, and then they'd come home, make dinner, and eventually fall into bed together, spending the night wrapped up in each other, both literally and figuratively. Zach's imagination had been a lifesaver growing up—his only escape from his lonely life.

There were so many choices in this world that sometimes it was a problem. Too much to choose from and not enough time to do it all.

He'd spent the afternoon studying but knew nothing more would sink into his brain right now; he was too consumed with thoughts of Cameron.

From his seat at the table where he studied, there was a clear line of sight to where Cameron usually sat in the evenings, watching whatever program interested him at the time. Often, Zach was easily distracted from the show by Cameron's strong profile or the way his mouth curled up into a smile whenever something he was watching amused him.

Zach suspected part of Cameron's hesitancy was because he saw him as almost a child, too innocent for him to be with. Zach was innocent, inexperienced, but he could change that. Zach usually used the Internet for studying, learning more about math and history and other subjects for his GED. Maybe now it was time for him to do some learning of a different sort.

Relationships, loving ones, were what he needed to learn about. How they worked, what would be expected of them, how to be intimate. Zach blushed at the thought. His father had never given him any kind of information on how men and women were together, how babies were made. As for two men together, Zach had next to no idea how that would fit. But according to everyone, you could learn absolutely anything on the Internet.

To start, though, Zach turned his attention to the fully stocked bar, which up until this point he hadn't gone near. If he was able to sit and share a whiskey with Cameron at night, it might help Cam to see the man behind the innocence. Zach traced his fingers lightly over the pile of books he'd been reading, made his decision, and then stood and walked to the bar.

The tall bottle with the amber liquid Cameron usually poured his drinks from was less than half full, but a cursory glance showed him there was another full bottle toward the back. Zach picked it up and looked at the label. There was cursive writing on the label, but Zach didn't bother to read all of it. He didn't much care what it was called. He knew it was whiskey from Cameron's many comments that he was pouring himself a whiskey, and that's all he needed to know.

He reached for one of the glasses kept at the bar and poured himself a small amount like he'd seen Cameron do many times. He took the glass and moved over to the large blue armchair Cameron usually sat in and wiggled himself onto it.

Once he was comfortable, Zach put the glass to his lips and allowed a small amount of the liquor to trickle onto his tongue. As soon as it hit his throat, a burning sensation chased the whiskey down to his stomach, choking and gagging him until he was spluttering. He wasn't even sure how much of the alcohol he'd managed to swallow, but a strange warmth was settling in his belly.

Stubborn. He thought about Dr. Warren telling him he was stubborn. He'd said people had to be stubborn to grow up the way he had and not let it destroy them. He used his stubbornness now to take another sip even though he'd hated the first. He didn't like the taste at all, but perhaps it was the same as beans. He'd hated them when he was little but when there was nothing else to eat he'd shoved them in his mouth as though they were the best-tasting food ever. He'd persevered until he'd gotten used to the taste. Whiskey might be like the beans.

The second sip burned the same as the first, but this time he managed to get all of it down his throat, rather than having it sputtered all over his clothes. His gut was more than warm now; it was hot, and his limbs were tingly and loose. He knew Cameron sipped at his drink, often taking close to an hour before finishing a glass.

What did he do in that time? Cameron usually watched the television or looked contemplative while he was drinking. Is that what people did? Sip their fine liquor while contemplating the mysteries of the universe? Or possibly nothing so grand. Perhaps they were just sad because of how their own lives had turned out or were congratulating themselves on living a better life than they'd ever expected.

Zach took another sip and thought about his life. What did he have to congratulate himself for? Everyone he'd met since escaping from his father had told him how brave he was, but he knew they were exaggerating. They had no idea. If he was courageous, he'd have taken care of his father the way Ben had. An honorable man would never have let his father marry off terrified young girls. A courageous man would have stopped him. If he was strong...

When he looked at his glass, Zach was surprised to see it emptier than he'd expected. He took the last sip and rose to pour himself another. He returned to Cameron's seat and took a drink. This one didn't burn as much as the previous ones, but it did make his legs feel even more like jelly and his mind a little fuzzier.

Maybe he wasn't doing this right, because he couldn't understand how anyone got enjoyment out of picking their lives apart. What the hell was he supposed to do with the knowledge he was neither brave, nor strong? Was that why Cameron didn't want him? Because he saw the real man Zach was and not the bogus person people thought he was?

Another sip and another and soon they were going down so much easier than the first. When he stood to make his third drink, he was decidedly wobbly on his feet. He couldn't help giggling when he tipped headlong into the wall. "Sorry," he apologized to it. Thank goodness the wall was strong enough to hold him up.

By the end of the fourth tumbler, he'd had enough contemplation. Cameron didn't want him, and he couldn't blame him—he wasn't the man people said he was. That was the sum total of his deliberations, and who better to share his newly acquired insights with than Cameron himself.

He fumbled with the phone Cameron had bought him, easily finding his number in the contact list. He only had four names in there. *Another proud achievement in your ridiculous life.* Twenty-two and only four contacts. He'd seen how young people relied on their phones; every TV series made some sort of comment on it, how their phones were practically glued to their hands, and yet his was rarely touched—it and its four contacts.

"Zach? You okay?" Cameron's disembodied voice floated to his ears, and Zach gave a pathetic little smile at the sound.

"Cam. It's me, Zach. Zachary Abraham Piper, you know, and I just wanted you to know I understand. I know now why you don't want me. I'm not brave or strong, and I have this weird birthmark on my chest that kind of looks like a turtle. So I get it, ya know." He'd had a much better speech in his head before he called, but the words he'd been meaning to say flew from his mind, so what he'd blabbered might have to do.

"Zach. Where are you?"

"I'm in your chair. I'm sitting right where that great ass of yours usually sits."

"And what are you doing?"

"Well, I'm trying that bookies, bookman, book-something whiskey drink you enjoy so much."

"Jesus." He heard Cameron whisper through the phone. "Stay there. I'll be right home... And, Zach, don't have another drink."

"Hey...hey," he called to Cameron, who had either hung up or was refusing to acknowledge him. "You're not my father," he thundered. "I had one of those, and he wasn't a very good one," he finished lamely. He threw the silent phone at the nearby couch and watched as it bounced and toppled to the floor. He absently wondered if he'd broken it but couldn't find anything in him to care.

"Telling me not to drink more," he muttered to nobody in particular as he swayed his way back over to the bar. With any luck, he'd have this bottle polished off before Cameron set one beautiful foot back inside this house.

It must have been only fifteen minutes, or half a glass later, when Zach heard the front door open and Cameron's quick footsteps on the tiles.

"Zach," he called. "Zach, where—" Cameron's words cut off as he rounded the corner and caught him sitting in his armchair, tumbler resting against his lips.

"Cameron..." he sighed. "Where'd you come from?"

"I was at the hangar; you knew that," Cameron replied as he edged closer to where Zach sat.

Zach allowed his gaze to track all over that perfect body, resting for some time on the bulge at the front of his jeans. "I meant where'd you come from, now, into my life? Sometimes I think you're too beautiful to be real."

"Zach," Cameron said, his eyes lowering to the glass Zach held in his hand. "How many have you had?"

"Well, I had one but some of that I spat out—it really burns, ya know—and then I had another one that made me all hot inside, and then I fell into the wall when I went to get another one, but I drank that one and another, and then you said I couldn't have more, but I've already got a father, and so I had another one because you can't tell me what to do," he finished with a smile, ridiculously pleased with himself because he'd been able to get the whole story out.

"I'm going to get you some water and an aspirin. You'll be—"

Zach lurched to his feet, effectively cutting off whatever Cameron had been going to say. He wobbled the short distance to where Cameron stood with his hands on hips and something close to fear in his eyes. He put his glass on the coffee table, but somehow the table must have got up and walked away because the glass fell to the shag rug instead.

Cameron didn't move at all, not even when Zach put his hands on his firm chest and allowed his fingers to trace small circles into his, unfortunately, covered-up chest. For a moment, he watched his fingers as they slid along the fabric, but then he raised his gaze to Cameron's face.

The blue of his eyes, usually so pale, had darkened, and his pupils were enormous, almost covering the blue. Cameron's heartbeat quickened beneath Zach's fingers and his breath ghosted over his face. He inched closer until their lips were almost touching.

"Zach." The sound of his name feathered over his lips a second before Cameron's lips were pressing urgently against his. He had no idea who had leaned in the last few millimeters, nor did he care.

If he thought the whiskey had warmed him it was nothing to the inferno burning through him now. His fingers left that hard chest and seemed to slide their way up and into Cameron's hair of their own volition, tugging on the soft wisps.

Cameron's arms were wrapped tightly around him, his hands moving incessantly over his back, and it was comforting and arousing at once. For a second, Zach assumed the whiskey must have killed him and he'd somehow, against the odds, landed in heaven. But then suddenly he landed right back in damn reality as Cameron pushed him away.

"No. Shit. Zach, I'm sorry. We can't..."

"Stop apologizing. We can..."

Cameron shook his head and took a few more steps back away from him. "You've been drinking and besides that I... I can't."

"Why?" Zach pleaded, needing to understand how Cameron could walk away from something that, even to his fuzzy mind, felt so right.

"Look, let's make a deal. You drink the water and take the aspirin, then go lie down, and when you wake up, I'll explain everything."

Zach looked at him carefully, trying his best to fight through the fogginess of his brain to judge if he was being truthful. His eyes were suddenly heavy, his body exhausted, and he didn't feel so good in the tummy anymore.

"Okay, deal. But you promised, Cam. You promised," he finished as he closed his eyes. He legs gave way and he sank to the ground. Something warm and strong was suddenly holding him and he was floating to...somewhere...he wasn't sure where, but he didn't get there before he was out.

Chapter Nine

CAMERON

"Hey, Cam, everything okay?" Ben asked as soon as he answered Cameron's call.

As brothers—twins—he and Ben were close, but Ben would be wondering why he was calling so soon after their last call two days ago. It was normal for them to go at least a week between contacts.

"I fucked up," Cameron quietly confessed. He had suspicions about how this conversation was going to go. Ben would give him an ass kicking and express his disappointment with him—and it'd be well deserved. He wished Ben could tell him everything was okay and what he'd done wasn't too bad, but he knew it was. And Cameron was still in a self-flagellating stage people often went through when they knew they'd messed up and wanted to be punished for it. He needed to hear Ben's disappointment in him; he almost wished he could physically experience the ass kicking.

"You fucked up? How?" Ben's voice held a trace of amusement as if he expected this to be another of those times where Cameron called to berate himself for a usually imagined offense. Cameron had been conditioned to find blame in himself for everything. It remained a work in progress to break that conditioning.

"I kissed Zach."

When his confession was met with nothing but silence, he continued. "Twice... And the second time he was drunk."

The shame of his actions washed over him for the hundredth time since he'd managed to get a passed-out Zach onto his bed. He'd left him there—fully clothed—too afraid to even remove the young man's shoes, terrified he'd lose control of himself once again.

"Fuck, Cam. What happened?"

"He told me he liked me. I tried to push him away, and then he kissed me."

"And then?" Ben asked after a few moments of silence.

"Then I left; he got drunk, and when I came home... I kissed him again, Ben. What the hell is wrong with me?"

"Cameron, who ended the kiss?"

"Me. Both times," he whispered.

"Then it's not that bad."

"Ben, I kissed him. He's twenty-two and all kinds of messed up. And when he was drunk... And then months ago in LA, we... Jesus, I let him touch me."

"Like on your dick touch you?"

Cameron jolted at the bluntness of his brother's words, though he should have expected nothing less from Ben. "It didn't get that far, but I was naked."

"Do you need me to come out there?"

"No. You've got enough going on."

"This isn't about Jimmy, Cam."

But Ben didn't realize that everything was about Jimmy—still. Jimmy was the one who'd taught him what a bad person he was. He'd drilled the lesson into him repeatedly, so whenever something went wrong, Cameron could always trace the blame back to himself. Cameron was always in the wrong.

"It's my fault," Cameron quietly stated. "I took advantage."

"Listen to me. Zach's naive, yes, but he's an adult. Is he fucked up? Sure, but who of us isn't. Cameron, Zach deserves to be treated as a man who knows what he wants, and if he says he wants you, then you have to trust that."

"He's so innocent, though. You know that, Ben."

"Look, I get it, Cam, but Zach's an adult. Let me ask you this. Do you want him?"

Cameron had exhaustively asked himself that question. On the surface, his gut reaction answer was always yes but... He closed his eyes and thought about it, twisting the question around in his mind once more. Physically Zach pressed all his buttons. His long runner's limbs were lithe and toned; his ass was round and tight. But as perfect as Cameron found his body, it was Zach's beautiful face that he often was hard-pressed to drag his gaze away from. The heart shape framed his enormous green eyes and his soft bow-shaped lips. Though he was undeniably all man, there was the barest hint of the boy left on his sweet face. Cameron suspected it was his innocence peeking through.

But physical attraction didn't define a relationship—not a normal one anyway. There had to be more, and the potential was there with Zach. Cameron thought back over the last several months they'd been living together. The memories were mostly all good. Zach was intelligent and kind, funny in a way he didn't even realize, and he was incredibly easy to talk to.

"Maybe," he finally replied. "But I can't shake the feeling I'd be taking advantage."

"Is it that or just an excuse because you've convinced yourself you don't deserve him—don't deserve to be happy? And you can't let yourself trust him?"

Sometimes his brother was too astute for his own good. Cameron knew he didn't deserve someone as good as Zach. He had nothing to offer him but the surety of dimming the light that shone from him.

"Look, I'm not saying to rush into anything with him, but I am saying to think about it. Explore what's between you. I'm aware of what Jimmy did to you, Cam, but you do deserve to be happy. Jimmy was so wrong about everything, but especially that you don't deserve to be happy."

"Thanks, Ben."

"You got it, bro. You call anytime you need."

"I will. How's Ethan doing?"

"It's rough. He tries to be up for the girls, but he gets so angry about the time he missed with Maggie. He's got a lot to hold against his parents, but the one thing he won't forgive them for is keeping Maggie away from him. It's a heavy load to bear."

"He's got you to shoulder it with him. You won't let him down, Ben."

"I sure as hell don't intend to." The vow in Ben's voice was obvious and Cameron knew his brother wouldn't fail. "The girls are a good distraction. Three-year-olds, man. I believe they're the toughest humans I've ever faced off against. Damn pixies run rings around us most days. But... Jesus, we love them."

Cameron was humbled by his brother. His strength and loving heart. Those little girls may have lost their mother, but they'd be okay because both Ben and Ethan would make sure they were.

"I'm here if you need me. I'll do whatever I can to help. Remember that."

"Sure will. I love you, Cameron."

"Love you, too, Ben," Cameron said as he ended the call. Their family had always been close, but they'd never been an "I love you" family, at least not until they'd lost both parents. It had taken those two tragedies for him and Ben to realize they had to take every single chance they got to say "I love you" to each other.

Cameron wandered to Zach's door and poked his head in. He was lying exactly where Cameron had placed him. Hopefully, he'd sleep for a good long time because Cameron knew he'd feel like shit as soon as his eyes cracked open. He wished he'd been able to get an aspirin and some water into him before he'd passed out. It would have made waking up so much easier.

He returned to the living room, to his comfortable blue chair and sank into it, head in his hands. How had it come to this? Cameron was going to flay himself open to Zach when he woke. He'd have to go that far to make sure Zach understood. Cameron couldn't fall in love with him—he didn't want to.

ZACH WAS HORRENDOUSLY hungover when he awoke in the morning. Cameron never saw so much vomiting and seriously considered taking him to the hospital. He spent the day cleaning him, trying to rehydrate him, and comforting him when Zach was sure he was dying. It wasn't until early evening Zach finally settled enough to get some decent sleep.

The morning after he knew Zach was still feeling the effects of his overindulgence when he got nothing but incoherent grumbles when he poked his head into Zach's room to tell him he'd been called in to join the search for a couple missing hikers. By the time the hikers were found, it was late that night, and Zach had been blissfully sleeping by the time he made it home.

This morning, though, when Cameron awoke, there seemed to be nothing to get in the way of the conversation he was dreading.

"Morning," Zach spoke quietly as he entered the kitchen. He took his usual stool across from Cameron and absently played with the hot breakfast Cameron put out for him as soon as he heard him get up.

"How're you feeling today?" This was the first time, since the day before yesterday when all Zach had been able to manage were declarations of his imminent demise, that he seemed capable of a more comprehensive conversation than grunts and groans.

"Alive. Did you find the hikers?"

"They were found."

Zach nodded and continued to push the food around on his plate. Cameron wasn't sure if he should leave him to come to what he wanted to say in his own time or if he should start the ball rolling.

"Cameron, I'm sorry."

"Don't apologize."

"No. I shouldn't have had so much whiskey, and I shouldn't be trying to force you into something you don't want."

"Zach, let me explain. I promised I would."

Zach looked up at him for the first time, and Cameron noticed his pallor and the whites of his eyes threaded with red. He looked at Cameron for a few moments before nodding. "Okay."

"Okay. You eat and I'll talk. Deal?"

Zach offered him the barest hint of a smile before answering. "Deal."

"Um...okay, so shortly after I lost my dad, around eight years ago, I met a man who swept me off my feet. He was handsome and intelligent and witty, a lot of fun to be around. I was so vulnerable at the time. I'd lost both my parents in a short span of time, and Ben was away in the army. I fell completely and utterly in love with him, and for a while it was good. Very good. And then it wasn't." Cameron swallowed and sought the courage to go on with his tale.

There was still so much pain, so much shame. Even when talking to people who knew what happened, Cameron always felt ashamed of what Jimmy did to him—at what he became because he fell in love with a monster.

Zach's hand gently touching him jolted Cameron back into his kitchen. "What happened?"

"He wasn't the man I thought he was." He said, in a giant understatement. "It happened so slowly, so innocuously I never saw it...not until after it was too late. He started monitoring me with constant phone calls, wanting to know where I went during the day, who I saw. I was doing joy flights then, and he'd get upset if I didn't answer—even though he knew I couldn't. When I got home, he'd want to know everything about my day and my passengers. Then he started showing up unexpectedly during the day at work, at home, everywhere. It seemed like interest in my life at first, but then he started getting angry, very angry, if I wasn't where I said I'd be, if I didn't answer his calls, or if he caught me talking to somebody, particularly men he didn't know."

Cameron stood and poured them both apple juice. His body began twitching as it often did when he spoke about Jimmy. He'd long ago stopped trying to keep himself from fidgeting when sharing this nightmare with anyone. He sat again once the drinks were poured and immediately began fidgeting with the cutlery, the placemat, his glass, anything that got in the way of his wayward hands.

Zach's warm hands closed over his, stilling them. "Go on," Zach encouraged.

"After we moved in together, it got worse. He hounded me at work so much they eventually let me go. Jimmy said it was probably because the business was going under, and I never got a clear answer from my boss. I let him talk me out of thinking his behavior was responsible. Before I realized it, he'd cut me off from everyone. And then other things started. He began criticizing everything I did. He wanted things done in a particular way, and if I didn't do it—" Cameron shook his head at the memories. "My dinners were too bland, the house was never clean enough, I ate too much, was too fat. I said the wrong things at social functions and embarrassed him. Anything—everything—I did was wrong, and I believed him when he said I was to blame for his behavior. If I'd have done better, been better, he wouldn't need to get so angry with me.

"I've read and heard about domestic violence, controlled and battered women...all of that, but I never realized what was going on with me. I'm six-foot-four, for god sake, how could that happen to me—how did I let it?"

"You never fought back?"

"No. Zach, I didn't even know there was something I should be fighting back against. I lost who I was entirely."

Cameron enjoyed the feel of the slight squeeze Zach gave his hands, ridiculously comforted by such a small gesture. Zach's hands on his had stilled the incessant need to fidget.

"It wasn't till he put me in the hospital that I woke up to what was going on. And it was like waking up—from a nightmare or a delusion."

"Tell me what happened."

Cameron closed his eyes and inhaled a breath. "Jimmy never hit me except for an occasional slap. It was always mental abuse, emotional, the occasional shove. I was at such a low point when we met he didn't even have to work hard to break me. He easily convinced me I deserved the way he treated me—I didn't deserve better. But this day...this one day he came home and we'd had some new neighbors move in next door, a couple about around our age—ironically a straight couple. Matt—the neighbor—had come over to borrow a hammer so he could hang up something, a couple of prints I think, as a surprise for his wife. Jimmy came home and he seemed fine when he found Matt and me talking on the porch. He came over and joined us, chatted for a while. Matt went home. Jimmy was still fine."

Cameron drew in another deep breath and took a sip of his juice. His hands started fidgeting again, but Zach reached for them and squeezed harder, stilling them once more. Cameron looked over at him. Zach's green eyes were watching him; a million different emotions burning there.

"Later that night, Matt brought the hammer back. Jimmy thanked him, and within minutes of Matt leaving, he took the hammer and he...he hit me with it—over and over. He'd never hit me like that before, and I remember him hissing at me that he'd teach me for flirting with the hot new neighbor. He wasn't screaming at me, but he spoke through gritted teeth, seething with rage. Most of the attack is, mercifully, a blur. They told me at the hospital, Jimmy, he uh...he sexually assaulted me at some point, and then he walked away, left me for dead. Matt found me the next morning. They said if he'd hit me with the claw of the hammer, rather than the handle, I'd have been dead.

"When I woke up in the hospital, Ben was there, and I really believe he would have killed Jimmy if the bastard hadn't already fled town. I sometimes wonder if he's still looking for him; he'll never tell me."

"I'm so sorry, Cameron."

"My body healed, but in here—" He tapped his heart. "—and in here—" He tapped his head. "—not so much. The thing is, Zach, he took my trust—every single bit of it, and I haven't gotten it back yet. So when I say it isn't you, I'm not just saying that. I mean it. You're a wonderful young man, and if I could..." Cameron shrugged his shoulders. If he could, he would, but he didn't want to—trying to find love was too big a risk.

"They never found Jimmy?"

"No. Police weren't able to get a lead anywhere. He was a wealthy man, so when he wanted to disappear, he did. I haven't seen him in over two years, but I know he's out there. I get calls sometimes; no one speaks, but I know it's him. I get letters, too, horrible ones. He promised me once he'd never let me go...and I believe him. Took a lot for me to convince Ben to leave my side afterwards, though, and I haven't told him about the calls or letters. I'm pretty sure he'd move in if I did," he said with a half smile. Ben having his back had always been a comfort. "Ben needs to have his own life."

"So do you," Zach murmured.

They sat quietly for a time, the weight of Cameron's confession settling between them. Their relationship would never be the same again; how could it be? Zach would always look at him a little differently now. Perhaps with disgust because Cameron had allowed another man to treat him the way he had. Possibly with bitterness that he hadn't turned out to be the man Zach thought he was.

"He was like my father," Zach murmured, his gaze downcast on the bench between them. "Your boyfriend was like him. Manipulating you into believing you weren't a good person, weren't worthy of the best. My father brainwashed people to believe he was god on earth and whatever he demanded they had to give him."

"I suppose in a way they are alike." Cameron had thought that once before. Zach was right. Both men were very good at manipulating people, getting them to believe they didn't deserve any better than the way they treated them.

"This is gonna sound crazy, but I'm glad my father hated me. I'm glad he neglected me or beat me if I stepped into his line of sight. I'm glad he showed me the monster he was right from the start. At least it spared me from believing he was a good man."

Again Cameron was surprised by Zach's insight. It would be better to have always known a monster as precisely that rather than seeing someone you loved and trusted suddenly unmasked as one.

He hoped their talk was over, that Zach would understand now. He cared about Zach and never wanted to hurt him, so he hoped he knew why Cameron couldn't give him what he wanted, couldn't be the man he wanted.

"So, um, I'm going up today to do some more surveying for the NPS. Are you up to coming with?"

He watched as Zach's eyes brightened as they always did at the thought of going up in the chopper. Flying really was a passion Zach embraced with unbridled enthusiasm. He easily remembered the joy on Zach's face when he sat next to him in the cockpit the day Piper's cult had been taken down. Zach's world was going to hell around him, but he'd been unable to contain his simple joy at flying.

"You bet. Give me fifteen minutes to shower?"

"You've got ten. Hustle."

Zach laughed as he stood and started to run from the room. He stopped at the threshold of the kitchen and turned back to Cameron, who was watching him with what he knew would be a ridiculous-looking smile on his face.

"He's wrong, you know. Your boyfriend was totally wrong. You're perfect to me, Cameron. And one day I'll get you believing that too." He vowed and ran from the room, leaving Cameron utterly stupefied in his wake.

THE SKY WAS heavily clouded today as Cameron flew them toward Wapiti Ridge a short time later, they admired the scenery below. Seeing the land from above was a completely different experience. It looked so serene and peaceful.

"You okay, Zach?" Cameron asked. Zach had been quiet since their talk, but then Cameron had dumped a lot on him to think about.

"Yeah. It's so beautiful up here. I'm just admiring the view." Zach's voice buzzed through his helmet speakers.

"You never get used to it. Every time I go up, I'm shocked by how beautiful our planet is."

"It is, isn't it?" Zach absently replied.

"Zach...it's not gonna be weird between us, is it?"

"Huh? Nah... No way."

God, Cameron hoped it wasn't going to be. He had more to say, but he suspected Zach, much like himself, wanted to leave it alone—at least for now.

They had been flying in silence for a while when suddenly Cameron flung his arm out in front of Zach, pointing to the forest floor. "Bear," his voice boomed. "No, bears. Looks like a mom and her cubs."

Zach turned to follow the trajectory of Cameron's arm as he pointed. They were flying as low as legally safe in this area so Zach should be able to easily make out a black bear with two little copies if itself ambling along the tree line. Zach reached for the binoculars and put them to his face.

Over the months, Cameron had pointed out many of the national parks four-legged inhabitants: bison, moose, deer, elk, and even wolves, but these were the first bears he'd seen. They were beautiful. The little cubs ran behind their mother, pushing and shoving at each other like typical siblings, the mother turning every so often and poking each with her nose in some kind of indulgent behave yourself gesture to her young.

Zach was laughing at the playful sight. Cameron turned the helicopter, bringing them around for another pass right as they threatened to overshoot the trio.

"Oh my god, did you see that?" Zach laughed as the cubs somersaulted over each other. Zach brought his hand down on Cameron's arm, giving it a gentle shake. Cameron answered with a laugh, his skin warming beneath Zach's fingertips. He loved this connection with another human and didn't want to lose it.

They circled and watched the bears until the mother started leading them into denser forest. Zach suddenly turned to Cameron, who was staring at him with a giant smile on his face. Cameron quickly glanced away, feeling as though he'd been caught with his hand in the cookie jar.

There was definitely something between them, but Cameron was fighting it with all he had because the alternative scared the hell out of him.

Chapter Ten

CAMERON

"Are you sure you want me in there?" Cameron asked, for probably the hundredth time. It was obvious Zach was losing his patience. It seemed that was a fairly common thing these days. Cameron was so determined not to upset Zach any more than he had that it was all he seemed to be able to do now.

Every night after dinner Zach joined him for a whiskey, and though Cameron had no real problem with it—in fact, quite enjoyed the intimacy of it—the time would have been more enjoyable if Zach liked whiskey. From the faces he made, it was obvious Zach merely tolerated every swallow. He suspected Zach was trying to prove he wasn't a child.

"Yes, Cam. I've already told you I want you in there," Zach answered and then went back to fidgeting with the loose thread on his shirttail.

They'd driven to Cheyenne early this morning, the almost six-hour journey feeling even longer, thanks to the tension in the car. Zach was meeting with the prosecutor on his father's case at two. Marco Cortez was a thorough man, and he'd told them both over and over he wanted to make sure he—as Ellen Ripley would say—nailed Arnold Piper right to the wall. Cortez had told a stunned Cameron that Ripley was the greatest heroic character of all time. Despite the seriousness of his work and his hardass demeanor, Cortez had an almost jovial streak running through him.

Zach had given Cortez, the FBI, and the police his story previously—enough to get the indictment anyway, but Cortez wanted all the juicy details. He wanted every single grubby, criminal detail Zach could provide. Cameron knew the basics of Zach's story, but he'd been preparing himself for days to finally hear the minutiae of the horror of Zach's childhood and young adulthood. Twenty years living under a tyrant's rule. And yet, as Zach had so astutely pointed out, at least he'd never believed his father was anything but a monster. Zach hadn't had to deal with the devastation of uncovering the devil hiding beneath the visage of an angel.

Cameron's knee bounced up and down as the minutes ticked on. He hated waiting, always the waiting. He wanted to get this done so he'd know and understand exactly what Zach had been through.

"Are *you* gonna be okay?" Zach asked as he put his hand gently on Cameron's bouncing leg. The wayward limb stilled immediately.

"Sure, of course."

Zach looked at him and raised his brow. "Really?"

"I will be. I'm just... I don't know what to expect. We've talked about your past, but I suspect you were holding back all those times."

Zach looked toward his own feet and shrugged his shoulders. "I never wanted you to know all of it, but I can't stop that from happening anymore. Everyone will know soon enough."

"I'm sorry, Zach. I wish you didn't have to do this."

"Not your fault. I'm sorry you have to hear it, though. It's not a pretty story, but I guess we've all got our ugly tales." He looked pointedly at Cameron.

Cameron thought of Jimmy and the ugly tales he had to tell about him. The familiar wash of shame shook him to his core, but his body remained still under the gentle hold of Zach's hand on his knee. He knew there'd be physical beatings in Zach's story, and the best he could hope for was that they were no worse than his. The emotional stories... well, they were a whole other ball game. He suspected there'd be similarities between his and Zach's, but Zach had been a child trying to fight off a monster. Cameron had been an adult. He wondered how Zach's dad had tried to break his mind. They'd both lived with evil, and though Cameron had escaped after only five years—it had taken Zach twenty.

"Mr. Piper. Mr. Cronin. Please go on in. Mr. Cortez is ready for you." The young man at the reception desk called to them.

They rose together. Cameron started to reach for Zach's hand as they headed into the prosecutor's large office—it seemed the most natural thing in the world to do. He quickly pulled his hand back and, instead, schooled his features and walked stiffly at Zach's side. Cortez ushered them into a couple of comfortable high-backed chairs facing his enormous mahogany desk.

Before any words were spoken, the young receptionist came in pushing a cart containing several hot beverages and a plate of fancy-looking pastries. They'd placed their beverage order as soon as they'd arrived, and Cameron had to admire the young man's efficiency in having them prepared at exactly the right moment. He handed a large mug of black coffee to Cameron with a small smile on his lips. It made him look even more handsome, but it was nothing to the beaming smile he favored Zach with when he handed him his equally large mug of hot chocolate. Cameron saw their fingers touch when the mug exchanged hands and didn't miss the slight brush of the receptionist's finger over Zach's. As if that wasn't enough to fan the unwelcome flames of jealousy, he had to endure the answering smile Zach bestowed upon the man. The man Cameron now thought of as an outrageous flirt—unfair though the title may be.

"Thank you, Kaleb. I think that'll be all for now." Marco Cortez's voice could only be described as seductive, smooth like honey. It should have had Cameron's dick sitting up and paying attention, but he was too busy obsessing over the look that passed between Zach and Kaleb.

Cameron took a gulp of his coffee to give his mouth something to do other than growl a territorial warning to the young man. Kaleb offered another giant smile in Zach's direction, nodded, and left the room.

"Thank you both for coming." Cortez began, his tone immediately all business. "Zach, today I only want you to walk me through your life with Arnold Piper. And I mean yours specifically, rather than the other crimes you may have witnessed such as the underage marriages. We'll come to those another time when we're prepping for the trial. I know this is difficult and time-consuming, but unfortunately, we'll need quite a few of these sessions so I can be sure I have all the facts I need. I want to make sure I understand Arnold Piper inside and out."

Zach nodded, put his mug on the table and settled back in his chair. Cameron admired the composed manner he was approaching this whole situation with.

"With your permission, I'm going to tape our meeting today so I can refresh my memory at any time..." Cortez looked to Zach and smiled when he gave a "yes" and nodded his approval. "Excellent, let's begin then. Now, tell me about growing up with your father."

It was quiet for so long Cameron turned to check Zach was still sitting beside him. He knew how hard it was to say the kind of shit you'd waded through out loud, and he wouldn't really have blamed Zach if he'd have run screaming. Uncertainty danced in the rich green of Zach's eyes when he glanced at him. He reached across and squeezed Zach's knee, mirroring his comforting gesture from earlier.

Zach blinked and cleared his throat and seemed to come back to the here and now at his touch. "Um...my father was strict. He set high standards—ones I never seemed to be able to reach. There were rules—for everything. For how we were supposed to behave, for how things were done in the camp, everything. I'm not sure what I did or what rule I broke; whatever it was, it must have been when I was too little to remember, but somehow it made him believe I wasn't good enough. He thought I was evil, an affront to god."

Zach paused and looked down. Cameron saw the tremble in his lip. He squeezed his knee again, reminding him he wasn't alone. Zach turned to look at him, his eyes sad, but a tiny smile on his lips.

"Sometimes he'd go for weeks at a time without speaking to me or even seeing me, and then, all of a sudden, I was all he seemed to see. Those were the worst times."

"When you say he'd go for weeks without contact with you, who would look after you during those times?" Cortez interjected.

"Nobody, not really. The others in the camp were warned away from me. They were told I was evil, and no one should go near me, or try to help me. If god wanted me to live, then I'd live. That's what my father said. But he said I shouldn't have anybody's help to live but god's. I'd hide when I could so I didn't attract attention. I'd steal food; it wasn't hard. There were plenty of vegetables to take from the garden. None of the cabins had locks, so I could slip in and take some bread or whatever food was handy. Sometimes Phia would steal me some scraps. I'd sneak into the laundry rooms at night when it got very cold and sleep in the dirty laundry. None of us had clothes of our own. There was a communal wardrobe, I guess you'd call it, so I'd just take clothes that fit. I survived." Zach finished with a shrug, as though living the way he had as a child was no big deal. Cameron's heart ached for the scared and lonely little boy he'd been.

"None of the adults helped you?"

"No. You have to remember, Mr. Cortez, they all thought my father was god's representative on earth. They thought god spoke directly to him, so his words were god's words. And he said I was evil—so I was evil."

"And when his attention was drawn to you?"

"He'd watch me like a hawk, I was hardly allowed out of his sight, and then he'd end up hitting me for some mistake I made. Mostly it'd be a slap or a closed fist as I got older. But occasionally he'd pick up...whatever was in easy reach and throw it at me or hit me with it."

Zach held up his left hand, the one with several fingers that sat at unnatural angles. "He did this with a mallet. I'd been helping to chop wood all day. It was one of the few men's tasks I was assigned. Normally, I worked with the women because my father said I wasn't enough of a man to do a man's job. Anyway, a few of the boys who were supposed to be chopping with me spent the day goofing off. When my father came to check on our quota, he was not happy with the work we'd—I'd—done. I told him about the others, but...he didn't want to hear it, told me I was a liar. He nodded to one of his men, who held me down while my father smashed my hand with the mallet. The next day, I was still expected to chop the wood to make up for what hadn't been done the day before."

"Jesus." Cameron couldn't stop the curse slipping from his lips. He knew it had been bad, but the cruelty and illogical actions of Zach's father knocked the breath out of him. For the first time in his life, Cameron wished one of his brother's bullets had hit true when Ben had shot Piper.

"Did anyone witness his attacks on you?" Cortez's voice was as smooth and steady as ever. Cameron suspected, as a criminal prosecutor, he'd heard all this, and much worse, many times over.

"Ah, yeah. Sometimes he'd gather the whole commune to witness as he tried to beat the evil out of me. There'd be a beating from him and then his followers were expected to come and lay hands on me and pray. Most put their hand somewhere on me and mumbled a quick prayer before fleeing. A few felt it would be better for my rehabilitation from evil to get their own whacks in before praying for *me* to be a better person." Zach laughed, and it sounded slightly manic to Cameron.

"Zach, can I ask where your mother was during all of this?"

Cameron edged forward, eager to hear Zach's answer. He knew his mom had left or died when Zach had been a young child, but as much as he'd tried, he never got more details from Zach. He didn't know *how* young Zach had been or how his mother had died, if she had. It was something Zach never, ever spoke about.

"My mother...my mother died when I was very young. I only remember her a little."

"Did you have any siblings?"

"Not from my mother, but as you know, my father had many wives, so yes, I have many step-siblings, all younger than me. I think my mother was my father's first wife."

"Zach, can you tell me your mother's name?"

"Annie."

"And do you know how she died?"

"I think... I think my father killed her," Zach whispered.

Every atom of air in the room was suddenly sucked out, leaving Cameron gasping as his chest tightened and he fought for breath. He couldn't have heard right.

"Can you repeat that, Zach?" Cortez asked, far more calmly than Cameron could have managed.

"I think my father killed my mother...though it may just have been a nightmare."

Cameron turned to Zach, no longer caring about Cortez or the recorder or what they were here for. All he wanted was to take away the pained look in Zach's eyes. "What do you mean?" he asked quietly.

"I have this memory, from when I was very little, of my mom," Zach began, his gaze never wavering from Cameron's. "I must have been around five and we were at the stream one day. I was bathing and she was there, watching me. The memory is very hazy, but I remember my father came out of the trees and he was screaming—at my mother. I'm not sure what was wrong, but I remember a rock and thinking that he shouldn't be hitting her with it. And the water all around me was turning red. I don't know what happened next or if it was real or a dream. I've had similar dreams since but... All I know is that I never saw my mother again."

Tears had started trickling down Zach's smooth cheeks, and Cameron didn't hesitate to stand, pulling Zach with him and dragging him into his arms. He crooned quietly to him while Zach let his tears fall. This was probably the first time he'd spoken the fear out loud. Could it be true? Had Zach watched his father kill his mother?

Before they managed to pull apart, Cortez's quiet voice interrupted them. "I think that might do for today. I'm not sure what we'll be able to do with this information, Zach, but I'm going to pass it on to the authorities. They can do a little digging and see what they can come up with."

Zach's head nodded against Cameron's chest, but he made no effort to pull away and Cameron didn't want him going anywhere.

"It could be nothing. It might have been a dream," Zach's words were muffled against his chest.

"Maybe, but it might be something." Cameron looked across at Cortez and caught his answering nod. It may be that Cortez had more on his hands with this case than they'd originally thought.

Chapter Eleven

ZACH

Zach splashed another handful of the cooling water on his face. He couldn't believe he'd spoken his darkest fear out loud. He hadn't planned to, but as soon as the prosecutor had asked about his mother, his suspicion had fallen from his mouth. He hadn't been able to help himself.

So many times over the years, his mind had flickered with images of that day—or dream—quick flashes of long ago. Sometimes he thought that thinking his father had killed his mother was simply his way of justifying his mother's absence. Wasn't it better she was dead rather than the alternative—she'd abandoned him?

"Are you okay?" A quiet voice asked as Zach closed his eyes to splash more water on his face. It wasn't the voice he wanted to hear, though.

Zach blinked and looked in the mirror at the man standing behind him. It was Mr. Cortez's assistant, Kaleb. He was probably only a couple years older than Zach and maybe three inches shorter. He had a thick neck and a stocky build. He was handsome, made even more so by his wide smile. He didn't come close to Cameron's beauty, but he was an attractive man.

"Hey, Mr. Piper... Zach? Are you okay?" Kaleb asked again.

Zach realized he hadn't answered and attempted a nod. He wasn't okay, but he didn't need to share that with someone who was more or less a stranger to him.

"Are you sure? You look a little pale."

"Yeah. It was a difficult meeting."

Kaleb stood behind him, and Zach watched him nod in the mirror and then nervously look around. He shuffled his feet a little, giving Zach the impression he had more to say but was finding it difficult to get the words out.

"Actually, this is probably a little inappropriate, but I was wondering if you'd be interested in getting a drink tonight...with me?"

Zach started and turned to face Kaleb. Was he asking him out? On a date? Could Kaleb possibly be interested in him? Zach didn't have a clue what to say. He'd never even considered the possibility that somebody might ask him out. The likelihood had seemed remote at best.

Did he want to go out for a drink with this man? He thought of Cameron waiting for him out in the hall. They were staying in Cheyenne tonight, so Cameron didn't have to drive back home overnight. They'd made no plans for how they were going to spend the evening, but would it be rude to take off with Kaleb and leave Cameron behind? He supposed he could ask if Cameron could join them, but would that work? Would Cameron be happy about him going out with Kaleb—and did he care?

Cameron didn't want him—he'd made that clear. So why shouldn't he go and have a drink with Kaleb? Maybe it'd help him forget his mother. He knew Cameron would want to talk about it when they got back to the hotel, and he wasn't sure he was up for that. He'd be able to avoid the conversation if he went out with Kaleb.

"Zach?"

"Sorry. I just… I've never been asked out before." Zach cheeks heated with his confession. Should he have admitted that to Kaleb? Did it make him seem like a big loser?

Kaleb took a step closer and lightly trailed his finger down Zach's cheek. "Well, I'm happy to be your first." He winked. "So is that a yes?"

"Yes, thank you. I'd like that." Oh god, what was he doing?

"Well, great. Where are you staying tonight?"

"Um, the Townplace Suites. It's over on—"

"I know where it is. I'll pick you up at seven."

Zach nodded as Kaleb stared into his eyes. He was a little uncomfortable with the scrutiny but tried not to look away.

"Damn, you are beautiful," Kaleb whispered and leaned closer. For a second Zach thought he was going to kiss him, and he suddenly realized he didn't want that. Fortunately, Kaleb pulled back before he got any closer and then walked out of the restroom door.

Should Zach call after him and cancel the drinks? Maybe it wouldn't hurt to go, just so he could see what it's like to go on a date, even if he didn't want his date to kiss him. If he had some more experience, Cameron might not be so afraid to be with him. And somewhere deep down where he didn't want to look too hard he wondered if perhaps all he was doing was trying to make Cameron jealous enough to claim what had been his for months.

"Hey, Zach, you done?" Cameron's voice floated to him from the doorway. That was the voice he wanted to hear, but he knew he wasn't going to get the *words* he wanted to hear out of Cameron.

"Yeah. Coming." He hurried out the door, hoping the flush on his cheeks had died away.

"You all right? Did Kaleb say something to you?"

"Um, he asked me to go out for a drink with him tonight."

Cameron stopped walking beside him, so Zach stopped with him.

"Oh. Did he? And what did you say?" Cameron wouldn't look him in the eyes; instead, his gaze flittered all over but never came to rest on Zach's eyes.

"I said yes," Zach practically whispered. He watched a battery of emotions play over Cameron's face, but he couldn't name one of them. "Is that okay? I mean we didn't have any plans, so I thought…"

"We better get to the hotel then. You'll want to shower before you go out and… We should get going." Cameron turned and walked away. Zach didn't know if Cameron was happy, sad, or angry that he was going out with Kaleb. But he knew right now he regretted saying yes.

KALEB WAS NOTHING if not punctual. He turned up at the hotel door a few minutes before seven. Zach let Cameron answer the door as he finished getting dressed. They hadn't spoken any more about tonight since they'd left the prosecutor's office. Cameron had asked him repeatedly if he was okay after his big reveal regarding his mother but he hadn't wanted to talk about it, so Cameron eventually let the topic die.

Through the half-open bathroom door, he heard Cameron and Kaleb quietly talking but had no real desire to know what they were saying. Zach had always hoped his first date would be something he'd be excited about, and he'd be full of nervous anticipation as he got ready, careful to ensure he looked as good as he possibly could. Instead, he was thoroughly unenthused and decidedly anticlimactic about it. Of course, for the nearly six months he'd known dates existed—and dates with other men—he'd always imagined his first date would be with Cameron.

Zach took a breath and walked out of the bathroom. Cameron and Kaleb both turned to face him, one with a huge smile on his face and the other with something between a frown and carefully schooled nonchalance.

"You look great," Kaleb enthused. "Are you ready to go?"

Zach flicked a glance to Cameron before answering, "Sure."

He and Kaleb moved toward the door, and it was only then, when the ache in his heart bloomed, he realized he'd been hoping at some point Cameron would stop him. He'd wanted Cameron to fight for him.

"Good night, Zach," Cameron called as he walked through the doorway.

Zach couldn't find it within himself to turn and look at him. Instead, he called a simple "Night" over his shoulder.

Kaleb led him to a sporty little car, which he could tell, even in the moonlight, was a deep red. The seats were leather, and Zach seemed to melt into them rather than taking his usual hop to get into Cameron's massive Bronco. It was a cool night, but he warmed up quickly, thanks to the heated seats.

They didn't go far, and much of the trip was spent with Kaleb chatting about this or that, pointing out the places to go in downtown Cheyenne. They drove past several bars and clubs, where hopeful patrons were spilling out onto the street, waiting for their turn to enter. Kaleb pulled around a corner and found a parking spot in the quieter side street.

"There's a great little bar just back there. Good atmosphere and great buffalo wings," Kaleb said as they exited the car.

"Sounds good," Zach replied as he noticed how close Kaleb walked to his side as they headed back onto the busier street. He half expected him to reach for his hand, but thankfully, he didn't.

Zach was nervous, though not nervous about impressing Kaleb. He seemed nice enough, but he wasn't the man Zach wanted. He was nervous because he suspected, before this evening was over, he was going to have to tell Kaleb he wasn't really interested. A nice burn of whiskey right now would both warm him up and fog his brain so his thoughts wouldn't be so harsh.

There was no line to get into the bar Kaleb led him to, and while he found a table, Kaleb went to the bar and ordered drinks. There was a single table left toward the back wall, so Zach gladly took it. From where he sat, he was able to see the entire room: bar, dance floor, and entrance to restrooms. There was a crowd of people dancing to a rock song that Zach, in his limited exposure to music, didn't recognize. Some danced in couples and others in small groups. There didn't seem to be any rules as everybody seemed to be dancing together. Zach scrutinized the way their bodies moved, some seductive, some with talent, and others seemed to be jerking their limbs in random, graceless movements.

"Whiskey rocks for you," Kaleb spoke loudly to be heard as he came to the table with two drinks in hand. "Manhattan for me." He dropped into the seat beside Zach and inched it even closer, close enough for their shoulders to scrape, and if he moved his legs at all, his thigh rubbed against Kaleb's.

"Cheers," Kaleb continued and knocked his glass gently against Zach's.

"Cheers." Zach glanced around searching for conversation. "Do you come here a lot?" He finally settled for.

"Why, Zach, is that a line?" Kaleb asked, with a smirk on his face, and his eyelids fluttering.

Zach didn't have a clue what he was talking about. It seemed like a fairly straightforward question to him. He remained quiet, hoping that Kaleb would just answer his question.

"I come here a fair bit. How about you? Is there a bar you frequent up in Cody?"

"No. No, actually this is the first bar I've been to."

"Are you serious?" Kaleb asked, looking totally flabbergasted.

"Yeah. Cameron's a homebody, and I guess I am too. I'm not used to cities or towns, yet." Truth was, until recently, Zach wasn't even used to actual buildings. He'd grown up in tents mostly, and though some of his father's followers had been allowed into the towns and cities, he never had been, at least not once he'd reached his teens. Zach knew now it was mostly the men who'd been allowed to leave. Their only mission had been either buying supplies or luring women into the cult.

"Wow, of course. I should have guessed with you being who you are." Kaleb seemed to fumble his words a little, but the confident smirk was soon back. "So is Cameron, like your boyfriend? Or maybe just your sugar daddy?" Kaleb leered at him.

Zach took a large gulp of his whiskey, totally unprepared for where this conversation had started heading. He glanced around the room, wondering if anyone noticed his discomfort, but nobody was even looking at him, except for an older-looking man at the bar. He looked as though he worked there, and he was unabashedly staring at Zach. More than staring, his eyes were narrowed, and he was hardly blinking. Zach was so mesmerized by the stranger that Kaleb's question had slipped his mind, until he was brought back with a thud.

"Not that I'd blame you. I bet he's packing," Kaleb was saying and Zach suspected he'd missed a few words beforehand.

"Packing? I'm sorry I'm not sure what a sugar daddy is." Zach hated showing his naivety but better to confess to it than make a bigger fool of himself by pretending.

"Oh, you really are that innocent, aren't you? Are you telling me Cameron hasn't tried for that sweet ass of yours? Man must be crazy."

Zach couldn't believe what he was hearing and had no idea how to extricate himself from this situation. He took another swig of his whiskey and found the glass empty. Another glass landed on the table in front of him, and the waitress gave him a wink as she sauntered away. He felt he'd missed something. How come she'd brought him another drink? His mind was foggier than it should be after one drink. Across the room, Zach saw the barman still overtly watching him.

Kaleb's hand was on his thigh under the table and his lips were even closer to his ear as he continued talking. Zach was struggling to focus on the words being growled in his ear. He opened his eyes, and his gaze met the barman's. His heart was thumping in his chest, and his body was shaking. Kaleb's hand was rubbing along his thigh now, and his pinky made contact with his groin on every upward stroke. Sweat began to bead on his forehead, and the entire room seemed to be spinning.

Kaleb continued whispering in his ear, but the words seemed unclear, almost as though Kaleb were talking underwater. Zach couldn't make sense of what he was saying. And yet he knew they weren't words he wanted to hear from Kaleb's mouth.

He took another sip of his whiskey, but rather than the courage he hoped to find, it only made him feel worse. He dragged his gaze to Kaleb, who was looking at him with a frown on his face, but he was still too close. Zach needed to get away from him—he didn't feel safe.

"I think you'd better leave." A loud, stern voice floated down to Zach. He looked up to find the older man from the bar, but he was looking at Kaleb now, with a scowl on his face. Kaleb glanced between them both.

"Yeah. I think I better get him home," Kaleb replied.

"No." The stranger leaned in closer to Kaleb. "No, you've done enough for him. I suggest you get going before I call the cops on your ass."

Cops? Police? Why did the police need to be called? Zach was feeling terribly ill now. He was going to be sick, but he knew he hadn't had enough whiskey for that. Everything was spinning too fast, even though he was sitting, and he shuddered at the thought of trying to stand to walk back to Kaleb's car.

He needn't have worried because Kaleb was going without him. Zach watched his retreating back. He should be concerned about that, and he should be concerned about getting home, but he just couldn't be bothered.

The stranger took the seat Kaleb had just practically run from and extended his hand. Zach looked at it, for a minute not knowing what he was supposed to do with it, until he realized he should be shaking it. His brains had apparently fled the building with Kaleb.

"I'm Mitch, the owner."

"Zach." He heard his response, which sounded sloppy to his own ears.

"Zach, I'm sure your date slipped something in your drink. How're you feeling?"

Zach liked Mitch's voice. It was calm and gravelly. He smelled good too. And, up close, Zach could see his eyes weren't cruel at all, rather a warm brown that looked dark because his pupils were so dilated.

"Zach?" Oh, and he loved the way Mitch said his name.

"Yeah."

"I asked how you were feeling."

"Funny...awful." It was the best and most concise answer he could give. Mitch's words from earlier came back to him. "What'd ya mean he gave me something?"

"I believe he drugged you, Zach."

"Why'd he do that?"

"You don't know why a date would drug you?" Mitch's eyes widened, looking completely perplexed.

"No," Zach whispered. He was either gonna die from whatever Kaleb had given him or from the shame of being so stupidly naive in front of Mitch. He just wasn't sure which would come first.

Mitch's fingertips stroked against his cheek, and Zach leaned into the touch, welcoming it. "I think we better get you home, boy. Do you live around here?"

"I live in Cody. And I'm not a boy."

"Well, that's an awful long drive. And to someone like me, you are a boy," Mitch smiled at him, and Zach gasped at the beauty of it. "Are you staying somewhere close by?"

"Yeah. I'm at the Townsuites something... No, the Place in Town. No, I—"

"The Townplace Suites?"

"That's it." Zach laughed, delighted Mitch had read his mind.

"Come on, then. Are you staying here with anyone?" Mitch helped him stand and, thankfully, didn't let go as he walked him to a door behind the bar. Zach was far wobblier than he expected, and now that he was standing, the nausea really hit his stomach.

"Cameron. He's here," Zach managed, though he was finding it hard to concentrate enough to answer Mitch's questions.

"He's here or back at the hotel?"

"Huh...?"

"Come on, boy, work with me," Mitch grumbled and dropped him into a seat. "What's his last name?"

"Cronin. Cameron Cronin and he's..." Oh god, this was awful, and his brain was a mess. Mitch had let go of him, and even though he was sitting, he felt like he was being tossed around.

Zach heard Mitch talking, he didn't know to whom, nor did he really care. He just wanted to die. The rolling and dizziness and sick feeling in his guts were even worse than the first time he'd tried whiskey. His eyes drifted shut, and he hoped when he woke up this nightmare would be over.

"Jesus, what happened?" A voice asked. Zach liked that voice—he knew it and trusted it.

"Bastard roofied him. I wasn't a hundred percent sure at first, but I watched him closely."

"Where is he?"

"I sent him packing, but don't worry, I'll have his face plastered all over by tomorrow. He won't be welcome in any clubs around here."

What the hell were these people talking about? He thought one of them was Cameron. The identity of the other man was picking at his brain, but he couldn't focus.

"Need a hand with him?"

"Please. I'm gonna take him to the medical center for a blood test and pass it on to that fucker's boss. He's a local prosecutor, so hopefully he'll go after him."

Ooh, if that was Cameron, he sounded so angry, but Zach couldn't remember why he would be. His stomach ached and rolled, and suddenly, he was wearing everything that had been in guts a moment ago.

"Cameron's gonna be pissed at me," Zach slurred. His mouth tasted foul and the stench of his vomit brought tears to his eyes. He wiped his mouth with the back of his hand, but somebody pressed a wet cloth to his face and wiped for him.

"Jesus, Zach, are you okay?"

"I'm fine," he tried the words out, knowing they were a lie.

"You were drugged," Cameron stated, and finally it clicked to Zach that it *was* Cameron who was here. How he was here, he didn't know, nor did he care. He was safe now Cameron was here and he felt a rush of relief.

"He told you?"

"What happened?" Cameron edged closer, and Zach saw the pain in his eyes. He didn't fully understand what had happened tonight, but he knew Cameron was upset by it.

"Stay away, I'm dirty," he whimpered. He was covered in vomit and god knew what else. Behind Cameron was the barman who, he remembered now, had gotten rid of Kaleb. He was leaning against the wall with his arms crossed.

"I don't care, Zach," Cameron leaned forward and rested his forehead on his. "Did he hurt you?" Cameron touched him then, just a gentle brush of the back of his fingers over his cheek, but it was enough.

"No. No, I'm okay," he whispered, leaning into the touch.

"Jesus, Zach." Cameron suddenly moved away from him and paced a little. There was indecision in his eyes. "I don't know what to do. Should I take you to the hospital? Call the cops? This is my fault. I should have warned you."

Zach wasn't entirely sure Cameron was even speaking to him anymore; it seemed more like he was saying his thoughts aloud or maybe asking Mitch.

"Cameron, I'm fine." To prove himself a liar, he vomited a little more. "Tired and embarrassed." He spluttered in between heaves.

"You did nothing wrong, Zach," Cameron said as he pressed a wet cloth to his head again.

"Neither did you."

They watched each other for a few moments, but Zach really was very tired. He wanted to lie down and forget—just for a while—about his mother and his father and Kaleb. But most of all, if only for a while, he wanted to forget his feelings for Cameron and how they would never be returned.

Chapter Twelve

CAMERON

Cameron observed Zach from behind his sunglasses as the young man swam laps of the pool. It wasn't a precise or graceful stroke as he'd never learned to swim correctly, but he could do enough to move through the water. He'd taught himself by mimicking the actions of swimmers he'd seen on television. He thought Zach probably mimicked a lot of things as he tried to sort out who he was in *this* world.

Every time he looked at Zach lately, he experienced a sharp punch of pure guilt to his guts. Zach had been alone and incredibly vulnerable in a dangerous situation because *he'd* been hurt Zach had said yes to a date with Kaleb.

Cameron had been upset so he hadn't bothered to warn him about things he should be wary of such as date-rape drugs and other nightmares that can happen as soon as you dip your toe in the big pool. He'd been fucking jealous and petty and mad, and he'd let Zach go out unprepared. Zach had placed his trust in Cameron and he'd failed him.

He'd never be able to thank the owner of the bar enough for stepping in when he did. Even now, weeks later, Cameron could picture the look on Zach's face when he'd explained to him in the Medical Center what had happened to him and how it could have been so much worse. He could have let the cops explain it to Zach, but Zach was his—his responsibility. He'd have given anything, though, not to have seen the look in Zach's eyes or hear the betrayal in Zach's voice because someone had wanted to do bad things to him.

"What happened, Cam? Why did he do that?" Zach asked quietly, as though he didn't want the cop who was still in the room to hear him.

"Oh Zach, I'm so sorry. There's some men out there who only want one thing from their date, and they'll do anything to get it." Oh, Jesus. He didn't want to have this conversation.

"One thing?" Zach looked so young and painfully innocent sitting there in the medical center waiting for the effects of the drug to wear off. He hadn't been able to understand why Cameron, the doctors, and the cops had all wanted him to pee in a cup. Cameron had battled the urge to cry throughout the whole ordeal.

"Sex, Zach. He wanted sex from you, and he didn't care if you wanted it or not." Cameron said it fast like ripping off a Band-Aid, though he knew it was going to hurt no matter how he told him.

Zach's jaw flapped open and closed, open and closed, like a fish out of water. He finally snapped it shut and did his best to conceal the little whimper that escaped him. *"But I'd have said no,"* Zach whispered.

"Zach..." Oh why did he have to do this? *"You probably wouldn't have been able to say no and it wouldn't have mattered if you had. He didn't care at all about you or what you wanted. I'm so sorry."*

"I'm sorry. I didn't know—"

"Nobody knows when they're being drugged, Zach. That's how it works. This is not your fault. I should have warned you." It wasn't Zach's fault at all, but Cameron couldn't let himself off the hook quite so easily. He shouldered the blame for this one.

"He was really going to hurt me." It wasn't a question. Zach's words were trailing off as another bout of weariness came over him. The doctor said he'd sleep on and off for a while and might not be feeling much better the next day. It depended on what he'd been given and how much. "Cam?"

"Yeah?"

"Can you...will you just hold me? You're the only one I can trust."

Cameron pulled Zach gently from his chair and helped him over to the small sofa. Both of them ignored the cop, who quietly slipped from the room. He squeezed them both on the sofa, placing Zach so he was leaning back against his body. He held him as tight as he dared.

"You really have to go tomorrow?" Zach called from the side of the pool and sent a little splash Cameron's way.

"I'll only be gone two nights. Pam said you could go stay with her or at least have dinner with her."

Zach gave him one of those exasperated looks he was so fond of giving whenever Cameron hinted that Zach was young or naïve or incapable of looking after himself. Cameron wasn't sure how much of that night Zach remembered, but it was enough that he'd been happy when Cameron told him Cortez had fired Kaleb and was pressing charges against him.

"Like you said, you'll only be gone two days. I think I'll survive."

"Oh I know you will. Pam offered, though, and I'm just passing on the invite." If Cameron thought for a second he'd have his wishes answered, he'd wish for Zach to take up Pam's invite or maybe for the training in Utah to be canceled.

Zach swam the short distance across the pool and hauled himself out. He stood at the foot of Cameron's lounge chair dripping wet and looking rightfully proud of his physique. Zach's body was perfectly proportioned now that he'd put on a bit of weight and muscle. His arms and legs had bulked up nicely, but he'd retained his trim waist. He might have been one of those classical sculptures that graced all the top museums and galleries. But Zach was so much better. His body was firm and chiseled, but he still had a softness that promised to be so willing and pliant if Cameron were to lick a trail all over...

Cameron coughed and looked away before he tented his fucking shorts. A war was raging within him between head and heart, and no matter the winner, it promised to be a bloody battle. Even now his heart was screaming at him, thrashing in its bonds. It wanted him to go to Zach, pull his firm, wet body into his arms, kiss the ever-loving fuck out of him, and then tell him he never had to worry about a date gone wrong again because he was Cam's. His brain, though, was a goddamn cold, methodical lawyer arguing all the reasons why he shouldn't—and could never—do that.

"I thought while you're gone I might look for a job," Zach declared, bringing Cameron back with a thud.

"I said you don't have to."

"I know. I need to do something to contribute, though. I can't rely on you and Lucas and everyone else forever. One day you'll want your house back, and I...I need to stand by myself." Zach grabbed the towel from his lounger and started drying himself. Cameron did his best not to watch.

"You can stay here as long as you need to, Zach. You know that." Cameron's heart thudded dramatically at the thought of Zach moving away. Damn manipulative organ. Not to be outdone, his brain began listing the pros for both him and Zach if Zach moved out. But Cameron didn't need his own space and Zach could still be his own man and live under Cameron's roof. This round was going to his heart. "Even if you get a job, Zach, it's very expensive living alone, and I really want you to stay at least until college and your father's trial."

Zach sat on his lounge and peered over at him. "Aren't you sick of looking after me? Aren't you sick of my bullshit?"

What? "What? No. Why would you think that?"

"Come on, Cam. You had to teach me simple shit any twenty-something should know. I've thrown myself at you when you're so clearly not interested. You had to hear all the crap of my life, and now I got myself drugged on a date. I've been nothing but trouble for you. You don't owe me anything." Zach gulped in a breath, and Cameron wondered if he was as close to tears as *he* felt. He had no idea Zach was thinking any of this.

"Zach, I love having you here." Cameron sat up and swung his legs over the lounge to give his full attention to Zach. "I've never thought of you as a burden or problem or anything like that. You may not be giving me money to be here, but you've given me something better. Companionship and friendship. And I need those things more than money."

"It's...it's hard being here," Zach whispered.

"I thought you liked it here." Cameron wanted Zach's gaze on him; he needed to look into his eyes to catch the truth, but Zach had his head down. "Look at me," he ordered. "What's hard about being here?"

"It's hard because I can't stop wanting you. I've tried. I went out with Kaleb to try, but it didn't matter and wouldn't have, even if it had been a perfect date. All I did was compare him to you, wish it was you looking at me the way he did. It hurts."

"I'm so sorry, Zach." Jesus, he was a selfish prick. He hadn't even considered it might be hard for Zach after Cameron had effectively rejected him—several times. Oh he ached; he ached and hurt so bad. He wanted—Jesus he wanted—to give Zach what he was asking for, because down deep in his secret places he never looked at, he knew it was what he wanted too. But his motherfucking brain kept harping at him; it kept nagging at him that he couldn't. He wasn't strong enough, wasn't good enough—he didn't deserve it—his brain hissed in Jimmy's voice.

"I know you are and that almost makes it worse. Because I know it's you holding back, and I understand why. But the why hurts too because he should never have done that to you. You are so good and kind and perfect, and he ruined that, but only in your head, Cam, because the rest of us see the best in you."

Cameron closed his eyes against the fierceness and sadness in Zach's vibrant green eyes. Cameron didn't deserve any kind of care and loyalty. Jimmy had taught him—No! Fuck Jimmy. It was Ben's voice, Dr. Peterson's, the doctors and nurses at the hospital, Zach's voice pleading with him. Fuck Jimmy. Why did he listen so intently to what Jimmy had told him? Why take notice of the one when so many others told him differently? And his mother, his beautiful, kind, strong mother—she would never have raised an undeserving son. He had to believe that over Jimmy because the alternative was to make a mockery of all the work his parents had done to give him and Ben a loving home and unconditional love. Fuck Jimmy.

"Zach, will you promise me something?"

Zach looked up at him sadly, probably expecting to be asked to promise not to bring this up again or try to forget his feelings or something else that would crush his heart just a tiny bit more. "Okay," he agreed.

"Don't make any big decisions about your future yet." It was cruel asking Zach to put his life on hold while Cameron sorted out his, but the balance was shifting and for the first time Cameron was rooting for his heart.

"Promise." Zach nodded. "But I can think about things for the rest of my life, and the one thing I'll always know is that you're the one I want. That's not gonna change." He reached out and gently stroked his fingers down Cameron's cheek.

Cameron shivered at the touch, wanting it—needing it—but still turned away from it. Not yet. Maybe one day, but not yet. He had to think. The maybe was a start but...not yet.

Zach sighed and walked away from him.

Chapter Thirteen

ZACH

"Sure, I can let you know if anything comes up, Zach," Ellery Jackson told him. Ellery owned Elli's Deli, a convenience store, where Zach bought a lot of his and Cameron's groceries. He much preferred it to the Walmart.

Ellery and his staff knew him by name and always asked how he was and how Cameron was. Zach liked that. He appreciated their care, even if it was only part of their job. Zach thought he'd enjoy working there.

"Thanks, Ellery."

"Of course. Why the sudden interest in a job?"

Ellery knew all about Zach and his past. He asked a lot of questions and Zach didn't mind giving answers. "I'm an adult and adults have jobs," he stated, trying to keep it as simple as possible.

"Sure, all right. If an opening comes up, I'll be happy to give you a go." Ellery smiled his huge smile and continued ringing up Zach's items.

He bought a few things for his dinner and more chocolate. He had dinner at Pam's last night but wasn't going to impose on her tonight as well. Besides, he needed to get used to being on his own. Living with Cameron had spoiled him for company, but it couldn't last. Sure Cameron had told him not to worry about working and he could stay as long as he wanted, but Zach had to plan for the worst. And the worst was Cameron rejecting him again.

If only Cameron let himself trust. Zach understood why he couldn't, but it hurt, and it was frustrating. He'd seen Cameron watching him, and though he may be innocent, Zach almost felt the want in Cameron's gaze.

"Hey, Zach. Haven't seen you for a little bit."

Zach turned to the voice and smiled. "Hey, Jared. Where've you been?"

Jared came over and took one of his bags as Zach finished paying for his groceries and wishing Ellery a good day.

"I've been out on the East Coast finalizing that big deal I was working on."

Zach had met Jared in town a handful of times. He was a big man, taller even than Cameron and he was gorgeous. Dark haired, in stark contrast to the paleness of Cameron's locks, and from a distance, his eyes looked black, though up close they were a rich, dark brown. He looked powerful, panther-like, and sometimes when they met, Zach's spine tingled and his hair stood on end as if he were the prey this panther was stalking.

"Are you home for long?" he asked as they began walking to Zach's, or really Cameron's, car.

"Not sure. It depends on a few things. What're you up to?"

"Um, buying some things for dinner. Cam's away again tonight so…"

Jared's lips curled up and his eyes flared wide. Zach's insides wobbled a little. "Look, I understand your unique situation, Zach, but I wonder if you'd like to have dinner with me? It'll just be dinner. I won't expect anything more from you. I like you, and I want to get to know you better."

Zach had foolishly accepted a date with a stranger, and it had been a disaster. Perhaps he should have dinner with

Jared, even if it was only once. He kept hearing Ryan in his head. *Make them jealous and keep them interested.*

"Okay, but friends only," he warned.

"Deal. So where is Cameron?" Jared asked through the huge smile on his face. He really was very good-looking.

"Training in Utah."

Jared nodded and handed Zach the bag he'd been carrying to put in the trunk. "Okay. What if I make us some dinner, and we just hang out—oh wait my kitchen's being remodeled. Damn, and I wanted to make my famous stroganoff..."

"You could come over to Cameron's. I'm sure he wouldn't mind. His kitchen's huge," Zach offered and immediately wondered if he'd done the right thing. Would Cameron mind? No, he'd told Zach plenty of times it was his home too. Surely that meant he was able to have his friends over.

"Perfect. I'll come by at six?" Jared was already walking away before Zach had even answered.

"Okay. Do you want the address...?" But Jared was already around the corner. Jared had told him he'd lived in Cody his entire life so it was possible he already knew where Cameron lived.

Suddenly Jared's head popped back around the corner, his smile was sheepish. "Forgot to get the address," he said, blushing right up to his ears. "Here give me your phone." Jared held his hand out as he neared Zach.

He handed over his phone and Jared pressed a few buttons. Zach heard Jared's phone beep. "There. I sent myself a text from your phone, so now I have your number and you have mine. You can text me the address."

Another contact. *Yay me.* That still made only five, but Zach was wildly delighted by the ridiculously small figure.

"All right. See you tonight then." Zach drove home, confused by his own behavior. Cameron might be weakening on the whole "must keep Zach out of my heart" thing, and he'd just agreed to have dinner with another man. No, he'd agreed to have dinner with a friend. Cameron had to see Zach as a normal, healthy adult. And they had friends, and dinners with friends.

By the time six o'clock came around Zach was a mess. He'd spoken to Cameron earlier and told him about Jared coming over. Cameron knew about Jared, though the two had never met, and he seemed okay with the idea, so Zach tried not to worry. But what if Cameron thought Zach was moving on from him? What if he assumed Zach had given up on him and so stopped thinking that he might be able to trust Zach enough?

Zach jumped at the knock on the door, and he was shocked he was actually wringing his hands as he went to answer it. "Hey, Jared, come in," he invited when he opened the door to a smiling Jared. He was carrying a couple of canvas bags, a delicious aroma coming from them.

"Hey, thank you. I've brought the ingredients for the stroganoff, but I cheated and bought dessert at the bakery."

Zach led Jared along the hall into the kitchen. "Wow, Cameron's place is terrific," Jared commented as they went. It was a beautiful home. Cameron told him it was a ranch style, but all Zach could see was that it was comfortable—and home.

"Now, Zach, you sit and talk to me while I cook," Jared commanded and immediately took charge of the kitchen. "I'll find my way around the kitchen, don't worry."

"Um, okay. Can I get you a drink first?" He'd already had a whiskey, just enough to help him relax a little.

"A soda, any flavor, please," Jared answered as he spread ingredients all across the kitchen island.

Zach poured him a cola and resumed his seat at the island. "What would you like me to talk about?"

"Oh, anything really. You, your past, Cameron... whatever you'd like me to know." Jared moved so efficiently around the kitchen Zach wondered if he'd been here before, but he and Cameron didn't know each other so he couldn't have. "Tell me how you came to be here—specifically in this house."

For a second, he wondered if he was maybe jealous of Cameron but then thought if Jared ever met Cameron it would likely be the other way around. Jared would be jealous Zach got to live with Cameron.

"Well, I told you a little about my father and his cult..."

"Uh huh. I saw a bit about it on the news too." Jared's gaze was intense as he watched Zach. He didn't think he'd ever been the recipient of such intense focus from anyone. It was a little intoxicating.

"Well, it was actually Cameron's brother, Ben, and his partner, Ethan, who helped get me out. I was escaping from the camp with some others, and we ran into them. They helped us and they also went back to stop my father from killing his followers. Cameron was involved too— He was flying the chopper. We met and Cameron offered to let me stay with him." Zach took a sip of his whiskey, the churned-up memories needing a bit of fuzziness to dull the pain.

"You didn't want to go with the rest of the cult members? Did you have siblings? Your mother? Friends?" Jared asked with the same unrelenting fascination in his eyes.

"I'd never believed in what my father did. I'd always known he was cruel, mean—not loving like he said he was. I never fit in with his believers. My mother died when I was young." Zach gulped, remembering the admission he'd made to Mr. Cortez about his suspicions around his mother's death. He wondered if anything would ever come of it—and he wondered if he wanted it to. Maybe ignorance was bliss in this case.

"Phia—the girl I escaped with—and her sister, Mary, were my only real friends in the cult. My father had everyone else convinced I was bad—evil. No one came near me, really." Phia hadn't wanted to see him since the escape, and Mary's mother had refused to let him near her. She'd blamed him for the ruin of his father—the loss of her prophet.

Jared reached across the kitchen island and covered Zach's hand with his own. He gave a gentle squeeze and shook his head. Zach didn't fail to notice his touch didn't come with the same crackle of desire Cameron's often did. If Cameron never came around—never gave them a chance, would he have to settle for being with someone who didn't ignite a fire in him? What kind of a life would that be?

"I'm so sorry, Zach. Your father was a fool. Anyone can see you are a terrific young man." Jared shifted his gaze back to the meal he was preparing. "So Cameron was a bit of a hero, jumping in and saving you?"

Zach did see Cameron as a bit of a hero but not quite in the way Jared was clearly thinking. Cameron was incredibly kind and giving. Instinct and inborn compassion led to the offer of somewhere for Zach to stay. Cameron's heroism was surviving Jimmy.

"Cameron's a good person. He wanted to help me, and he'd never see himself as a hero," he stated simply.

Jared was quiet for a time while he cooked, and Zach was content to sit and watch. Jared must have been a fair bit older than him, perhaps even older than Cameron, but he didn't seem to have any family. The few times they'd met in town he'd seemed lonely, so Zach assumed that probably accounted for his eagerness to have dinner with Zach.

"Do you have family, Jared?" Zach had asked him this once before, but Jared had kind of danced around the answer, and then Zach's phone had rung and they'd never got back to it.

"My parents live up in Boston. I don't see much of them. They never really accepted me."

"Oh, I'm sorry." Zach understood not having the acceptance of a parent.

"Their loss. I have a sister, but I haven't seen her for almost three years now. I like to surround myself with friends and the occasional boyfriend," Jared said with a wink.

He didn't feel uncomfortable exactly, but he also didn't want to get into a talk about dating and boyfriends and such. With Cameron, he'd have jumped right in, but with anyone else, he was going to take his time.

They talked a little more while Jared cooked, mostly of trivial things. Their likes and dislikes, small things that told them a little bit about each other but no more of the important stuff. Zach wanted to keep his significant personal stuff for Cameron.

"This is great," he complimented Jared around a mouthful of his stroganoff.

"Thank you. I can't cook much else this well, but I can survive without needing to rely on takeout. Speaking of takeout—that must be new for you?"

"Yeah. We don't have it much. Cameron and I both prefer simple home-cooked food, but we have it maybe once a week."

"Cameron cooks for you?" Jared's eyebrows rose as though shocked he would do such a thing.

"Yeah. He's also taught me to cook a bit. Cameron's had to teach me a lot." Zach noticed the conversation with Jared often circled around to Cameron. He got the impression Jared was poking around trying to figure out if they really were just roommates or if possibly he'd have to compete with Cameron for Zach's affections.

Later that night after Jared left, Zach lay in bed thinking over the night. It had been pleasant. He liked Jared and had fun with him. But never once during the whole night had Zach felt the butterflies or the little throb in his heartbeat that he experienced so often with Cameron. Dating Jared would be like settling for eating beans the rest of his life when what he really wanted was the rich, comforting taste of the chocolate Cameron had introduced him to. Would he have to settle for the beans if the chocolate took himself off the table?

Chapter Fourteen

CAMERON

"Was that Jared, again?" Cameron tried to keep his tone even as he asked the question, but if he really wanted to prove to both Zach and himself that the phone calls with Jared didn't bother him, then he probably should have left the irritated "again" off the end.

"Yeah. He gets back the day after next and asked if I wanted to go to out with him on Thursday." Zach replied with a small smile on his face. *God, he was gorgeous.*

Jared had been calling Zach for over a week now, ever since the day they'd met up in town when Cameron had been away, and Jared had come to dinner. Cameron still felt sick to his stomach every time he thought of that night with Kaleb and the danger Zach had been in. He hoped Jared was no Kaleb, though he'd been alone here with Zach and hadn't hurt him, so that was a good sign.

He'd have to finagle a meeting with him so he could see for himself. There was no way he was going to straight-out tell Zach he wanted to do that, though, and have Zach thinking he didn't trust him. It wasn't Zach he didn't trust. Wait. *It wasn't Zach he didn't trust.* Cameron trusted Zach. The revelation had come so innocuously he almost missed it. He *trusted* Zach.

"I won't be around to meet him, which is a shame because I'd really love to." Cameron needed to meet Jared and make sure he'd look after Zach because he'd failed so spectacularly at that.

A part of him wanted to tell Zach not to go on the date, but he was his own man, capable of making his own decisions. Besides, Cameron still hadn't given Zach what he wanted, so why shouldn't Zach look for it elsewhere? Cameron had been so close, but then Zach had told him about Jared, and his conniving brain saw it as an out and overruled his heart.

"You have nothing to worry about, Cameron. The thing with Kaleb was my fault," Zach murmured, once again reading his mind.

They'd already fought over this, but Cameron was happy to do it again and again until Zach realized he was not to blame. "It wasn't your fault, Zach. It wasn't. You couldn't possibly have done anything differently."

"I could have known more of this world."

"That isn't your fault either. Your father kept you from it. And I could have—should have—told you about things like that. I should have warned you."

"Maybe. But I've been free of my father for months. It's time I learned more about this side of the real world."

Cameron couldn't help thinking Zach was already on his way to learning more about the seedier side of the world. If he could, Cameron would stick Zach in a bubble, where none of the evils of the world could harm him, but really he was twenty-two years too late for that. Zach had already suffered at the hands of his own father, a man who should have protected him. And in all the mess of Kaleb and with Jared coming along they'd barely had a chance to talk about Zach's mom.

Zach had been carrying the weight of his mother's disappearance around for years, and Cameron wanted to help shoulder the burden; he just wasn't sure how to do that or if Zach even wanted him to anymore.

"And you think you can trust Jared?" Cameron asked.

"I do. I'm happy to be friends with him. I'm comfortable around him. Not like with you, but that's...you're special." Zach looked up at him from beneath his lashes. Sometimes the things he said to Cameron left him speechless.

"Well, you don't want to date him, then?" An ache pressed upon him at the renewed idea of Zach on a date, but if he would not give himself to Zach—he could not—then it would not be fair for him to be anything but supportive as Zach went out to find someone else.

"I'd rather it was you." Zach's voice was so quiet Cameron barely heard the words. He closed his eyes against the wavering in his gut. He couldn't give in—he mustn't.

"Zach..."

"I know. I know what you said, but I can't help how I feel. And you're the one I want, Cameron." Zach shrugged and shook his head a little in apparent exasperation. "It's that simple. Jared's a friend."

Cameron nodded. Zach was clear about what Cameron meant to him. It was Cameron who was struggling to figure out his feelings.

Zach shifted his feet, his head bowed and Cameron waited. He knew Zach well enough to understand he was trying to find the words he wanted before he spoke again.

"Can I ask a favor?" Zach finally managed.

"Sure. What's up?"

"Will you take me on a date?" Zach's eyes never left Cameron's as he asked.

Zach amazed him every day. His trust in others should have been shredded to ribbons because of his father and yet every day he placed his trust in Cameron. He had more guts in his little finger than most people had in their entire body—Cameron included.

Before Cameron formed an answer, Zach continued, "Not a real date. I...I want you to show me what a date should look like so I know. I trust you, Cameron, and I need to know what a date should be, so if it isn't...at least next time I'll know."

How could he possibly say no—how could he possibly say yes? "All right. I'll take you out to dinner, but you have to know that—"

"I know. It won't be real. I know, Cam." Zach drained the rest of his glass, smirking a little as he finished. "Though if you wanted it to be real, you have to know I'd be okay with that."

Some days it was best to ignore the little hints and flirts Zach threw his way, brushing past them as though they were nothing when of course they were not. "Go change. Jeans and a button-down," he ordered lightly. Zach smiled and ran out of the room

How much longer could things stay this way? How much longer could he dance around the issue of *them*? The very last thing Cameron wanted to do was hurt Zach, but that seemed to be all he was doing. Maybe if Zach did start dating Jared, it would change everything.

Cameron wandered toward his own room for a quick shower and change. Every second, while he chose his outfit, or stood under the hot spray, or dried and dressed his body, he instructed his mind not to think of this as a real date. And every time his traitorous heart led him to thoughts of how to make the date romantic or how easily this could be real, he conjured up images of Jimmy—the emotional damage so much worse and more painful than the beating he'd taken from him. He knew Zach was nothing like that—but hadn't he believed the same about Jimmy? Wouldn't he have sworn on a stack of bibles that Jimmy had been the best of men?

"Cam? You ready?" Zach's voice rumbled through the quiet of his room, but Cameron barely heard it over the thunderous noise in his head. He quickly pulled his jeans up over his hips, tucked in his shirt, and turned to answer.

He found Zach standing in his doorway, his gaze fixed on Cameron's groin, the tip of his tongue peeking out to lick at his bottom lip. It had been a long time since someone had looked at him with such obvious desire—or at least a long time since Cameron had let himself notice.

"Just about," Cameron answered as he bent to slip his shoes on. "Let's go." He hustled past Zach as he walked toward the garage, doing his best to forget the lust on Zach's face—and was no doubt reflected in his own. He wanted Zach, no point in denying his attraction, and he suspected this fake date tonight was going to fucking kill him.

THE CODY CATTLE Company was pretty quiet, but then it was a Tuesday night. Cameron sat at the end of one of the long benches with Zach opposite. He left plenty of room between them and the next diners. Country and western music played softly in the background, but he knew the live music would start up shortly and drown out any conversation. Another reason, besides the food, to pick this place. He wasn't sure how to do this fake date—he barely knew how to do a real date—it had been that long.

"This place is great," Zach enthused, coming to life after the stifling silence of the car ride here.

"Food's wonderful and the music is usually terrific." Since Zach started living with him they'd tried many different foods: Italian, Mexican, Chinese, even a little

French cuisine, but Zach was used to plain foods, and not much of it, so even though he was building up his tastes Cameron knew he still preferred plain meats and vegetables.

"So how does this work again?" Zach asked, eyeing the buffet.

"Well, you grab your plate and pile on whatever looks good. You can go back for more. It's called an all-you-can-eat chuck-wagon buffet. Cowboy food." Cameron grinned. He loved the food here—his waistline not so much.

Zach picked up his cola and swallowed a large mouthful. "Shall we?" he asked before placing his glass back on the table and standing up. He held his hand out to Cameron. It was the most natural thing in the world for Cameron to take it as he stood.

"Let's," he replied and led Zach to the buffet. They piled their plates, Zach grabbing a variety of things Cameron suggested he might enjoy.

They ate quietly for a while as Cameron let Zach savor the new flavors and foods on his plate.

"So this is a date?" Zach asked around a mouthful of cornbread

"Well, yeah. Dates are for getting to know someone. There's usually a lot of questions and answers about your lives: jobs, hobbies, family. That sort of thing. It's wise to steer clear of topics such as politics and religion. Those two tend to cause arguments, like Dr. Warren said."

"I don't know anything about politics, and I'm not a fan of religion after my experience with Father, so I'm happy to stay away from them. Um, let's see. I know about your family and your job—that leaves hobbies."

"That's true. We do know an awful lot about each other. Comes from living together I guess. But typically on a date, you won't know as much, so what if you ask me questions?

Ask ones that will tell you the type of person I am. Then you'll know whether or not you'll want to see me—I mean your date—again."

Zach watched him steadily, a little smirk gracing his lips when Cameron slipped up and mentioned seeing him again. "Okay. Tell me, Cameron; I know you work hard, long hours and when you're not doing that you're working around the house—or you're with me. What else do you like to do that makes you happy?"

"I like working around the house, and I enjoy spending time with you, but something I really love to doing but I don't do often enough is gardening. My yard's huge, but it's all lawn. I haven't had time to put in a proper garden. A big one I can plant a variety of vegetables in." Cameron looked away, hoping Zach hadn't noticed the sudden sadness settling in him.

"If you love gardening, why did you look so sad just then?"

Damn Zach's almost freaky ability to read him. Only Ben had ever been able to see through Cameron so easily before. "I haven't had a garden since Jimmy. I had a beautiful one back then, spent hours in it. Until one day when Jimmy came home. I hadn't answered his calls—I'd left my phone inside while I was out in the garden. Anyway, he was furious, and he tore up my garden, pulled out every plant, trampled the seedlings, got the hoe and hacked everything apart." Cameron couldn't finish the story, couldn't bring himself to tell Zach what had happened afterward, how he'd degraded himself and pleaded with Jimmy to forgive *him*.

"I'm so sorry, Cam." Zach reached across and squeezed his fingers, stilling their trembling.

"My fault. I forgot the rules." He knew he'd said the wrong thing the instant the words were out of his mouth. Sometimes, even after years away from Jimmy, he forgot, still thought it was all his fault and not Jimmy's.

"How can you say that? How can you think that, Cameron? You told me it wasn't my fault what my father had done to me, and it wasn't my fault someone had drugged me. Were you lying? Is it my fault?" Zack's eyes narrowed, his lips pulled into a hard line.

"No, I wasn't lying. I know it wasn't my fault either, it's just sometimes I forget." Cameron shrugged. "Jimmy conditioned me, programmed me to believe everything was my fault."

"Well, don't forget—ever. You mean everything to me, Cameron, and I can't stand the idea of you blaming yourself for what that man did to you."

Jesus, sometimes Zach knocked the wind out of him. "How can you be so together? I mean you had twenty-one years of your father telling you that you were nothing, treating you like shit and you're way more together than I am. How?"

"It's like I said before, I guess. I always knew he was the bad guy. I never trusted him. You thought Jimmy was a good guy. You trusted him. And he broke that trust."

Maybe that was exactly it. Cameron had believed Jimmy was a good guy. And if he'd been so wrong about him, then how could he possibly trust himself to recognize another monster?

Chapter Fifteen

ZACH

Zach was having a good time. Sure, it wasn't as great as his "date" with Cameron had been, but he was having fun.

"Another?" Jared called to him over the din of the club. Zach looked at the glass in his hand and was surprised to see it was already empty.

He still didn't especially like the taste of whiskey, but he liked how it took his mind away from reality, made everything fuzzy, so his memories weren't so sharp, and didn't hurt him quite so much.

He nodded and watched as Jared signaled to the bartender for more drinks. Zach didn't take his eyes off the man who made them. Cameron had spoken to him about predators and how they drugged their victim's so they could take advantage of them. He had no intention of allowing a repeat of what happened with Kaleb.

"I'm sorry I didn't get to meet Cameron tonight. Where did you say he went?"

"Late training course. He went this morning. He'll probably be back by now." Zach replied as he noticed the little pull of longing, knowing Cameron was at home now without him. It was stupid; Cameron had already rejected him, but Zach couldn't help it. His rational brain didn't call the shots when it came to Cameron.

"He's still teaching you to fly?" They'd talked about this a little over dinner the other night, but Zach loved any opportunity he got to talk about flying, and how Cameron was teaching him. He was proud of both himself and his teacher.

"Yeah. I love it and Cameron's a great teacher. He's patient and knowledgeable. He's an excellent pilot."

"Rescue pilot, right?"

Zach nodded. "He works for the local sheriff, but he also does other work for National Parks, does some wildlife monitoring, stuff like that. He used to do joy flights, but he says...um...he says he got bored only flying tourists around. Said it was the same thing every day but with different people." Zach wasn't going to get into Cameron's past with a stranger. Zach took a little sip of his whiskey, determined to slow his intake.

There was silence for a while and Zach wondered if he should fill it. He was comfortable with silences around Cameron, but he was starting to feel a little awkward with Jared. Perhaps he'd freaked Jared out with talk about his past. He wouldn't blame him if he had.

"So what's your plan for the future?" Jared eventually broke the silence.

"Well, I'm almost finished with my GED, and then I want to get my pilot's license and go to college. Actually, what I really want to do—" Zach gulped. He couldn't believe he was about to share this with Jared. No one knew this, not even Cameron. "I'd like to work with Ben and Ethan," he practically whispered and waited for the scorn to come from Jared, but of course, he didn't know what Ben and Ethan did.

"Doing?" Jared encouraged.

"They run a business tracking and rescuing missing and kidnapped kids. There'd have to be times when a helicopter pilot could come in handy, or maybe if I do become a therapist, I could go in to help keep the kids calm. They were amazing when they rescued Maya and Riley."

"The nieces?"

"Yeah...I haven't told Cam that yet. I'm not sure what he'll say."

"How old are you Zach?"

"Twenty-two."

"Then Cameron's not your guardian, and you don't need his approval." Jared shrugged as though it was that easy. Yes, Zach was an adult, his own man, but in some way, he was connected to Cameron, and he didn't think that'd ever change. It wasn't Cameron's approval he was seeking—it was so much more. He wanted Cameron to respect him, to be proud of him, and if he was making wishes, he still wanted Cameron's heart.

"I know, but Cameron means a lot to me. He's been there for me, helped me, sacrificed for me."

Jared huffed, his lips quirking. "Sounds right. He sounds like a great guy. I wonder why he doesn't have a girlfriend—or is it boyfriend?"

"He doesn't trust easily. He had a boyfriend a while ago, and he um...he didn't treat him well. He abused him—badly." Zach cut himself off; it really wasn't his story to tell, but as always, the whiskey was loosening his lips, relaxing him probably too much.

Aside from that, he hated thinking about Cameron's ex and what he'd done. Zach had little in the way of real physical strength or muscles, but he knew if he ever got that monster in front of him, the fucker wouldn't stand a chance. Zach would tear him apart.

Zach noticed Jared visibly tense, his fists clench, and his lips draw tight, and he wondered at the strong reaction.

"Sorry," Jared gritted out, obviously noticing Zach watching him. "That kind of thing really burns me. People who believe they can treat other people so badly, especially when they do it to people they're supposed to care about or love."

It crossed Zach's mind that perhaps Jared knew someone who'd been abused or possibly he'd even been a victim himself. "I know what people who mistreat others are like. For my father, and I suspect for most abusers, it's all about power. My father wanted to be god on earth, worshipped and obeyed. I never toed his line, and he made me pay for it."

Jared shook his head. "Human nature never ceases to amaze me."

"Yeah. I don't get that guy, though. If Cameron was mine, I'd... Oh, sorry." Zach winced and lowered his gaze.

Rather than a bitter or nasty reply, he heard Jared chuckle softly. "So you like Cameron then?"

Did he go with honesty or did he try to distract Jared from this line of thinking? He was out with one man—he refused to call it a date, and he'd warned Jared that he only wanted friendship—and he was talking fondly about another. He sucked at this. Of course, he had no experience.

In the end, he went with honesty. "I kind of do, but he's um...he's not interested in me, anyway, so it doesn't really matter."

"He cares about you, though?"

Zach considered the question for a moment. "Yes, he definitely cares about me...but as friends only." He shrugged. Cameron had told him he cared, had proven it in the way he treated Zach. It just wasn't in the same way Zach felt about Cameron.

"It's okay, Zach. Cameron's your hero. How could you not have a little crush on him? I understand." Jared smiled. Zach appreciated his effort, but he was so wrong. It wasn't only a crush and it wasn't some kind of hero worship.

"Dance?" Jared surprised him with his one-word invitation.

Cameron definitely hadn't mentioned dancing when they'd had their fake date. Zach didn't have the first clue how to dance. There was no way...

"Come on," Jared encouraged. "I can't dance either if that's what you're worried about but look at the dance floor...half of them can't dance. We'll just move a bit and pretend. It'll be fun." Jared stood and looked expectantly at Zach. Something about the small grin on his face and the confident way he held himself told Zach Jared fully expected him to say yes to the dance. And he was right.

Zach followed Jared onto the dance floor. It was crowded but not oppressively so; they were still able to find a small corner of it to themselves. Zach looked around and saw other men dancing together and sighed with relief. Cameron had also warned him there were people who didn't approve of gay couples, and it could be dangerous for them to show affection in public.

Jared started moving as soon as they got on the floor. His hips swayed back and forth and side to side in time to the music; it was coordinated, and it was sensual, and Zach could hardly pry his gaze away. Jared was a very good-looking man. Zach remembered thinking of a panther when he'd first spotted him, and he was moving that lithe body of his now with all the grace of the big cat.

Jared's full lips tipped up at the corner, and he reached out and put his large hands on Zach's hips, moving them in sync with his own movements. After a moment, he pulled

Zach in closer, so their bodies were almost touching as their hips rolled to the sensuous beat. Zach was mortified when his cock hardened.

The feeling he was somehow betraying Cameron pressed down on him and yet how could he be? He was doing nothing wrong. And it was exhilarating to see Jared was watching his every move, licking his lips as he clearly enjoyed the way Zach's body was moving.

Cameron may not want him, but he was certain Jared did. Would it be so wrong to chase happiness in a different direction to the one he truly wanted if what he wanted simply wasn't an option?

Jared moved in even closer. He tilted his head forward so his lips were lightly skimming Zach's ear as he spoke. "You look so fucking hot moving like that."

Zach's entire body shuddered, and he wasn't sure, but he thought he felt Jared's tongue lick at the shell of his ear. He was hot and shaky, feverish all over and didn't know if it was the whiskey or the dance. The only thing he was certain of—and it was like having a bucket of cold misery thrown over him—was that if it was Cameron he'd been dancing with, he'd have been so turned on he might have come right there on the dance floor. How could he ever settle for less than that?

Jared dropped him home a little before midnight, but Zach was feeling too buzzed to sleep. Sure he'd realized going out with Jared was settling for less, but what was he supposed to do if Cameron refused to let him any closer?

At a loss for what to do and feeling the absence of Cameron's company, Zach meandered toward Cameron's bar. He'd had plenty already tonight but one more... He poured himself a drink and something else caught his eye.

On the dining table, Cameron's laptop was still set up and begging for Zach's use. He remembered his idea from months ago when he'd considered using the Internet to learn how to be gay—or rather what to do with another man if he ever got the chance. He walked over, pulled out the chair, and made himself comfortable. He took a few sips of his drink while the laptop booted up.

He opened the web browser, as he'd been taught, once the screen was available and stared at the Google search page. What did he look up? How to be gay? Maybe. What to do with men? No. He needed specifics. He typed in men having gay sex and hit search. As usual, a long list of options was presented to Zach and he briefly perused them before clicking on one near the top of the list. He was taken to a site called Pornhub. He had no idea what it was, but his screen soon filled with rows of thumbnails, each containing a tiny image of two mostly naked men together.

Zach took a gulp of his whiskey, his brain registering he'd emptied the glass already. He quickly stood and poured another, deciding he needed more of the liquid courage to click on one of the images.

He settled back into the chair, took a sip, and clicked. It led to a bigger screen with still more thumbnails. Zach clicked on the play arrow and was immediately greeted with the sight of two men kissing. Neither wore a shirt and one man's shorts were unbuttoned while the other man had nothing but a pair of briefs on. He leaned forward, mesmerized by the almost savagery of the kiss. It was nothing like the sedate kisses he'd seen on the TV. The men pushed and pulled at each other as though each was trying to consume the other. Their hands were roaming all over, tugging at whatever clothes were left, their grunts and groans going straight to Zach's cock, filling it until he was hard.

There was nothing gentle or soft about what the men were doing; it was more animalistic than he'd expected. Unable to look away, he blindly reached for his tumbler, taking yet another sip of the burning liquid.

Once the men on screen were both completely naked, one of them began trailing his lips down the other's torso, stopping to give attention to each nipple before making his way farther south. Zach watched, wide-eyed, as the man— now on his knees—nuzzled his face into his partner's crotch.

He took another sip and jumped a little when the kneeling man opened his mouth and swallowed the hard cock in front of him. The standing man groaned long and low and let his head fall back against the wall, his lips parting as moans and whimpers fell from his mouth.

Zach had never really imagined such a thing, but watching these men on the screen now, their pleasured faces, the sounds they were making, Zach's mouth went dry. What would it feel like—taste like—to have Cameron's hard cock in his mouth? He vividly remembered the size of it and wondered how he could possibly get something of that size to even fit in his mouth? And how would it feel if Cameron's lips were wrapped around his length?

Zach's hips started to roll as though they were searching for his pleasure. A tingle spread through his groin. An overwhelming feeling of something building flooded him, but he had no idea what he needed.

He'd had orgasms before. Zach didn't think anyone needed to be taught how to touch their own dick; there was nothing more natural. But there was a feeling that he was missing something every time. And he strongly suspected a partner—more specifically Cameron—was that something.

Suddenly, on the screen, the man on his knees surged up and pulled the other man to him, their ferocious kissing resuming. They manhandled each other toward the sofa in the background. The video clearly jumped ahead when one of them was suddenly on his knees with his arms resting on the back of the sofa. The other was standing behind him holding his own cock and tracing the blunt tip over his partner's ass cheeks. With his other hand, he pulled one cheek, giving Zach a view of the man's hole for just a second before it disappeared beneath the cock now rubbing back and forth.

Zach paused the image and stared at the two men on the screen. Both frozen, one looking intently at the spot where his cock was touching another man's ass and the other looking over his shoulder with nothing but pleasure written all over his expression. Were they really going to do what Zach thought? How could it work? He jumped up and ran for the whiskey, bringing the entire bottle back to the table. His hands trembled as he refilled his glass before resuming the video.

His own pleasure was long forgotten as Zach watched the man on the sofa pant and squirm as the cock was slowly pressed inside. They both stilled once they were groin to ass, and the man behind trailed kisses softly down his partner's back. It only took a moment before he grabbed the man's hips and pulled back. Zach saw his cock almost come right out before he surged forward, forcing it back in. Over and over he did this, and louder than the sounds of their groans and gasps, Zach heard the men's skin slapping together.

The man kneeling on the sofa seemed completely overwhelmed as he took the pounding being given to him. His head thrashed from side to side as he panted and called out "yes, yes, god yes" repeatedly. Both bodies were slick with sweat, their muscles flexing as they moved. Zach had never seen anything more amazing—and a little scary—in all his life. How could they make themselves so vulnerable to each other?

Zach's gaze was glued to the screen. The two men were really moving now, and Zach admired the strength of both to keep up such a punishing pace. They must be exhausted.

Finally, the man with his cock in the other called out "I'm gonna come." He pulled out of his lover and stroked himself a handful of times before spilling his seed all over his partner's ass. Zach blinked at the screen, completely engrossed in what he was seeing.

"Zach?"

Fuck. Zach never jumped so high in his life. He was used to being startled by his father, but this was so...so much worse. Cameron's voice came from behind him, so he must see what Zach was watching on the laptop.

He swallowed, delaying turning and facing Cameron until he'd found his courage. But it took less time than he thought, thanks to the whiskey in his veins, and he fumbled around, his line of sight directly level with Cameron's waist. With a quick glance, he could see the outline of Cameron's cock, nestled in the loose support of his boxers. His mind flew back to the kneeling man who'd taken his lover's cock into his mouth so enthusiastically. He wanted to do that—he wanted to do that to Cameron so badly.

"Zach...um," Cameron tried, gesturing helplessly to the laptop where Zach knew the image was still playing.

"I didn't...I don't...I...um...I don't know how it all works" was his rather lame explanation. "Sex. I don't know how it works, and you said I could find the answers to anything on the Internet."

Neither moved as they continued watching each other. Cameron said nothing. Zach felt the red boil of anger flooding his veins. "I'm an adult and I can watch this if I want to. It's none of your business." He smirked in satisfaction as Cameron flinched at his words.

Zach stood, defiantly facing Cameron. He wasn't sure if it was the shame of being caught driving him to bogus confidence and unwarranted outrage—or the whiskey.

"Of course, Zach. You're right. Um, but..." Cameron's face flushed and he glanced nervously around the room. "If you have any questions, you know you can ask me. Okay?"

Come to him with questions? Zach wanted to go to him for answers, yes, but he wouldn't be asking the questions Cameron wanted to hear. He wanted Cameron to be the answer to what he felt missing every time he took his own pleasure. He wanted Cameron to be the missing piece of his heart; the one who would make even his darkest moments feel so much lighter. He wanted Cameron to answer how another man's cock in his mouth tasted or how it felt to be inside another man.

Zach nodded and saw Cameron's gaze flick to the whiskey before he turned and walked away. Was he more disgusted with Zach for watching the men having sex or for drinking the whiskey? Would Cameron ever see him as an equal and not the innocent, pathetic, damaged son of a monster? Would Cameron ever see *himself* as worthy again?

Chapter Sixteen

CAMERON

"So your date went well, then?"

"We're not dating, but yeah, we had a good time. I guess. Jared's nice. Easy to talk to and we had fun."

"That's a good start. And um..." Cameron shifted uncomfortably; not quite believing what he was about to say, but after what he'd caught Zach watching after his date with Jared the other night, it probably should be said. "Um...so there's no rush you know. I mean it's okay to take your time...get to know each other before..."

Zach flicked a quick glance at him but was, thankfully, too distracted by handling the cyclic and fiddling with some other controls to be able to fully turn and glare at him.

Today was his day off, which worked out for the best because Marco Cortez called last night wanting to see Zach this morning in Cheyenne. Rather than drive there way too early this morning, Cameron—well Zach really—was flying them in the R22. This was the craft he used to teach Zach, because the pilot had to do the work in this one, unlike the rescue chopper, where the computer more or less flew it.

It had taken Cameron a long time to spend the insurance money from his mom and dad, but every time he went up in the R22, he knew he had made the right decision. His parents would have approved of spending the money their deaths provided him on the helicopter. Flying was his bliss, his sanctuary from the madness of the world.

"So, do you think you'll go out again?" Curiosity burned through him, forcing the question out. Zach and Jared were none of his business, but he couldn't stop himself from wondering. Zach had been tight-lipped ever since their first non-date date, only telling Cameron he'd had a good time but little other details.

He'd also seen Zach watching porn a few more times since the night he'd caught him. He seemed fascinated by it, but Cameron supposed it was similar to someone who'd been denied food, gorging themselves on anything edible when they suddenly came across it. Zach must have questions, but so far, he'd been completely unwilling to ask any.

"He said he'd call me when he's back from New York." Zach's response was short and lacked any sort of excitement—and Cameron was disgusted with the little fist bump going on in his head at the idea the relationship with Jared was fizzling out already. He should be hoping for Zach to find happiness, even if it wasn't with him.

They flew in silence for a while, Cameron watching proudly as Zach shifted the cyclic and maneuvered the pedals and collective skillfully. Some people were just born to fly.

"What do you think Mr. Cortez wants?" Zach asked after a while.

"No clue. We had an appointment to go down in two weeks for another briefing, so I'm guessing something unexpected has come up...something that couldn't wait."

Zach didn't look away from the clear sky in front of him, but Cameron knew he'd see worry in his bright green eyes if he did. "Maybe my father has decided to plead guilty and save us all a trial."

"That'd be great, but don't get your hopes up."

"Oh, I'm not, believe me. My father will never think he's done anything wrong unless he snaps out of his delusion." Zach pulled at the cyclic and depressed the left pedal to swing the nose left, assuring the R22 was on the correct course. This was the longest flight Zach had piloted, but he was doing beautifully.

"Thanks for coming, Cam. I know it's your day off and all. I'm sure there are lots of places you'd rather be."

"Can't think of one." Cameron grinned, hoping to cheer Zach up, but he remained subdued and quiet, completely unlike his usual self.

They talked little for the remainder of the flight and drive to Cortez's offices.

Cameron was not surprised to see a middle-aged lady now occupied Kaleb's seat. He itched to ask Cortez about his former assistant as he and Zach were ushered into his office. There was no way Cortez would have fired Kaleb if he hadn't been sure of his guilt. Damn, he'd love to get his hands on the little creep. His anger at Kaleb distracted him from the anger he felt toward himself for not warning Zach about the dangers of dating.

"Thank you both for coming. I'm sorry for the short notice," Cortez said as he gestured for them to take the seats opposite him. Cameron didn't miss the third seat sitting empty next to theirs. "We're just waiting on Detective Marshall. She'll be here in a few—" The phone on his desk buzzed, but Cortez made no move to answer it. "Well that'll be her now," he confidently pronounced. Cameron wondered if the buzz was simply to signal his client or whoever he was waiting for had arrived.

Detective Marshall strode into the room oozing the kind of confidence police had to have. She shook Cortez's hand and then turned to him and Zach, not waiting for introductions. "Mr. Piper and Mr. Cronin," she stated and shook their hands and then took the empty seat. She was exactly the kind of no-nonsense cop represented on television.

"Detective Marshall, Zach and Cameron have just arrived so if you'd like to go first…"

"Thanks, Marco." She rifled around in the file she held in her hand and pulled out a photograph. She held the eight by ten image right in front of Zach's face, and Cameron heard a small gasp escape his lips. "Mr. Piper, can you confirm this is your mother?"

Zach reached out and gently touched the smiling face of a teenage girl. His hand shook and Cameron desperately wanted to do something to ease the tremble. "Yes. I think it is her. That's how I remember her, anyway. It was a long time ago, and I was only about five, but in my memories…that's her."

Detective Marshall and Cortez glanced at each other and exchanged a small nod, but otherwise remained quiet.

"Who is she?" Cameron burst out, unable to keep quiet.

"This is Anna Malcolm. She was reported missing, possibly kidnapped, almost twenty-five years ago. She was only fifteen at the time."

"Fifteen," Zach spluttered. "My father took her when she was only fifteen?"

"That's our working theory as of now. We've spoken to a few of the other cult members who are willing to talk to us. One of them confirmed she was your mother and also corroborated your story that your mother simply disappeared one day when you were very young."

Zach's body folded and his head went between his legs. Cameron stood immediately and leaned over him, gently rubbing soothing circles into his back. Zach's body shuddered as jagged breaths were ripped out of his lungs, the trembling in his body worsening as the news sunk in.

"Could we get some water, please?" he whispered to Cortez who immediately picked up his phone and murmured something.

Cameron knelt beside Zach. He kept up the circles as he tried to get Zach to look at him. "Zach? What can I do?"

Zach raised his head a fraction, but Cameron saw the stark fear and sadness that had overrun the usual levity in his gorgeous eyes. "I hoped it was a nightmare," he whispered brokenly. "She was real, though, and he might have...he might have killed her."

"He might have, but we don't know for sure yet. Would you like some water? And then we can listen to what else the detective has to tell us."

Zach nodded and sat up, reaching for the glass of water Cortez held out for him. The room was quiet as he took a few sips and then rested back in his seat. "Sorry. I'm okay now," Zach said to the room in general but kept his focus on Cameron. Cameron did his best to show Zach he had his full support through his touch and the look in his eyes alone.

"Are you all right if I continue, Mr. Piper?" The detective asked.

"It's Zach. Please call me Zach," Zach said as he nodded for her to continue.

"Thank you, Zach. I'm Helen." She smiled. Cameron saw the human behind the tough detective for the first time. "We haven't contacted Anna's family yet. We've been waiting for confirmation, but you should know you have grandparents, Zach, and lots of cousins from what we understand. Anna's parents never stopped looking for her—never gave up. It may be possible to do a DNA screen to confirm you're their grandson if you're both amenable to that idea."

Zach looked to Cameron, confusion on his face. At some point, one of them had reached for the other's hand, but Cameron wasn't sure who. Not that it mattered. The important thing was, hopefully, his touch was now offering comfort to Zach. "It's a test they can do to confirm you're related. If Anna Malcolm is your mom, then her parents' DNA will match in part to yours," Cameron explained.

"Yes. Yes, I'd like to do that, please," Zach said as he turned back to Detective Marshall.

"Okay. Well, I'm going to fly out to see them shortly. We just want to get as much information as we can before I speak to them. Unfortunately, they've had their hopes built up and crushed before. So, I want to be as sure as I can be before I go to them. I'll be going to see your father tomorrow. I want to see if he can offer us anything."

"Like what?" Zach asked.

"Well, a confession would be nice, but I'm hoping he'll at least confirm the ID and perhaps even tell us what happened to her. Whether your memory turns out to be correct or not, we'd like to know where Anna Malcolm is."

"Can we do something about what he did to her?" Zach turned and addressed his question to the prosecutor.

Cortez shook his head. "At this point, no. We'd need a lot more evidence, more information. We don't know what happened when Anna went missing, or if Piper did anything to her. With some basic math, she'd have been nineteen when she had you, so we can't even go after him for rape of a minor. Unless other cult members start talking, we've got nothing."

"Zach, do you know if your father kept any kind of record of where his camps were located and when? Any way for us to be able to work out where the camp might have been around the time your mom disappeared?"

"I don't…no, I don't think so. The only ones who might have known or kept records were Mr. Watson and Mr. Lloyd. They were his second in charge."

Detective Marshall made a note in her pad and then stood. "Zach, I'm going to do the best I can to find out what happened to your mom. I'll keep in touch, okay?"

He and Zach stood and shook the detective's hand. She exchanged a quick "be in touch" with Cortez and then left. Cameron's head was spinning so he could only imagine the whirlwind that must be sweeping through Zach's.

"Zach, do you have any questions?"

"No. Not yet. I don't know what to think."

"Understandable," Cortez replied. "Detective Marshall is an old friend who works on cold cases. I contacted her about your mom after your last visit, and she's been searching through missing persons and any um…Jane Doe bodies that have turned up over the years, trying to match the timeline. Anna Malcolm seemed to fit. When she took the photo to the cult members, and she was recognized…" He didn't need to explain any further.

"Thank you, Marco. For helping Zach." Cameron stood and offered his hand.

"Of course. I hope it's helped. I wish we'd found out more, but it's a start. Now as to the other matter. The police have charged Kaleb. Unfortunately, he did make bail. It should be a fairly cut-and-dry case, but I will need to depose you before trial, Zach. We can do it when you come in to talk to me about your father. After that, I won't need anything from you until the trial."

"Thank you, Marco."

"Of course, and to be honest, I'd be surprised if he didn't plead guilty—he knows better than to take me on." Marco stated. Cameron thanked him again and they shook hands.

Cameron led Zach from the building to their rental car. There was no time frame they had to stick to, and Cameron was fairly sure Zach wasn't up to the flight back to Cody just yet. He drove them to Cahill Park, hoping to find a bit of quiet for Zach as he parsed what had happened in Cortez's office.

The parking lot was empty, which was a good sign for the solitude he was after. Once they stopped, Cameron got out and walked around to the passenger door, opening it for Zach and ushering him out.

"What're we doing here?" Zach asked.

"I thought we could take a moment before we headed back." Cameron walked to a cluster of trees, Zach following closely behind. He lay under the largest tree, his back on the soft grass, and his hands clasped behind his head. He squinted up at Zach who still stood over him and then uncurled one arm to pat the grass next to him.

He closed his eyes and smiled as Zach huffed and lay beside him.

"You okay, Zach?" he murmured.

"No."

"What can I do?"

"I don't know."

"Whatever it is, when you figure it out, I'm here for you, Zach."

"I know... And that helps."

It was only a handful of words, but it was enough. Cameron had Zach's back always and now he knew Zach understood that. In a perfect world, they could have had more, but Cameron was so broken he refused to even try. But somewhere, in the back of his mind, an itch was starting, a whisper that perhaps he was strong enough to attempt to find love. Maybe, just maybe, he did deserve someone like Zach.

Chapter Seventeen

ZACH

He wasn't having a good time at all tonight; he was out of sorts—upset by the news of his mother. He'd been moping for three days since the detective had shown him the photo and told him she may have found who is mother was. Not even Cameron had been able to pull him entirely from his dark mood, though his company helped soothe his aching soul. He'd give anything to be home with him now but somehow Jared had talked him into coming out tonight. Zach had been nothing but a wet blanket most of the night, though, his mind consumed with his mother and Cameron.

The only two people he'd ever loved—and Zach believed he loved Cameron—and both of them were out of his reach.

Jared had dragged him out onto the dance floor again, but it wasn't like other times they'd danced. The music was louder and the tempo faster. There was no seductive swaying of their hips; instead, it was more a thrashing of their limbs as they let go and allowed the music to move them. Zach was glad of the change because he didn't think he could endure sexy dancing with Jared tonight.

As one song ended, another rolled straight into it, not allowing the dancers a moment's rest. Zach lost track of time passing as he tipped his head back, closed his eyes, and let the beat thunder through him. He'd already had a bit to drink but suspected the alcohol was probably seeping out of his pores as his exertions and the heat of the dance floor made him sweat.

He was aware of Jared moving somewhere close by. Even with his eyes closed, he felt the intensity of Jared's stare roaming over his body. Jared had been different tonight—flirtier and more handsy.

They'd talked a little at dinner, but Zach hadn't told him anything about his mother and he wasn't quite sure why. He'd always found Jared easy to talk to, but his mother was too private—too intimate—and Zach wasn't ready for that.

A hard, bony elbow nudged into his side, and Zach's eyes popped open. Jared's smiling face was close to his own as he flicked his head to indicate he was leaving the dance floor. Zach followed close on his heels as Jared led him to a table in a different area of the club, a quieter section less full of bodies.

As soon as he sat, Jared moved off to the bar without even asking Zach what he wanted. In truth, he probably should have gone after him and insisted on water, but another whiskey might make his brain so fuzzy it'd be incapable of forming the image of his mother or picturing what may have happened to her. Maybe his brain would be sloppy enough so he could pretend Cameron loved him back while he was at it.

When he returned to the table, Jared passed Zach his drink and clinked his glass against Zach's calling out "Cheers" with a big grin on his face. Zach tried to find a returning smile but knew from Jared's expression he had failed miserably.

"You okay tonight, Zach?" Jared squeezed his hand as he asked the question, and though the touch wasn't at all repulsive, Zach knew it wasn't the one he wanted.

"Yeah. Tough week. I'm sorry I'm not much fun tonight."

"Hey, now, you're great company anytime." Jared took a sip of his drink, watching Zach closely. "Anything to do with Cameron?"

Nothing and everything. Everything was so tangled up. His life was a jumbled mess of wool with every thread somehow coming back to Cameron. "Not exactly. I just had some surprising news recently, and I can't quite wrap my head around it."

"Something you'd like to share?"

"Another time maybe. Actually, if you don't mind, I'd really like to go home..."

For a second, Zach thought he saw a flicker of something—something not quite right in Jared's eyes, but it was gone just as quickly, leaving the warm brown eyes he was used to behind. "Of course. Finish your drink, and I'll take you home. Will Cameron be there by now?"

Zach didn't even need to check the time to know. "Yeah, he'll have gotten home not long after you picked me up. We should have stayed for you to meet him I guess." Zach had wanted to, but Jared had seemed keen to go, so he'd left a note for Cam letting him know they'd left early.

"Sorry I was early. I guess you'll just have to blame it on my eagerness to see you again."

Zach took a large gulp of his drink, hoping to finish it quickly so they could leave. Before he'd completely drained it, though, another turned up at the table. Zach looked questioningly at the waiter.

"Oh, sorry, my fault. I left a standing order for them to replace our drinks when we were finishing them up. I'll cancel it when the waiter brings my next one over." Jared smiled and Zach did his best not to be angry. None of this was Jared's fault: not his mood, or his mother, or Cameron.

"Your dancing is getting better," Jared said after a short silence. "I can see you're really letting yourself go around me. I wonder if you're that relaxed around Cameron."

Zach didn't see the link in what Jared was saying. He was more relaxed around Cameron than anyone, and he thought Jared understood that. Maybe he was jealous.

"One more dance?" Jared encouraged as they finished their last drinks. Zach's body was already moving to the beat before he'd even given his answer, and Jared smiled—wolfishly—and pulled him onto the dance floor.

It was even more crowded now, so Zach had no choice but to press his body up close to Jared's. They moved much as Zach remembered from his first dance with Jared, with the other man's hands caging his hips and their lower bodies rubbing against each other as they swayed.

Zach didn't even register when Jared moved closer and his lips brushed his ear again. It was a different kind of shiver that raced up his spine this time.

"Do you have any idea how much I want to fuck you right now?" Jared pulled back and looked into Zach's eyes. Zach tried to focus his gaze, but everything was fuzzy and wobbly. He didn't reply—had no idea how to. He wanted to relax and enjoy this—enjoy Jared's body so tight up against his own and the feeling of being desired. Jared's question pinballed around in his head and Zach desperately wanted to nod and tell him yes. He wanted to desire Jared the way he craved Cameron. He wanted to say yes and hope that Jared's body could make him feel good enough so thoughts of Cameron never broke through his defenses again.

"You are so fucking gorgeous, Zach, and Cameron is a bigger fool than even I assumed if he lets you get away without even sampling that tight ass of yours," he growled into his ear again when he leaned in close.

Something was wrong, very wrong, and Zach wasn't sure if it was with him or Jared—or perhaps both. His whiskey brain wouldn't fire, wouldn't let him think clearly. There was something there—some thought was scratching at the edge of his mind, and it was getting louder and harsher as though demanding to be let in and looked at. If he let that thought in, everything would change. He didn't know how or why, but he knew.

"I really need to—" His words were cut off by the press of Jared's lips to his own. They'd kissed hello on the cheek before, but this one was different. It was on the lips and was almost violent, proprietary in an overwhelming way, and Zach's first thought was that he wasn't Jared's, had never been, and he'd been a fool to try to be.

He squirmed in Jared's arms, doing his best to push him away. Jared only pulled him closer, and Zach couldn't understand why. Was he misreading Zach's squirms as passion rather than an increasingly desperate attempt to free himself from the unwanted kiss? And if not, why wasn't he stopping if he knew Zach didn't want this?

From behind him, Zach felt a large body collide with his own, hard enough to dislodge him from Jared's vicelike grip. He turned and looked into the eyes of an enormous middle-aged man with the bushiest beard Zach had ever seen. Beside him was a younger, much smaller man who wasn't allowing much space between him and the giant.

"Sorry, man," the giant smiled at him and then sent a terrifying glare in Jared's direction. Zach wondered if he'd noticed his distress and done it on purpose. Regardless, he was just glad of the chance to get away.

Zach moved quickly, heading toward the bar. What was he doing here? This wasn't what he wanted. Jared wasn't who he wanted.

Cameron had told him to either call him or grab a cab if he needed to leave a date and the man he was with couldn't or wouldn't take him. He asked the barman to call him a cab, planning to stay right where he was until it arrived.

Jared wasn't far behind and began spluttering apologies as soon as he caught up. "Zach, I'm sorry. Are you okay? I assumed it's what you wanted... I thought you were enjoying it." He was saying the right words, but Zach had no idea if they were sincere or not. There was none of the usual warmth to his tone. It was as though he thought of the apology only as something perfunctory—something he had to do whether he believed it was needed or not.

Zach shook his head, not quite trusting himself to speak. They'd both had a bit to drink. Had Jared really done anything that bad? Maybe Zach *had* wanted to kiss him and do more with him, but when the crunch came, it all felt so wrong. Should he blame Jared for that?

"It's fine," he finally managed. "I'm just going to go. I'm really not up to this tonight. I shouldn't have come. I'm sorry." Zach looked up and saw the barman point to the doors. Zach turned and fled without waiting for a reply from Jared or even saying goodbye. He didn't miss the giant man and his smaller partner standing right outside the door. They watched him as he stepped into the cab, neither moving until he was in the cab and safely on his way.

Zach had no idea what time it was when the cab pulled up to Cameron's place a short time later. It couldn't have been too late, though, because the whole house was lit up like a Christmas tree. He paid the driver and made his way inside, doing his best to keep the noise down.

He kept one hand on the wall to steady himself as he stumbled along the hall, the extra whiskeys taking their toll on his coordination.

"Zach?"

Damn, he wanted to make it to bed without running into Cameron. He really wasn't up to answering questions about how the night went—simply because he just didn't know.

"Yeah, it's me. Sorry I woke you." He doubted he'd woken him as he heard Cameron coming toward him from the living room, but still it was something to say.

"How was—Zach, are you okay?" Cameron asked as he rounded the corner.

"Of course," he snapped, unreasonably irritated Cameron could read him so well. And why did he always ask if he was okay as though he was incapable of looking after himself? He watched as indecision turned to determination on Cameron's handsome face.

"Are you sure? You don't look so good."

"Thanks," he spat and then softened at Cameron's obvious flinch. "It's late and I'm tired."

Cameron studied him for a moment and then smiled. "It's only nine thirty, but I don't doubt you're tired after this week."

"What's that supposed to mean?" The snippy tone returned to his voice but couldn't stop it.

Cameron started at his uncharacteristic ill temper, but it only made the anger already smoldering in Zach burn hotter.

"I know you think I'm some useless kid, and I know *you* don't want me, but that doesn't mean I *am* useless or that no one else wants me."

"Goddamn it, Zach, I do want you, but I can't have you." Cameron's eyes widened with his unexpected confession.

"Why not, Cam? Why can't you have me?" he pleaded, but when Cameron turned away from him without giving an answer, Zach's anger flared into an inferno. He walked closer toward where Cameron stood with his back to him, his heavy steps thumping on the tiled floor. He waited until Cameron eventually turned.

"Did you know Jared wanted to fuck me tonight?" he thundered. "And do you know how close I came to saying yes?" Cameron remained silent, but Zach saw something ripping its way through his eyes. Was it fear? Sadness? Anger?

"But it's not him I want, Cam. It's not his hands I want to feel all over my body. It's not him I want to share myself with. And it's not him who I want to show me what it's like to be with someone. It's you, Cam. Always you and it fucking hurts that you don't want me back."

"Zach...please."

Zach wasn't sure what Cameron was pleading for, but he'd never seen him look so heartbroken. He shook his head, leaned over, and placed a gentle kiss on Cameron's lips.

"Night, Cam," he whispered, "I love you." His words were spoken so softly, a mere puff of breath, so he wasn't even sure if Cameron heard him, at least not until he heard Cameron's breath hitch and his entire body shuddered.

Zach turned and headed for his room, surprised when Cameron followed him.

All he managed when he got there was to kick his shoes off and fall onto his bed. His eyes were closed before he even hit the mattress. He felt Cameron move farther into the room and then sank into the warmth of the blanket he laid over him. Cameron's fingers gently carded through his hair, but Zach was so very close to sleep.

"Night, Zach." He heard Cameron whisper but he must have been dreaming because he also thought he heard him say "I love you too."

Chapter Eighteen

CAMERON

"Jesus Christ, Cam, I told you to be careful with him."

"I am… I was," Cameron argued.

"Really? Because you just told me he came home rolling drunk, told you he loved you, and your response was silence, followed by standing at the end of his bed watching him sleep for hours like a creeper. And *then* taking off first thing this morning, before he woke up, so you could avoid him for a while longer." Ben's voice rose with his exasperation. Cameron couldn't blame him. He was just as frustrated with himself.

"I didn't know what else to do, Ben. I'm lost here. I can't give him what he wants."

"Why?"

"You know why. How can I possibly give him anything when I'm so broken myself?" Cameron whispered, hating the weakness he heard in both his voice and his words. The weakness he suffered every single time he remembered what Jimmy had done to him.

"Jimmy didn't break you, Cam. He bent you the hell out of shape, but you are not broken."

Cameron let Ben's words lie for a moment and then rolled them around in his head for sense, tasting them on his tongue for truth.

"You don't think I'm broken?"

Jimmy had isolated him, beat him, mentally tortured him, and raped him over a period of five years. Cameron hadn't even been aware enough to realize that every time Jimmy made him have sex with him when he didn't really want to—when he'd told him no—had been rape. The nurses at the hospital had been the first to point that out. It had taken James Reilly five short years to rip away every tiny bit of self-esteem and respect Cameron had possessed and pulverize it under his boot.

"No. And I never have. I know—at least I'm guessing I know—only a fraction of what that bastard did to you, Cam, but you beat him. You got away."

"So did he," Cameron murmured, wondering if Ben would admit he was still hunting him.

"Not forever. One day, Cam…"

The familiar lump bulged in Cameron's throat, but it had been a long time since he'd cried over Jimmy. His sorrow this time came from the revelation slowly beginning to form in his mind—if he refused to grasp onto possible happiness when it was slapping him in the face, then he was continuing to allow Jimmy control of his life. He was letting Jimmy win.

"How could I be so weak? How could I let him do that to me?"

"You were strong enough to survive. Strong enough to get away and rebuild your life. He got to you at a time when you were alone and vulnerable. You aren't weak, Cam. You trusted him, and he shit all over that. But if you keep pushing happiness away… Look, this is really simple. How do you feel about Zach?"

"I care about him," he hedged.

"*I* care about him, Cam. That's not what I'm asking. Could there be more than just caring about him?"

"I think there could be. I think I could love him, Ben, and that scares the hell out of me."

His brother remained silent for a while and Cameron shifted nervously. Ben thought fast on his feet and that was devastating enough, but when he really stopped and considered something all the way through, his insights could flay a person open.

"Do you remember Mom and Dad?" Ben finally asked.

"Of course, I do."

"No. Do you really remember them? Do you remember how Dad used to put his arm around Mom and never leave her side when they had to go to a social function because he knew how anxious Mom got about them? Do you remember how Mom used to rub Dad's arms when he started getting worked up about something and how quickly it calmed him down? Do you remember how we could never ever divide and conquer them when we were kids—because they were such a team? Do you remember that?"

Cameron walked through his memories of his parents. They'd adored each other, but more than that. They were, as Ben said, a team. He never saw either parent break because when one faltered, the other was always there to prop them up.

"Yeah, yeah I do remember."

"You could have that, Cameron. I know you could because Mom and Dad taught us how. I have it with Ethan, and you can have it too. Jimmy was—well, I hate that he hurt you so much—and is still hurting you," Ben said, confirming the idea crystalizing in Cameron's mind. It was time to take that last little sliver of power back.

"You're right, Ben. You are so fucking right—and you know how I hate telling you that 'cause, ya know, your head is already way too big." He laughed, trying to bring some levity into the heavy conversation.

"Asshole." Cameron heard the smile in Ben's voice. "Look, it might not be with Zach, but you can find it and you will. And, yes it broke Dad when he lost Mom, but even if I lost Ethan tomorrow, it's worth it. It is so fucking worth it."

"When did you get so wise, baby brother?"

"Eh, you know we all have to wise up sometime. Listen, its Maggie's birthday soon, the first since we lost her. When that's passed, why don't you and Zach come on out for a visit? I'm sure the girls would love to see you both again, and Ethan could do with the distraction."

"I think we will. Zach's got a bit of prepping to do for his father's trial, but I'm sure we can squeeze in a trip out your way. Thanks, Ben."

"No problem. Oh, and hey, Alec's looking into Zach's mom too. He's gonna see if he can use his FBI contacts to see how far back the Piper cult was being observed; maybe they've got a record of locations. I'll let you know, anyway."

The brothers talked for a while longer, mostly about the twins Ben was now raising with his partner, Ethan, but under all the griping over lack of sleep, tantrums, and the exorbitant cost of a couple three-year-olds, Cameron could tell his brother loved every second of it.

As much as he wanted to race home and see Zach now that he'd talked things out with his brother, he looked at the time and realized he'd just clocked on duty and couldn't leave—but there was nothing stopping him from calling Zach to see if he wanted to have lunch together.

"Yeah," Zach mumbled, through the phone. Cameron had clearly woken him up, but he'd have to blame excitement for that.

"Hey. How're you feeling?" Cameron hoped his question wouldn't start an argument.

"Tired. What time is it?" Zach's voice was muffled and drifted in and out, and Cameron pictured him tossing around in his bed, probably trying to find the time.

"A little after nine. Hey...um if you're interested, I was wondering if you want to have lunch with me today?"

There was silence from Zach's end, nothing but crickets.

"Zach?"

"Yeah. Lunch?"

"Yes, lunch. You know the meal you have in the middle of the day. I thought we could have it together. I'd like to talk to you about...something."

More silence followed his words. Cameron wondered if he should call back later, give Zach more time to wake up properly.

"You're not angry?"

"No. There's nothing for me to be angry about, Zach."

"But I—"

"Not now. Just...have lunch with me."

"Okay," Zach whispered back.

"I'll pick you up at one. If I get called away, I'll call you." This too was met with silence, and Cameron couldn't stop himself from chuckling. "Go back to sleep, Zach. Sorry I woke you."

One o'clock came quickly. He'd spent the morning doing a few flyovers of a small fire that had broken out. It had been quickly extinguished, but police were now involved in searching for the arsonist they believed responsible. Cameron was still on call if needed but he'd be able to slip away for a quick lunch with Zach.

Zach met him at the door, apparently eager to go out to eat. There was a diner not far from the helipad that served the best burgers in town, so he'd be close enough to work if he got called in on his lunch break.

"Hi," Zach greeted him with a shyness Cameron hadn't seen in months.

"Hi," he replied with a confidence he hardly felt. "Ready to eat?"

"Starving... Cameron, I'm sorry. Last night I was—"

"We'll talk at lunch, Zach. But it's not... Don't blame yourself."

Cameron could feel Zach watching him as he drove to the diner. He'd made a mess of things with Zach and now he had to fix it. He hoped Zach would give him one last chance.

They took a table toward the back of the diner, away from the other customers. It wasn't exactly a romantic setting for what Cameron wanted to say, but at least they had privacy. His usual waitress, Meghan, approached within seconds of them taking their seat and they ordered quickly. As soon as Meghan walked away they were left alone—their gazes unwaveringly locked on each others.

Who would break first? It had to be Cameron. Zach had already done the hard work, admitting to his feeling for Cameron for months. It was Cameron's turn.

"Zach, I—"

"Cam, I'm so—"

They both exploded into laughter when they tried to speak at the same time. "You go." Zach laughed.

Cameron nodded and the seriousness of what he was about to say cut his laughter off.

"Zach, I've been thinking about things...us, I mean, and I can't promise you anything, but I wondered, if you're not serious about Jared, of course, if you'd like to go out with me...on a date?" *Well that was smooth.* Zach simply stared. Had he messed this up too?

He watched Zach, who remained silent while gazing at him with an intensity Cameron had rarely felt. Cameron's stomach rolled with nerves, and his body trembled with anxiety. Despite Ben's encouragement and his own determination to give this a try, Cameron wasn't a hundred percent sure he could do this.

"A real date?"

"A real date." Cameron nodded. "I've been so stupid. I know you and Jimmy are nothing alike. I know you'd never hurt me, but I was just so scared. It's hard to forget...to let go."

Zach reached across and laid his hands over Cameron's fidgeting ones, once again calming the incessant need to move whenever he remembered those horrible days with Jimmy. He wasn't sure if Zach was even aware of what he was doing, the comfort his simple touch gave him.

"I'd really like that, Cam. You know I love you. Jared's nice enough, but he's not you." Zach surprised him then by pulling one of his hands toward him and pressing his lips to Cameron's knuckles. He kept the hand close to his lips as he spoke so his breath ghosted over Cameron's skin. "I know how hard this is for you. I'm so proud you're trying. I won't hurt you, Cam. I won't."

"I won't hurt you either, Zach."

Zach nodded and smiled, a lightness coming into his emerald eyes. "So, where are you taking me?"

"Actually, I haven't even thought about that."

"Okay. When are we doing this?"

Cameron smiled ruefully and looked away, embarrassed by his utter lack of organization. "Umm..."

"Let me guess, you don't know when?" Zach laughed. "One step at a time then, Cam."

"One step at a time, Zach."

Chapter Nineteen

ZACH

Bob Seger was playing softly through the speakers as Zach put the finishing touches on dinner. The potatoes were almost done, and the steaks were searing nicely. Cameron would be out of the shower any minute, and their night together could begin.

After Cameron had asked him out for a date two weeks ago and then been unprepared with answers about when and where Zach had decided to take charge. They'd been to the movies and out to dinner a few times. No dance clubs or heavy drinking, but lots of sweet kisses and hand holding.

Tonight he was preparing a romantic evening for Cameron. Surely you didn't have to go out to date—anywhere they were together could be romantic, could be turned into a date. Even though they had quiet dinners together most nights, this one would be different. The candles were new, as was the soft, slow music.

He let his body sway to the music as he turned the steaks, and he couldn't help thinking of Jared. He liked Jared and he knew Jared liked him; he'd made that very clear, but it wasn't in the same ballpark as what he felt for Cameron. Jared wanted more from him than he was able to give. And after their last date...

"Smells good." Cameron's deep voice always cracked a little whenever he tried to keep it soft, making Zach wonder what it would be like if he ever whispered things in his ear—dirty things, things like he heard when he watched porn. Just the thought of it sent a shiver up his spine. "You okay? Cold?"

"Not at all." Zach kept his face turned from Cameron, knowing it would be flushed red because he'd been caught having dirty thoughts about Cameron. "Um, go and sit and I'll bring dinner out."

Zach still didn't turn, but he heard Cameron leave the kitchen and make the short walk to the dining table.

"Wow, Zach, this looks amazing," Cameron called. Zach had covered much of the large dining table in candles, leaving only a space large enough for them to comfortably eat. They needed no other light in the room, and Zach knew it looked magical in there.

He quickly dished up their meals and carried them into the dining room. Neither he nor Cameron were fancy, both preferring simple meals with little extravagance, so his modest dinner would be well received.

Cameron sat at the table, whiskey in hand, watching him as he walked into the room. The candlelight flickered across his features, highlighting Cameron's strong jawline and the stubble that covered it. His damp hair was a little longer than usual and looked like he'd only run his fingers through it after his shower, leaving it to dry wild and shaggy. Cameron's eyes were normally pale, but in this light, seemed even more so. He never blinked as he continued to watch Zach approach.

Zach's hands trembled slightly under the intense scrutiny, the plates he held shaking as he lowered them to the table.

"Thank you." Cameron kept his voice low and husky, the sound making butterflies flutter in his stomach, his pulse kick up, and his heart thump madly in his chest.

"You're welcome," he answered as he took his seat opposite Cameron—who looked right at him.

"My god, you look beautiful in this light," Cameron whispered. If Zach had been standing, his legs might have dropped from beneath him.

Should he say something similar to Cameron—because he looked beautiful, too, more than beautiful, really. He didn't know the right word to describe how good Cameron looked.

He searched his mind for a suitable reply, but eventually settled on a simple thank you and began cutting into his steak. He and Cameron had countless dinners together over the months, but Zach was unaccountably nervous at this one. Their dynamics were shifting; they were dating, and they were going to explore a relationship. He guessed that was the cause of his nerves.

Zach was lost for something to say while he cut into his steak. He had to calm down and remember it was Cameron sitting across from him. The man who had become the best friend he'd ever had—the man he adored.

"So what number date is this?" he asked.

Cameron looked up from his meal with an amused look on his face. "Definitely fifth. Our first date counted, Zach... I just didn't realize at the time."

"What happens on a fifth date then?" he asked before putting another forkful of the marinated meat into his mouth.

"Well, I'm not sure about regular people, but this date is going to involve a fair bit of kissing because as delicious as this meal is, it's your taste I want on my lips tonight, Zach."

"That's um...well...I think... You're not going to fight me on this anymore?" Zach hadn't known what to expect after

Cameron said he wanted them to date, but he loved the direction they were heading, and if Cameron was going to go all out, it was only fair he did the same.

Cameron lowered his cutlery and reached for Zach's hand across the table. As soon as Zach slipped his hand in Cameron's, he closed his fist, locking their hands together. "I was never fighting you. I was fighting myself. I knew from the second I saw you that you were special...were going to become very special to me. I was fighting myself because I didn't want that."

"Why?"

"It hurt so much with Jimmy and cost me so much. I didn't want to ever fall in love again... It was too big a risk."

"What changed your mind?"

"Ben...if you can believe it. Our parents had a wonderful relationship and he reminded me of that, reminded me I could have one, too, and it was worth trying to find someone."

"You think I'm worth it?"

"I do, and I'll tell you why. You grew up in a horrible way. You had no love around you, nobody to show you how to love or be kind or treat people the right way. A lot of people would rage against the world and the people in it after what you went through, but you...you only want to embrace it. You are so open and loving and kind. Every day you amaze me with your resiliency and your capacity to care even after you were treated so carelessly."

They kept their gazes locked on each other for a few moments and then Cameron pulled away, returning to his meal. "Now eat so we can get to the kissing," Cameron smirked.

Little was said for the rest of the meal aside from a few compliments from Cameron about how good the food was. Zach had no idea how to follow a speech like the one

Cameron had given. He'd had no idea Cameron thought anything close to that about him and he was humbled by it.

When they'd finished, Zach stood and reached for the plates. Cameron was quicker, though, pressing up behind him, his strong arms wrapping around his waist before Zach managed to pick up one plate. Cameron's breath ghosted over his ear as he leaned close. "Leave those." The whispered words did exactly what Zach expected as his body shook and his cock filled.

Zach turned in Cameron's arms, which loosened just enough to allow the movement but tightened again as soon as he was facing him. They were so very close Zach could only see Cameron as a blurred image. He tilted his head and searched for Cameron's soft lips.

Their kiss was easy, slow, but it affected Zach as much as previous, more searing kisses. Cameron's lips were soft and warm as they gently moved against his own. Zach's parted on a little sigh, and Cameron took the opportunity to slide his tongue into his mouth.

A song Zach didn't recognize was playing softly as he followed Cameron's lead while their bodies swayed to the slow melody. When their kiss broke, Zach put his nose to the hollow of Cameron's throat as their dance continued. Cameron quietly sang the words about sweetness and love and Zach felt like his heart might explode. As the song ended, Cameron ducked his head and found Zach's lips again.

There'd be no holding back the inferno now as their tongues met again, dancing together as their bodies had just been. Cameron pulled him even tighter against his chest. Zach's hands swept all over Cameron's broad back, leaving no part untouched. Cameron's body heat seared through the soft cotton of his shirt, his muscles bunching as he pressed closer and harder into Zach.

Zach felt Cameron's heart beating strong and fast against his chest—or maybe that was his. He reached up and tangled one hand in Cameron's hair, his long, thin fingers sifting through the shaggy locks. His body sang with pleasure and yearning; he was contented and surprisingly relaxed. For a moment, he wondered if this was all just an amazing dream.

As he took a forceful step forward, Cameron took one back until Zach had manhandled him away from the dining room table, and he had the backs of Cameron's legs pressed against the large sofa. Only out of necessity did they break apart then as Cameron lowered onto the couch, Zach following quickly after. They both turned so they were facing each other, their thighs touching, their fingers entwined. He wasn't sure about Cameron, but Zach was finding it impossible to keep his hands to himself.

Zach tracked his gaze slowly up Cameron's body, enjoying the bulk of his thighs, the bulge that was incapable of being hidden beneath his jeans, the flatness of his stomach and the barely contained power in his arms. But it was when he got to Cameron's face—the raw masculinity of it offset by the tenderness in his eyes—he lost all control. He'd been crazy to even think any other man could come close to Cameron—he had no equal.

"You taste so fucking good, Zach."

Those simple words were enough to fan the flame, and he leaned forward to smash their lips together again, not soft and gentle this time. It was hard and fierce, their lips gnashing together as the lust between them exploded. Zach forced Cameron's body back until he was lying almost flat on the couch. He wriggled his body, so he lay on top of Cameron, his legs resting between Cameron's spread thighs.

The kiss went on, and time was lost—irrelevant. They barely broke apart to take in air, too consumed with each other. The sensation of their hard cocks sliding together even through the layers of denim as they squirmed in their pleasure was amazing. He wanted more—needed more.

Ever since his escape from his father, Zach had made a habit of figuratively shutting his eyes and jumping into the unknown—after all, this entire world had been practically unknown to him. It was what he'd do now.

"Cam?" he whispered as he reluctantly pulled away from those lips.

"Mm." Cameron pressed his mouth to his throat and trailed soft kisses down its length.

"I want...more," he gasped as Cameron nipped at his skin.

"What do you want?" The words were a whisper, a mere puff of air blowing over his heated skin.

"You." His lust-addled mind couldn't manage anything more specific; he only hoped Cameron would understand.

Cameron pushed up from beneath him, dislodging Zach and forcing them both to stand. Cameron's gaze was locked with his. Hands were fumbling at the fly of his jeans, but he suddenly grabbed Cameron's fingers, stilling them. This might not be the right time, but if he didn't say what he needed to now, he might burst.

"Do you remember when you took me to buy these clothes?" he whispered, and Cameron shot him a questioning look before nodding. "You were so angry when you found out I had no clothes of my own—never had. I remember following you to the car, and I thought you were mad at me, but then you explained how you were angry *for* me. That was the first time I ever remember feeling like it was okay for me to believe I was important, I mattered, and

I didn't deserve the way I'd been treated. I remember thinking that if someone as wonderful as you believed I mattered then I must. That, more than the home or the food or the flying lessons or anything else is what you've done for me."

Cameron watched him carefully and then brushed his thumb across his bottom lip before cupping his neck and pulling him in for another kiss. It was agonizingly slow, as though Cameron refused to rush to the end. Cameron's big hands cupped his cheeks and held him still and tight as he kissed him breathless.

Eventually Cameron pulled back and stared into Zach's eyes. It wasn't uncomfortable in the least. "I've been such a fool," he murmured.

Zach saw the passion building again in Cameron's eyes and felt it in the thrum of his heartbeat. Cameron kissed the tip of his nose before moving back to his lips. It only took a matter of seconds before they were both back in the ocean of rising passion threatening to drown Zach.

Cameron's large hands pushed his jeans down, his boxers going with them. Then those hands were on his shoulders, gently pressing him onto the sofa. Cameron followed him, his big body forcing Zach's legs apart as he knelt before him.

There was a moment of hesitation as he realized the vulnerable position he was in, with his pants down and Cameron fully clothed. But a glance at Cameron's pale-blue eyes was enough to assuage any fears or nerves. Cameron would never hurt him. He hoped Cameron knew the same about him by now.

"Tell me to stop any time...if you need to," Cameron said and then immediately lowered his head, sucking Zach's cock to the back of his throat in one swallow. The tight wet warmth of Cameron's mouth was so much better than his hand.

Zach's body convulsed at the sensation, like a bolt of lightning had struck him. He didn't know what to do with himself as Cameron continued to suck him hard and dirty, wreaking havoc on his lower body. As Cameron dragged his lips up his shaft, the tight heat of his mouth pulling on his dick had Zach canting his hips forward, chasing more of that warmth. Cameron's tongue swirled around his tip and then licked a trail down to his balls. And on and on it went.

Licking, sucking, teasing.

Zach had seen the mechanics of this act a hundred times on Pornhub, but he was thoroughly unprepared for the reality, the sensation of Cam's mouth on him.

He was frantic, his body completely uncontrollable as he writhed and thrust, all the while sitting right on the precipice—wanting to go over and yet at the same time frightened by the fierce reaction of his body to Cameron's touch.

"Cam," he groaned, needing something to ground him. As though he could read his mind, Cameron pulled off his aching dick with a wet pop and stared up at him. His pale eyes were shrouded by the black of his pupils, his tongue licking at his lips as though he were savoring Zach's taste.

"Hold on to me, Zach. I've got you," he murmured before lowering his mouth back to Zach's full to bursting balls and licking his way back up to the tip of his cock.

Zach reached out and grabbed onto Cameron as he'd been told. His fingers curled in his shaggy hair, holding on as Cameron's head bobbed up and down, up and down, over and over.

It didn't take long after that. A familiar tingle spread from the base of his spine, this time more intense than anything he'd felt before. He tugged at Cameron's hair in warning, completely unable to formulate words beyond the increasingly loud groans and whimpers falling from his lips. Cameron ignored him and only intensified his attention.

"Oh fuck," he hissed as his body jerked and spasmed, and he came down Cameron's throat. The slurping noises as Cameron swallowed his load and then licked his cock clean had Zach's body twitching in the aftermath, already on its way to new arousal.

Zach flopped back on the sofa before Cameron had finished cleaning him up, throwing an arm over his eyes, totally worn out and spent. Cameron moved between his legs, and then he was right there kissing him thoroughly. Zach tasted himself on Cameron's lips—his tongue, as it pushed inside to tangle with his own. His body trembled, completely overawed by what had just happened.

Finally, Cameron sat back on his heels, giving him a reprieve from the sensations wreaking havoc on his overly sensitized body. He peered at Cameron through his half-closed lids and only then noticed the flush on his cheeks and the wildness in his gaze. Perhaps Cameron was as overcome as he was.

"You okay?" Cameron whispered.

Zach nodded, still struggling with words. Cameron smiled and reached forward to cup his cheek, his thumb brushing over Zach's damp skin.

"Let's get you to bed, huh?"

Was Cameron ending the night? Didn't he want more from Zach? Didn't he want Zach to touch him and set him ablaze like he'd just done to him? He didn't want to go to bed—he wanted to stay with Cameron.

"My bed, Zach. Let's get you into my bed. I'm not letting go of you tonight."

Zach smiled and managed to find his tongue. "Yes. Yes, please. Don't let me go, Cam."

"I don't think I can," he murmured the words so softly that Zach barely caught them.

Chapter Twenty

CAMERON

Sleep eluded him as he lay with Zach curled in his arms. Cameron had hardly moved during the night but Zach...Zach's body had been restless. He'd twisted and turned, but still he'd never moved too far away from Cameron and he'd never woken. He was lying now with his face pressed into Cameron's neck, one arm thrown over his chest and one leg between Cameron's.

Cameron pressed kisses into Zach's soft hair sporadically, unable not to. He'd had a taste of Zach now, and goddammit he wanted more—so much more. Cameron's breath stuttered when Zach's lips pressed against the skin of his neck as he'd done several times during the night, though he never truly woke while doing it.

He did his best to keep his thoughts away from last night: the decadent sounds Zach made, the sensual way he moved his body, the sinful taste of him on Cameron's tongue. All of it was perfect, beyond anything Cameron imagined. He tried not to think about it, because each time he did, his dick hardened, and he had a difficult time keeping his hips from rolling, seeking out relief.

Zach's face, with eyes wide and lips in a small circle of shock, popped into his head as he remembered telling him he'd come in his pants like a damn teenage boy just from the sight, sound, and feel of going down on him and a few well-timed strokes with his own hand. The expression of shock and awe had never left his face as Cameron had stripped Zach and then himself and then led him into the shower, eventually tucking them both under the covers.

They hadn't spoken much at all, spending the time before Zach drifted off to sleep exchanging gentle kisses that occasionally flared into more heated ones. Cameron had never kissed someone so much during one night of passion. Jimmy had never been much of a kisser, doling them out as though Cameron should be honored he'd condescended to allow his lips to touch Cameron.

He didn't want to think of Jimmy—not here, not now. But, as always, the memories came unbidden. It had all been such an awful mess: the pain and humiliation of knowing he'd been unable to please the man he thought he'd loved, not knowing at the time that no matter what he'd done he'd never have been able to please Jimmy. The harsh rebukes shouted at him or sometimes spoken so quietly and with such distaste they'd ripped a piece of Cameron's soul away every single time. The shame and degradation he'd felt, rather than the pleasure he should have, when Jimmy had roughly pushed into him after brutal words had been used to tear down the good man he'd always believed himself to be. The punishing thrusts meant to tame and hurt rather than pleasure. Hands closed into fists to make him cower, threatening rather than embracing him.

Cameron began to fidget as he always did when he remembered those days. He wondered if his body was getting ready for flight. He hadn't been able to fight back then even to defend himself—by the time Jimmy had finished with him, he hadn't thought himself worthy of being protected, anyway.

Beside him, Zach wiggled again, pushing his body closer so he was covering more of Cameron. He was warm, soft, and yet hard at the same time. Perfect. He'd do anything to protect Zach, including fight for him if he had to.

Could he do this? Was he strong enough to put not only his heart but everything he was on the line again? The notion of harsh words and humiliating punishments coming from Zach sucked the breath out of him. It wouldn't happen that way again—it couldn't. But what if?

He'd believed Jimmy was good and kind; he'd loved him, never seeing the monster lurking beneath. What if Zach was the same? What if Zach—

Cameron had to move, had to get out. He needed air. He needed to think but away from the body that called to him like a siren on the rocks singing to passing sailors. Zach groaned when Cameron slid out from under his grasp, but he didn't wake.

He grabbed his jeans and shirt from the floor, where he'd shucked them last night, and quietly left the room. He stopped outside the door and pushed his weary body into the clothes, all while his heart was aching and his brain was spinning. The two organs fighting: his heart screaming at him to trust and love, his brain arguing he must run to safety.

He needed air and there was none in here. He walked through his house, passing the dining table where the dinner leftovers and burned remnants of the candles remained. The flames, having long died, left nothing but a mess to be scraped off the table, never to be whole again—much like he'd been after Jimmy.

Air. If he could just get some air, he'd be able to think clearer—better. As much as he wanted to, he knew he couldn't get in his chopper and fly in his frenzied state but being around his helicopter usually worked to calm him. He found a notepad and quickly scrawled a message to Zach. As terrified as he was right then, he wasn't simply going to walk away, leaving Zach to wonder where the hell he was. None of this was Zach's fault.

It was only a ten-minute trip to the helipad, especially at this time of the morning with the sun barely peeking over the horizon. He went straight to work once he arrived. There was always maintenance and upkeep to do on his chopper, and it helped to ease his disorderly mind.

Zach is good and kind and sweet and would never hurt me. Cameron repeated the mantra over and over as he worked, not allowing his distrustful brain to creep back in with memories of abuse and pain.

After an hour or so he considered calling Zach, though he knew it was still too early. When his phone started ringing, Cameron lunged for it, expecting Zach. Instead, it was the sheriff.

"Cam, you up?"

"Yeah, I'm at the shed."

"Good. We need you in the air. We've got a missing kid. Eight years old. Head over to Dubois. Little boy went missing from there. The family and locals have done a ground search of the immediate area. He was last seen when the parents went to bed around midnight, so that's about a seven-hour window. Given his age, he couldn't have gone more than twelve miles. Start at fifteen miles and work in. We'll work our way out and meet."

"Got it." Cameron hung up immediately and prepared to go. A missing child...Jesus, he hated these cases. Dubois was a tiny town on the edge of the national park. If the boy had wandered off into it...

Paul Hoover pulled into the lot moments after he'd hung up, having obviously been called in to be Cameron's eyes. They were in the air in less than fifteen minutes.

The day was shaping up to be crystal clear so that'd help, but spotting an eight-year-old child in thick bush from the air was never going to be a piece of cake.

"You okay, Cronin?" Paul's voice crackled through his earpiece.

"Yeah. Just hate it when it's kids."

"Me too," Paul answered. Cameron wondered if he was thinking of his own three kids and how he'd be feeling if it was one of them missing. He couldn't imagine the anguish.

"How's Zach doing?"

Paul's question slapped Cameron's thoughts immediately back to the man he'd left warm and naked in his bed. And that image had him questioning why he'd ever left. Zach was like the best kind of fruit: soft and sweet on the outside but with a hard and tough core. How could he have doubted him for even a second? Fuck Jimmy. It was past time for Cameron to stop letting him win.

"He's good. GED almost done, and he's prepping with the prosecutor for his father's trial. Truth is, Paul, I've never met anyone who can keep going no matter what shit is flung at him the way he does." Cameron heard the pride in his voice, mixed with the growing feelings of love he felt for Zach.

"He's a good man...a lucky man he got out when he did, from what you told me."

Zach was a good man—the best of men and Cameron had to stop running from him. Just because he'd encountered one wolf in sheep's clothing didn't mean he'd meet another.

It didn't take them long to reach the fifteen-mile radius. Sheriff Begay had called in twice, but there was no news on the missing boy. Cameron flew and surveyed the ground as safely as possible. Paul had the binoculars out and was carefully scanning as much of the terrain as he could while Cameron flew low and slowly over the search area in a grid pattern. Thoughts of needles and haystacks came to mind, but they'd do their best and Cameron knew every one of them, both in the air and on the ground, would keep trying until...

A little over an hour later Cameron was starting to think about refueling. Riverton would be closer than heading back to Cody. Jackson Heatherton had refueling facilities at his place, and he'd okayed it for their use.

"Air one, come in."

"Air one. Go ahead," Cameron replied to the call sign.

"We've got him, Cam. Little boy's safe. Not a scratch on him. Wandered off and got himself lost. Found him hiding in a shed."

"Thank god. We'll head on home then, Sheriff."

"Thanks, boys," the sheriff replied before signing off.

Cameron didn't know the boy or his family, but he still felt an enormous sense of relief that he'd been found. He could only imagine how the boy's family must feel. To have a loved one go missing, not knowing if they were alive or dead—he just couldn't imagine.

The flight back to Cody passed quickly; most of it spent listening to Paul's proud tales of his children. The eldest was approaching teenage years, and Cameron looked forward to watching how his friend would handle that.

It was barely lunchtime by the time he'd shut down the chopper and worked through the postflight checks and balances. Paul offered a trip to the diner, but he only wanted to get home to Zach. He wanted to hold him and reassure him everything was okay. He'd panicked and run but he was going back, and he wasn't going anywhere again.

The house was quiet when he entered, so Cameron wondered if Zach was still asleep. Having sex for the first time could be overwhelming and exhausting, especially with how hard Zach had come. And just the memory had him hard again, wanting more of Zach.

As he passed through the kitchen, he noticed his note was gone but had been replaced by another. He picked it up and read Zach's almost illegible handwriting. His father had made sure he was able to read, but writing hadn't been quite so important to the cult leader.

> *Dear Cam,*
>
> *Jared called and I thought I should go and see him to explain.*
>
> *I'm meeting him at the Cody Hotel for lunch. Be back in the afternoon.*
>
> *Zach.*
>
> *PS Can't wait to see you again, hold you, touch you. Well you know...*

Zach had sketched a little smiley face at the end, and Cameron's heart thumped at the simple affection in the note. He wasn't quite so pleased with the little prick of jealousy nicking at his brain when he thought of Zach going to see Jared.

Well, maybe he couldn't have lunch with Zach, but perhaps he could plan a special evening of his own for the two of them. He threw together a sandwich with some leftover chicken and salad and headed back to work while trying to reignite the romantic part of his brain he'd let die off years ago.

But, when Cameron returned home nearly six hours later with great plans for a romantic evening, Zach still wasn't home.

Chapter Twenty-One

ZACH

Zach pinched himself as he made waffles for breakfast that morning. It was after nine and he'd only just woken—in Cameron's bed. His jaw ached from his continual smiling. Had last night really happened? It seemed more like a dream.

Granted, it would have been infinitely better if Cam was still in bed with him when he'd woken, but he'd read the note, and he understood Cam's need to work on his helicopter. He knew how much it relaxed Cameron, and he'd need that calm today. They'd both taken a big step toward each other, and for someone like Cameron, who was more used to running from others, it was a big deal.

He had the radio playing in the background as he cooked and had heard the report ten minutes ago of a missing child. Cameron would be in the air looking for the boy, so he'd be unable to talk to him for who knew how long. He'd be up and down in the helicopter until the child was found. His dedication was something more to love about him.

Zach allowed the music on the radio to seep into his body and gently rock it. Cameron had an eclectic taste in music, so he'd introduced Zach to a variety of styles: rock, country, rap, even something Zach had been amazed to hear was called heavy metal. His favorite station, the one Zach was listening to now, played mostly what Cameron called old-school rock. Zach didn't have a favorite band or style, for that matter, yet.

He did recognize Fleetwood Mac as the next song started, though. Stevie Nicks's gravelly rendition of "Landslide" was a song he'd heard often on this station so he could sing along to parts of it. Knowing the house was empty, he sang at the top of his lungs, flubbing a few words but not caring, until his waffles were ready. Food trumped singing, especially today. He was extra ravenous and wondered if last night's activities contributed to his hunger.

He'd had sex. Cameron had given him a blow job, and it was so much better than he'd imagined—and he'd imagined it a lot. He could almost feel the wet warmth of Cameron's mouth as he remembered last night. The way his lips had closed so tightly around him, sucking with such force he finally understood the expression of having your brains sucked out through your dick, which he'd heard often during the porn he'd watched.

Just thinking about last night had him hard and desperately wishing Cam was home. He couldn't wait to return the favor. He was dying to know how Cameron tasted, what he'd feel like in Zach's mouth.

From somewhere deeper in the house, he heard the tone of his phone. Zach dropped his waffle and ran, hoping Cameron would be on the other end of the line. Where the hell had he left his phone? He heard it but couldn't see it. Following the noise, he finally found it shoved under the sofa. Had it been in his jeans pocket last night when Cam had...? Jesus, he had to stop thinking about it.

He shoved his hand under the sofa and pulled it out. Though it had already stopped ringing, a quick look at the screen told him Jared had called. His butterflies started up again but not the good ones this time. He was nervous, not exactly afraid, but he wasn't looking forward to telling Jared about Cameron.

It couldn't be put off, though. That wasn't fair to Jared, so Zach palmed his phone and called Jared's number. He picked up on the third ring. "Hey, Zach. Where were you?" He didn't sound angry, exactly, but there was something off in his tone. Maybe it was wariness, as though he wasn't sure of the reception he'd get. Understandable, given how their night had ended two weeks ago.

"Sorry," he apologized though there was a niggle somewhere in the back of his mind warning him that he probably didn't need to do it. He didn't need to be at Jared's beck and call. "I couldn't find my phone." He continued on, wanting to stop but his polite brain just kept the words going.

"You should keep a better eye on it." Jared's tone was still terse, so Zach remained quiet, waiting to see where this was going. "Anyway, I've got you now. I'm back in town, and I thought we could have dinner and talk about the other night..."

They did need to talk, but it wasn't dinner with Jared that Zach was interested in. He'd much rather share that meal with Cameron again. He brutally shut that line of thought down before memories of last night flooded him and he was left with a raging hard-on and no Cameron around to help him out with it.

"Actually, could I meet you now? Dinner's no good, but we do need to talk." There was no immediate response from Jared, and he wondered if he knew what Zach wanted to talk about. It was never nice hurting someone, but even with the zero experience he'd had with relationships, he knew he had to tell Jared how he felt.

"That will be fine. I'm at the Cody Hotel while my renovations are being done, room twelve. Come on up when you get here. Shall we say half an hour?" Jared's tone was still off—suddenly so distant and formal. Zach suspected he knew what was coming.

Twenty-five minutes later, he was standing outside of room twelve. He was five minutes early and was mystified to realize he was a little concerned that Jared might be angry with him for being early. Perhaps Jared's behavior the other night had affected him more than he'd first realized.

His palms were sweating and his heart thumping as he knocked on the door. He put his hands in his pocket to stop them from trembling as he heard Jared moving around behind the door.

When it opened, Jared stood before him, without even a smile to greet him. Zach struggled to conjure a smile of his own so settled for a simple hello instead.

"Hello, Zach. Come on in."

Zach brushed past Jared as he entered the large room. A giant bed took up much of the space, and a burgundy cover lay over it with an assortment of pillows stacked at the head. The bed faced a cabinet topped with a medium-sized television. The thick blackout curtains were pulled shut, leaving the room lit by the artificial light of the bedside lamps. There was a small round table, with two accompanying chairs along the window, set with a small tray of food and what smelled like coffee.

Zach wasn't sure what to do. Should he sit at the table? He didn't want to sit on the bed.

"Sit down, Zach." Jared was behind him, his breath tickling his ear, his lips so close his words vibrated on his neck.

Zach sat on the nearest chair, his nerves snowballing rather than easing. Jared had been kind to him, though, so deserved to be treated well. His nerves about telling him what had happened with Cameron were the reason for his discomfort. Nothing more. Jared sat across from him, and for a moment neither said a word.

"So...what do you have to tell me, Zach?" Jared pushed a coffee across to Zach as he spoke. Absently, Zach took several sips, letting the hot liquid burn a trail down his throat, delaying the words he needed to say.

"I wanted to apologize for the other night. I wasn't in the best mood and I wasn't very good company. I didn't mean to ruin our night." Zach let that sit, wondering how Jared would react. It might give him an indication of how things would go when he confessed to Jared about Cameron.

"Was Cameron there to console you when you got home?"

It hadn't been the question he'd expected, but he answered anyway. Jared deserved the truth. "He was there. We fought, actually."

"About?"

"I'd had a lot to drink, and I jumped down his throat when he asked if I was okay. It didn't go well after that."

Jared stared at him for a while, his hand fiddling with some of the slices of cake on the table, the silence settling like a heavy fog.

"And did Cameron fall into line?" Jared eventually asked, the question completely throwing him. Fall into line? He had no idea how to answer. This wasn't how he wanted this conversation to go, so rather than fumble an answer, Zach decided to blow right past the question and explain to Jared what had happened.

"Um...well, this is very difficult, Jared, but...you've been very kind to me, and I'm very grateful to you. The thing is, though, that Cameron...Cameron and I—"

"Cameron finally had a taste of your sweet ass, then?"

Zach liked dirty talk but there was a time and a place, and he didn't care for the crudeness coming from Jared. He was at a loss how to respond. He figured his silence was answer enough.

"I'll take that as a yes. Tell me, Zach," Jared leaned in closer, a slice of cake held in his fingers and resting inches from his mouth. "Have you had a taste of Cameron yet?" He bit into the slice, a cruel smile on his lips.

This wasn't right. All he wanted to do was run. Jared's hand slammed onto the table, the crack of contact echoing through the room.

"Answer me!" Jared thundered, making Zach jump even more than the slap on the table had.

Zach stood and peered down at Jared. "I'm sorry I hurt you, Jared. I think I'd better go." He turned and started to head toward the door.

"You really should you know...have a taste of Cameron, I mean." Jared's words and spiteful tone brought Zach up sharp. "No one tastes better than Cameron. His ass, his come...his tears."

The blood in Zach's veins turned to ice, and his stomach dropped to the floor. He was going to be sick. A trickle of sweat trailed down his cheek, hooking under his chin and into the collar of his shirt. His hands were trembling badly, and he was completely unable to focus his vision.

Zach had lived most of his life in fear of the monsters that circled him in the cult, but the shards of dread now were more akin to terror—and it wasn't fear for himself. He heard

Jared moving behind him and wasn't surprised when he came and stood in front—between him and the door—his body close to Zach's.

"You know, Zach, I don't think I quite introduced myself properly. My full name is *James* Jared Reilly. Cameron called me Jimmy."

Whatever strength, hope, happiness he'd had inside faded as the revelation from Jared's—no Jimmy's—words sank in. This man who he'd been friends with and gone out with and kissed was the monster who'd nearly destroyed Cameron.

The place where all good feelings had swelled and grown after last night, was now replaced with a seething anger burning through him unlike anything he'd experienced since he'd overheard his father's plans for the mass suicide—murder—of his followers. He'd been helpless then but still had planned to do something. He wasn't as helpless this time.

"You bastard," he began while feeling the rage burn him from the inside out.

"Yes. Yes. I'm a bastard, and you're going to kill me for what I did to Cameron and blah blah blah." Jimmy took a step closer, and as his face twisted into an ugly snarl, for the first time, Zach got a glimpse of the true evil that lay beneath the otherwise handsome appearance. "But understand this, Zach, Cameron is mine. Mine to do with as I please. Mine to hurt, mine to control, mine to punish. Always mine." He spat.

"You're wrong," Zach gasped out, surprised at his ability to form words in the midst of the tumult currently having its way within him. "Cameron's not yours anymore. He hates you. He knows the monster you are."

"Hates me? Don't you understand the fine line between love and hate? It's no thicker than a spider's web. He may believe he hates me, claim he hates me, but *I* know he loves me. I've felt how he loves me. When we're alone again, he'll confess his love. He'll prove it with that body that belongs to me—only to me."

Zach took a step back for the first time. He hadn't wanted to show fear or back down an inch from this monster, but the full weight of what he was dealing with suddenly settled on his shoulders. Jimmy didn't live in reality. He existed in a world of his own creation, just as Zach's father had—and he knew how dangerous that could be.

He'd have to be smart, think carefully if he was going to get away from Jimmy, and if he was going to save Cameron from him. His stomach hadn't stopped roiling, and his legs were weak despite the passing of the initial shock. He didn't feel right.

"Something wrong, Zach? Don't worry; it won't be long now, and you'll have nothing to worry about."

What had Jimmy done? There must have been something in the coffee. But what? Was Jimmy trying to kill him or maybe he'd given him something to knock him out, giving him a head start? To what, though? Escape or go after Cameron?

He was feeling very dizzy now, his vision was dimming. He was eased onto the bed, but he tried to fight. He didn't want Jimmy's hands anywhere on him. He fell back, lying prone, cringing as Jimmy sat at his side, his foul hands caressing his cheek.

"I gave you a strong dose, Zach. I can't have you making a fuss when we leave here. You know, when I came back and found you'd moved in with my Cameron, I originally planned to kill you. But the situation with you and Cameron intrigued me, and I wanted to know more. I enjoy knowing Cameron's pain." Jimmy dropped his head so Zach could feel his lips brushing over his cheek as he continued to speak. "I can't tell you how pleased I was to hear Cameron was unable to find anyone after me. That is the love I'm talking about, Zach. That is the love you will never have from Cameron."

When Zach tried to refute his words, tried to explain how wrong Jimmy was, he was terrified to realize he couldn't get his lips to cooperate. In fact, he seemed to have lost control of his entire body. His eyes began to close as he drifted away. His last image was of Jimmy's twisted features as he hovered over him, that hateful grin firmly in place.

Chapter Twenty-Two

CAMERON

Where the hell was he? It was rapidly approaching 9:00 p.m. and Zach still hadn't returned from seeing Jared. Nor had he answered any of the calls Cameron made. Cameron was pacing the length of his long hallway as he tried to rein in the worry growing for Zach.

The unwanted idea that Zach had changed his mind—perhaps he'd decided Cameron wasn't good enough after all—had already popped into his head several times. But the even more unwelcome thought that something was terribly wrong was also knocking at his door, and Cameron was fighting it with everything he had.

He wasn't sure what to do. Zach was an adult and had every right to be out as late as he wanted and go wherever he pleased. It was the lack of contact that kept niggling at him, though. It gnawed away at him, feeding the growing concern that something was wrong and Zach needed him.

Another circuit of the hall and Cameron couldn't take anymore. He stalked toward his garage, grabbing his keys on the way. His hands shook as his fingers worked to get the key in the ignition. His truck eventually roared to life, breaking the silence of the otherwise quiet night. He backed out and turned toward West Yellowstone Avenue. He didn't know where else to go other than the last place he knew Zach had gone, The Cody Hotel.

Cameron parked quickly once he arrived, taking the first spot he came to. The hotel was a three-story building with a slightly rustic look to it. Most of the rooms at the front were either darkened or had the curtains drawn, but he could make out a sliver of light around some of them. He hadn't parked far from the entrance but ran inside nonetheless. He was quickly losing patience as his concern grew.

A woman, surely no older than forty, manned the front desk. Cameron thought he recognized her from around town but didn't know her to speak to. Her smile was slipping as he quickly approached her. He could only imagine how he must look with fear seeping out of every pore. He saw her quickly glance to her left and, obviously noticing her coworker engaged in conversation with a guest not too far away, seemed to relax a bit.

"Good evening, sir," She smiled, her professionalism not skipping a beat.

"Hi. I'm Cameron Cronin. Could you please tell me if you have a Jared staying here?" Even as he asked, it registered he had no surname to give when she no doubt would ask for it. He also wondered why Jared was staying at the hotel when Zach had told him he'd lived in Cody all his life.

"Jared? His surname, please?" Her fingers hovered over her keyboard as though waiting for action.

"I don't know it." He watched her brows furrow as the confirmation that he was going to be a problem seemed to hit her. "Look my...the man who lives with me came here to meet his friend Jared, and I haven't seen him since. That was at least nine hours ago. He isn't answering his phone either. I'm worried about him."

"I'm sorry, sir, but we can't give out guest details. The best I can do is call the room for you so you can speak to him. But without his surname, it'll be difficult to track him down."

"I don't know it. Damn. I don't even know what Jared looks like. I never met him," Cameron mumbled more to himself than the lady across from him. "Do you have a restaurant on-site?"

"Yes, and a bar area. If you go straight through those doors and turn left, you'll come across them. Perhaps your friend is in there." She smiled, seeming more pleased because she might be getting rid of him than that she believed what she'd said. Cameron gave her a quick nod and then took off in the direction she'd pointed out.

The hotel wasn't huge, so it didn't take long for him to find the restaurant and bar area. A quick walk around both showed no sign of Zach. Yes, there was a chance they'd gone somewhere else but for this long? It seemed implausible. Something was wrong and it was becoming clearer with each agonizing second.

Cameron couldn't stop thinking of the parents of the young boy he'd been searching for this morning. He remembered how bad he'd felt for them that someone they loved was missing. If what he was feeling was a tenth of what they had felt while their son was missing, he had no idea how they'd survived it.

He wandered over to the large window, which took up a considerable area of the wall. What was the next step to take? He could call Sheriff Begay. Even though Zach was an adult and technically no one would look at his disappearance until at least twenty-four hours had passed, Roy Begay was his boss and a friend. He'd take it seriously.

Was Cameron ready to go there just yet, though? He'd go back and speak to the woman at the desk. He could show her a photo of Zach from his phone and hope she'd seen him. Not that he needed the photo because he'd be able to describe Zach in exact detail; after all, he'd spent the last months doing nothing but cataloging every inch of Zach's perfect body and stunning face.

He could describe the tiny gold flecks dotted throughout the green of his eyes and how the gold matched the highlights of his light sandy-brown hair. He could describe how the right side of his lips turned up higher when he grinned, but when he favored you with a genuine, beaming smile, both sides were even. He could describe how the pinky and ring finger on his left hand were oddly out of alignment, both turning unnaturally away from the thumb. He could describe the musky and slightly salty taste of him or the slightly citrusy scent of the shampoo he loved that sometimes was drowned out by the far better earthy smell that was naturally Zach.

Cameron pressed his forehead to the window as he looked out into the dimly lit parking lot. His hands twitched at his side, clenching as though they wanted to reach out for something—or someone. Allowing the sadness and fear to take over wasn't going to get him anywhere. He gave the memory of Zach's face a small smile and then stood and turned back toward the lobby. He was going to get answers, or something, from the woman there.

"Find him?" she asked as she watched Cameron approaching.

"No. Listen, I know you have rules and policies, but something's wrong. Please, can't you look through your guests and see if there is one with the name Jared? You don't have to give me any information, but you could call the room and speak to him." Cameron heard the pleading in his tone, but he didn't care. He'd beg if he had to.

"Actually, sir, I've already looked. If you'll wait over there a moment, I'll call the room."

"Thank you. Thank you so much." Cameron sagged with relief and made his way over to the small group of seats she'd gestured to. He took the seat facing her and watched as she made the call. As the seconds passed, he realized she was getting no answer to her call, and he wasn't sure if that was a good thing or not.

When she hung up the phone, Cameron jumped up and walked back to her desk, knowing what she was going to say.

"No answer. I'm sorry."

Cameron nodded, wondering if he'd hit a brick wall. "Could I ask one more favor?"

The lady, Cheryl, as he read on her name tag, nodded and Cameron continued. "Would you please pop up to his room, maybe if you can see the lights are on, you could knock on the door? I know it's a big ask, but I'm so worried."

"I really shouldn't." Cheryl looked nervously around, so Cameron wondered if he'd asked too much of her. Though where Zach was concerned nothing was too much to make sure he was safe. "Look, just wait here and I'll quickly run up. Bill?" she called over to the employee who was still talking with, presumably, one of the guests. "Can you come and watch the desk for a few minutes please?"

Bill murmured something to the person he was standing with and then walked over to the desk. Cheryl already had a keycard in hand and was moving out from behind the counter by the time Bill arrived. He gave Cameron a short nod and took Cheryl's place.

Cameron went back to his seat as Cheryl headed toward the bank of elevators. He was rocking back and forth, no longer able to keep his body still. All he wanted—the only thing he wanted—was to see Zach's face. Even if it was only to hear he desired Jared and not him. It would gut him open, but at least he'd know Zach was safe.

He didn't look away from the hallway Cheryl had disappeared into moments ago, and it must have only been five minutes later when he saw her step back into sight and head toward him. There was a nervous frown on her face and a large sheet of paper in her hand. Cameron stood, preparing himself for whatever she'd found.

"There was no answer," she began before Cameron could say a word. "This was taped to the door, though, and it's for you."

Cameron looked at the paper she held out toward him. It wasn't paper at all but rather a photo. It must have been ten by fifteen inches and was black-and-white. Scrawled across it in red pen were the words "For Cameron."

Cameron held the photo in shaking hands as he looked at the image of Zach, his heart aching for the real thing to be before him instead of this inferior facsimile. He was clearly asleep on a bed and next to him, with his arm wrapped under Zach's shoulders and a smile on his face was Jimmy.

"Jesus, oh god," Cameron cried before his knees buckled and he sank back into the chair. His entire body was violently shaking, and he knew he was going to be sick. "I'm gonna be sick," he moaned, hoping Cheryl heard and would act fast.

She did, and a wastepaper basket was shoved under his nose. Cameron brought up what little he had in his stomach.

His sweat-soaked body continued to shake as finally the heaves ended. A wad of tissues was pressed into his hand, and he looked gratefully at Cheryl. "Thank you," he said before wiping his mouth.

"I'll be right back," Cheryl said before turning and walking away. She returned after a few minutes with a fresh basket and a glass of water, both of which Cameron took gratefully. His stomach was still rolling, so he had no idea if he was finished being sick.

Jared was Jimmy. And he had Zach. Of that, there was no doubt. The question was: what did he want with him? Nothing good was the only sensible answer. Cameron had to find them.

"Cameron," Cheryl softly called, "can I do anything for you? Call someone?"

"No, but thank you," he said, though in truth he felt like he was out of his body and looking on. It didn't seem real or possible that this could be happening. "If I could just sit here for a minute."

"Of course," she replied. "Are you feeling a little better?"

"No," he answered honestly. "How come you helped me? Most people would have told me no."

"I saw your face. You looked more than simply worried. And then when you saw that photo...you looked terrified."

Cameron nodded. He bent forward, resting his head between his legs as he tried to decide what to do. He should call the police, but something held him back. What he needed was Ben. His brother would be able to find Zach, probably quicker than the cops. He also wouldn't have to bother with any red tape they might come across.

He needed to get home and see how quickly he could get out to San Francisco. It was Maggie's birthday tomorrow, and he didn't want to call and drag Ben away from Ethan tonight. Jimmy was playing with him, so Zach would be safe until the time and place of his choosing, and he knew nothing was going to happen to Zach until Cameron was there to witness it—he understood Jimmy's cruelty.

"Thanks for your help, Cheryl. I'm feeling much better." Cameron shook her hand as he stood.

"Do I need to call 911?"

"No. No thank you. It's really nothing like that. Just a shock that's all. Seems my boyfriend was cheating on me after all."

"Are you sure?"

"I'm sure. I've always been a little dramatic." He tried a smile, doing his best to fool her into thinking he wasn't, in fact, scared out of his wits. Cheryl nodded and let him go, but he wasn't at all sure he'd convinced her.

Chapter Twenty-Three

CAMERON

Cameron flew out of Salt Lake City on the first flight available. He knew he wouldn't have slept a wink last night so had driven to Salt Lake City instead. From there he was able to get a direct flight to San Francisco.

Once on board, he tried to nap, even knowing the flight was only a little over an hour. He knew he needed to keep his strength up but every time he closed his eyelids, Zach's smiling face beamed back at him, and he couldn't stop thinking about what he might have lost.

He tried not to think about what might be happening to Zach. Just the idea of him being in Jimmy's presence made him both sick to his stomach and terrified out of his mind.

Sleep wasn't coming, despite his exhaustion, so instead, he looked out the window and remembered the last time he'd been on a plane. Zach had been with him as they'd flown out to spend a weekend with Ethan and Ben, both of whom were dealing with Maggie's death and the fatherhood it had thrust upon them. But they were getting better—together. Maya and Riley were chatting up a storm and running his brother ragged.

He closed his eyes and let memories of Zach having fun with the twins play behind his lids. He'd chased them around the park, pushed them on the swings, and swum with them in Ben's pool. The three of them had laughed and laughed the whole weekend. The two little girls so clearly adored Zach. Even though he never tried to get away from them, they had followed him around as though they couldn't bear to let him out of their sight. Getting them away from Zach so he could shower or use the toilet became a three-man job. It wasn't easy distracting a couple of three-year-olds from something or someone they'd become besotted with.

Cameron couldn't think of anyone who'd met Zach who hadn't been delighted by him. He had to get him back. Zach had so much to offer. It was way too soon for the world to lose him—too soon for Cameron to lose him.

Cameron allowed himself happy memories of Zach for the rest of the flight. He took a cab to the cemetery from the airport, far too tired and strung out from stress to drive safely. He knew exactly where he had to go, Ben had texted him two days ago to say he and Ethan would be at Maggie's grave this morning for her birthday. He hated interrupting, but he needed his brother's help—needed all of their help desperately.

He paid the cab driver and made his way from memory toward the gravesite. He hadn't quite made it there when he saw several figures walking toward him. Two adult-sized and two toddler-sized. He watched them approach, Ethan talking quietly to Ben with the barest hint of a smile on his face, but for once, Ben wasn't smiling back. He was watching Cameron intently.

"Cam, everything okay?" Ben called when they were closer.

"No. I need your help... I need help from you all."

"What's happened?" Ethan asked, the faint smile gone.

"I need you to find Zach."

"Zach? He's missing?" They were standing right before each other now, and Ben reached up to put a hand on his shoulder as he spoke.

Cameron nodded. "Jimmy has him." The words came out pained and crackly. Cameron's body trembled and the sick feeling he felt every time he thought about it came sweeping over him again threatening to send him to his knees.

"Jimmy?" Ben asked. Cameron saw both incredulity and anger on his face.

"Jimmy was the friend Zach was seeing. He was Jared. Zach's known him for months and I didn't know. I didn't bother to find out. I can't—" His chest was so tight he had to drag each breath in and out. For a second, he wondered if he might be having a heart attack.

"Let's go."

This was why he'd come to his brother. Ben knew what he was doing in situations like this and he'd take control. He'd fight as hard, and as long, as Cameron to get Zach back.

Ben and Ethan each picked up one of the girls as they hurried to their car, Cameron right on their heels. Both of the men in front of him already had so much on their plates, but he knew they'd help. They were family, all of them, and it was painfully clear to Cameron now that Zach was family too. He just hoped it wasn't too late to tell him.

Ethan had the girls quickly buckled into their car seats like he'd done it a million times already and Ben roared out of the parking space almost before Ethan had even made it into his seat. Cameron sat in the back of the seven-seat van. Talking over the top of the twins didn't seem an option, so he remained quiet.

He didn't recognize the house they pulled up to twenty minutes later, but he knew it wasn't Ben's. A stern "wait here" from his brother told him this wasn't their final destination.

Ten minutes later Ben and Ethan returned without the girls, but Cameron had just about gone crazy in that time. Ben drove once again, the family van seeming to strain under the pace he put it through now the children were safely out.

"Tell us everything," Ethan commanded, and so he did.

By the time they arrived at Ben and Ethan's place, Cameron had shared everything he knew and suspected with them. As far as he was concerned, all that was left was to come up with a plan to get Zach the hell back.

Ben was on the phone to Alec Banner before they'd even made it inside. As an ex-FBI agent, now working for Chasing Hope, he'd be a great help. He and Ben had met when they were both in the army, and though a good ten years older than Ben, they got on like a house on fire. He was family to Ben, and that made him family to Cameron.

Cameron didn't know much else about Alec, but he'd always come across as a good man the handful of times they'd met, and if he could help find Zach, then Cameron was more than happy to have him on board.

"Can I get you something? Tea? Coffee? Cold drink?" Ethan offered.

Other than a coffee and muffin on the plane earlier Cameron couldn't remember the last time he'd had a real meal or drink. "Ah, coffee thanks. Black, no sugar."

"What about something to eat? You look a bit wobbly there."

"Please," Cameron replied feeling more than just wobbly. "I haven't had much in the last twenty-four hours." And what little he had he'd thrown up at the hotel.

"I bet." Ethan fussed around in the kitchen making Cameron's sandwich and coffee. "I remember when the girls were taken; I hadn't even met them then, only just found out they existed, but as soon as I knew they were missing...it was the most awful feeling."

"I want him back so badly. And knowing he's with Jimmy..." Cameron felt those tendrils of terror that had momentarily eased suddenly come alive, sliding and coiling themselves throughout his entire body. How long before they squeezed enough he couldn't breathe?

"Um...Ben told me a little about Jimmy, not all of it I'm sure, but enough. I'm sorry for what he did to you...and that he's got Zach now. Neither of you deserves this."

Zach certainly didn't, but Cameron wasn't so sure about himself. He'd made great strides in the last few years but still... Jimmy had all but destroyed his confidence and sometimes the feeling of being useless and pathetic could easily knock him on his ass.

"Zach doesn't deserve it. God, he's so...amazing. So sweet and kind. Intelligent. I can't imagine where he'd be if he'd had a half-decent upbringing. If there'd been someone around to care, to love him. He certainly wouldn't be looking at me twice."

"I don't buy that, Cameron. I don't buy that at all. I know you pretty well, and everything I've seen is good." Ethan passed the sandwich and coffee over. He didn't offer him a seat, and Cameron wondered if it was because he recognized Cameron's twitchiness. He knew it wasn't his flight response kicking in this time. No, this time he was ready to fight.

"Can I give you some advice, Cameron?"

He wasn't sure what kind of advice Ethan was going to offer, but the man had more than proven himself to

Cameron. He didn't have to worry about Ben being hurt, he knew Ethan would die before he let that happen, and Cameron couldn't ask for more than that for his brother.

"Sure."

"I was in love with Ben for months before I'd allow myself to admit it. I didn't think I was good enough. But Ben loved me, and if a man as wonderful as him chose me—believed I was good enough—then who was I to argue. So when you get Zach back—and you will—you hold on to him with everything you've got because it is so worth it."

"Believe me, Ethan, when I've got him back in my arms I won't be letting go for anything. If I'd have just…" There was no point looking back, the what-ifs wouldn't do him or Zach any good. More likely they'd slow him down.

"Okay. So Banner's going to meet us in Cody," Ben began as soon as he walked into the room. He immediately went to stand at Ethan's side, tangling their fingers together. "He'll give Jacey a call en route to see what she can do. He's also going to get in contact with some of his old colleagues—ones who can keep quiet—to see what they can do. But, Cam, I think it's best to keep the real law enforcement out of this as much as possible." Ben gave him a look as though assessing whether or not he understood what Ben was getting at—he did.

"I agree. This is going to go one of two ways. Either Zach's already…already dead, or Jimmy's got him stashed somewhere so he can kill him in front of me. I think it'll be the latter, but either way, I want him taken out, Ben."

"That's the plan, Cam. I let him go once, and I'm not gonna make that mistake again." Ben nodded and then turned to his boyfriend. "Ethan, how do you wanna do this? Banner and I can manage if you need to stay with the girls."

"Ryan and Lucas said they can have them for a few days. I'll come out with you now, and if it's not—" Ethan grimaced and quickly glanced at Cameron. "—if it's not over by then, I'll come back."

"Okay, but when the time comes, you can't be around if we can help it. If it all goes to shit, the girls can't lose both of us."

Cameron noticed Ethan tensing—he didn't like what Ben was saying at all, but he was a smart man and knew they had to put the children first, so Cameron believed he'd ultimately agree.

"All right. I don't like it—not one little bit, but I'll do it." He finished by lightly pressing his lips to Ben's, his hand gently wrapping around the back of Ben's neck. The kiss and the way they were so obviously a team was so loving and intimate that Cameron had to swallow past the lump in his throat and look away. Ben and Ethan had exactly what he wanted for him and Zach.

"Who's Jacey?" Cameron eventually thought to ask.

"Jacey Locklear. She's this tech wiz Banner knows. She can hack anything. He's going to see if she can get into security cams, CCTV to see if we can track them. She'll try to find any cars registered to Jimmy. That kind of thing. She's helped us out on a few cases already. Really knows her stuff."

Cameron nodded. This had to work. They had to find them, and they had to stop Jimmy. It was clear to Cameron it was the only way he'd ever be able to live a normal life. It'd been more than two years—closer to three—since Jimmy had been around, since they'd seen each other, and yet it was clear Jimmy was still obsessed with hurting him. Cameron couldn't let him go after the people he cared about, though— he wouldn't let him. He'd do whatever it took.

They didn't get back to Cody until after one in the morning. Their only option had been a flight to Billings and then an hour and a half drive to Cody. But they eventually made it and found Alec Banner resting against Cameron's front door. His knees were pulled up, his head resting on them as he slept. At least Cameron assumed he had been asleep, but just as he'd seen Ben do, he came awake instantly as soon as they approached. He wondered if anyone who'd ever been in the military managed to sleep deeply.

"Cronin—s, Ethan," Alec greeted them and shook each of their hands.

Cameron opened the door and they all followed him inside. He offered Alec a thank you for coming to help which he merely brushed off. Alec Banner was a good-looking man with a wild shock of ginger hair, which had grown considerably since he'd left the FBI. His eyes were hazel and warm, his lips thin and with scarring on the left side that Cameron had always suspected came from a repaired cleft lip. His skin was pale and flawlessly smooth with a smattering of freckles on the bridge of his nose. He wasn't as tall as Ethan and him, but he likely reached six foot one and his body was fit.

"So," Alec began as soon as they'd settled onto the sofas. "I got an update from Jacey. She went through all the footage from the hotel security—told me it was 'piss easy'—and Zach is definitely with Jimmy. She got them on camera leaving the room. Jimmy's room was at the rear of the hotel right beside the fire exit door. Zach was out cold, must have been drugged, and Jimmy carried him right out the fire door. Parking lot cameras recorded him shoving Zach in the back of an old Dodge. It was definitely premeditated. He had his car pulled up close to the exit."

Drugged. Out cold. Shoved in the back of a car. Every word was an ice pick to his heart, but he held it together. Zach had suffered, so the least he could do was hear about it. He couldn't sit still, though, so he got up and paced around the room.

"Jacey pulled the surrounding CCTV. The last sighting she got was Jimmy's car heading south on I-120. She's tracking footage into and out of Meeteetse. It's the next town with CCTV. She'll have to track Jimmy town to town."

"Cam?"

"Yeah?" He looked across at his brother whose frown was even more pronounced now.

"You need to sleep. Come on. You're dead on your feet, and I'm gonna need you for this one. Bed...and that's an order."

He desperately needed sleep, he'd been awake for close to forty hours, but he just didn't think it'd come to him. He was too wired. Too damn scared. Ben was right though, so he had to at least try. He nodded and murmured good nights.

"Hey," Ben called after him. "We'll get him back. I promise you. And that fucker's not getting away this time."

Cameron knew Ben would do everything he could to keep that promise and that knowledge helped. It helped enough that he was able to get a few hours sleep.

IT WAS ANOTHER thirteen hours before they actually did something Cameron considered constructive. Alec had spent most of the day Skyping with Jacey. They had located Jimmy's car in Shoshoni, and as far as they could tell he hadn't left—unless he'd switched cars. There was a municipal airport there and they'd considered flying down, but there was no local car rental available to them. Instead, they drove there in Alec's car, arriving at dusk on the third day of Zach's disappearance. Ethan had stayed behind. His job was to run interference with the sheriff's department if it came to that, with the added bonus of him being out of the firing line if the situation went to shit.

Sheriff Begay had received a concerned call from Cheryl at the Cody Hotel because of Cameron's distressed visit the other night. So far Cameron had managed to stick with the Zach cheating on him line, but Begay hadn't sounded entirely convinced. If the Sheriff got one look at that photo, he'd know exactly what was going on. Ethan would do his best to sidetrack the sheriff if he showed up at Cameron's door again.

Frantic didn't even seem a big enough word to encompass how he was beginning to feel. Ben and Alec were altogether too calm for his liking. So as they pulled into a local motel, he was doing his best not to get too irritated with them.

"Sit tight while I go get us a room," Alec said, tossing a nervous glance at Cameron as though he knew he was about to boil over.

Cameron watched him stride toward reception and concentrated on clenching and unclenching his fists, the only comfort available to him.

"Cam, you need to relax. And before you rip my head off, I know it's easier said than done, but believe it or not, this is going well. We've tracked them quickly. Alec's confident they haven't left the area. This is a good thing." Ben spoke slowly and calmly as though he were talking to some kind of bull about to wildly buck around in a china shop—which in truth was how he felt.

"I can't get the what-ifs out of my fucking head...or the guilt."

"It's not your fault. Never was."

"Zach wanted me. Had the fucking guts to admit it, but I was too much of a coward to try with him, too fucking gutless to even admit to myself that I wanted him back. If I'd have been a better person...braver, none of this would have happened." The truth of his words stole his breath. He knew logically Jimmy was to blame but still...

Ben surprised him by replying, "Maybe you're right, but I suspect it was always gonna come to this. With you and Jimmy and any new man you ended up with. Jimmy was never going to let you go and be happy. So I figure you've got two choices here. You can either sit around whining and blaming yourself, or you, me and Alec can come up with a way to get your Zach back and get rid of that fucker for good. Which one's it gonna be?"

Cameron saw the glint in his brother's eyes and knew already which way Ben planned to go. He offered his brother what he hoped was his best evil grin and knew he'd succeeded when Alec came back to the car, looked between the two brothers and asked with a wary expression if he'd missed something.

Chapter Twenty-Four

ZACH

By Zach's count, this was the third day Jimmy had him. That is, of course, if he'd woken the same day Jimmy had drugged him, so really it could be longer. He might have lost innumerable days. His head was still achy, but otherwise he was unharmed—at least physically.

He wondered how Cameron was. Was he frantic? Did he think Zach had run off with Jimmy? Did he even know Jared was Jimmy? How badly was he hurting? Zach ached to be there with him, to do any little—or big—thing he could to make him feel better.

He had no idea where he was, only that he was no longer in the hotel room. Since he'd woken, his entire time had been spent in this one small unremarkable room with a locked door, barred windows, a narrow bed, connecting bathroom, and nothing else. Jimmy brought him meals, occasionally talking to him, but otherwise leaving him alone. He was bored and scared and just wanted to go home.

Home to Cameron—wherever he may be. Ryan had been so right. Zach had mostly grasped it all those months ago when Ryan had told him Lucas was his home, but now he understood it to his very core. Cameron was his home. With Cameron was where he felt safest.

When he got out of here, he was going to make sure Cameron understood it too.

What he'd give to have Cameron here with him now, even though he recognized the selfishness in that wish. If Cameron were here where Jimmy was, then… No, better he be here alone. At least Cameron was safe.

Wherever they were was eerily quiet. Zach hadn't even heard traffic noise since he'd been here. The silence made it easy to hear Jimmy approach. He heard the floorboards groan under his footsteps now, giving Zach precious seconds to prepare to come face-to-face with Cameron's monster.

As with every other time, Zach pressed himself as far back as he could get against the farthest wall from the door, but there'd never be enough distance between him and this man.

"Good morning, Zach," Jimmy said as he pushed the door open. He held a small tray in his hand with what looked to be coffee and toast. He put it on the bed as he'd done before, and then he stood back, leaning against the wall opposite Zach.

Zach watched him, his gaze flicking to the still open door, but he knew he'd never make it. He saw Jimmy's mouth curl up into a snarl as though daring him to try.

"You'll be pleased to know that Cameron will be here today. I expect he's already pretty close on our tail. He'll have done such hard work to find you, but if he'd have just waited, I was going to text him where we were anyway."

Zach's feelings were a tempest swirling around him. His heart fluttered at the thought of seeing Cameron today and then stopped in terror when his brain caught up to what Cam's arrival actually meant. Whatever Jimmy wanted with Cameron was going to happen today, and he couldn't imagine it'd be anything good. Was he going to hurt Cameron? He'd said Cameron needed to be punished. And Zach couldn't stand by and let it happen.

"You're a sweet man, Zach, and very good-looking, but I'm sorry, it's always been Cameron. He's mine, he belongs to me, and nothing can change that."

"He doesn't love you. You did nothing but hurt him." Zach knew it was useless to argue with a madman, but he couldn't help himself.

"I had to hurt him. It was the only way to make him better. How can I make you understand? Cameron is beautiful, but he could be perfect if he'd have stayed with me."

"Cameron is perfect to me, and I don't have to change him or beat him or make him feel awful about himself—"

"But he will never be yours," Jimmy thundered. "Never. All I did," he continued in a calmer tone, "was love him and try to make him better."

"By nearly killing him? By making him believe he's worthless? He doesn't even need to be better, and if you really loved him, you'd know that."

"Is that so? Doesn't need to be better? Do you need me to list all the ways Cameron needs to improve? Let's see... He'd eat too much of the wrong things, spoiling what could have been a perfect body. He could never clean anything properly. Is it so unreasonable to expect things to be done a certain way? And yet he could never manage to do that for me. He lied to me over and over. Telling me he was at home, but when I called, he never answered. He belongs to me. He answers to me."

The more Jimmy talked, the lower the curtain fell, until Zach clearly saw the madness Jimmy had successfully hidden away from him for all those weeks. Zach should have recognized it sooner—he'd grown up with a similar crazy.

"You don't deserve him," Zach whispered. "If I could wipe away every second you had with him, I would, because you don't deserve any of them."

Jimmy tilted his head, appraising Zach in such a way that it made his skin crawl. "You really are in love with him, aren't you? You know, Zach, it is very impolite to be in love with another man's man. And if I didn't want to punish Cameron, I'd kill you now for it." Jimmy looked him over as though imagining doing exactly that and Zach cringed even farther away. "Eat your breakfast. I'm going to let Cameron know where we are. I really can't wait any longer to see him, to get my hands on him again. Perhaps I'll even let you watch before…"

Everything Jimmy just said was so wrong, so unhinged, it left him feeling sick to his stomach. Jimmy couldn't be reasoned with—he knew that much now.

He thought about Cameron, remembered what kind of man he was. Cameron was strong, and he was honorable and brave. He'd fight, and Zach would damn well fight with him. Enough with letting men like his father and Jimmy have things their way; he was not theirs to tyrannize and control. His life was his own, just as Cameron's was his, and it was past time Jimmy understood that.

Jimmy left the room and Zach debated whether or not to eat the food he'd left. On the one hand, he wanted the strength it would give him, but on the other, Jimmy had drugged him once already, and he didn't want to risk a second time when he needed to be at his best today. In the end, he settled on eating the toast only. He suspected any drugs were likely to be in the coffee, so he left it untouched. Instead, he drank water from the bathroom sink to hydrate himself.

In the absolute silence around him, Zach tried to imagine how things might go today and what he could do to help. He suspected Jimmy's ultimate plan would see him dead by the end of the day, but Zach had no intention of letting that happen. How was he planning to do it? It would be in front of Cameron, part of his punishment; at least that much he did know.

What could Zach do? He didn't want to die, especially not now, and he refused to allow himself to be used to hurt Cameron. He had to do whatever it took to get away, even if it meant he had to kill Jimmy to do so.

Nervous tension had him pacing the room for what felt like hours. So many scenarios looped in his head, he was lost in them and didn't hear Jimmy approach until the door snicked open.

"Well, he's here. I was correct—he was right on my tail." Jimmy's body shuddered and a broad smile broke over his face. "I don't mind telling you, Zach, I'm a little bit excited. It's been too long since I've seen Cameron up close—since I've spoken to him."

Jimmy spoke as though all of this was completely normal. What was so terrifying was he seemed to have no understanding at all of how wrong this was.

"Zach, I'm going to need you to come with me."

The moment was here—too soon. Decision time. Even now he had no idea how this was going to go or what he was going to do, but he did know he wasn't going to let Jimmy win. Somehow, he was going to get himself, and more importantly Cameron, out of this.

Zach stood and immediately noticed the small gun in Jimmy's hand. He'd anticipated a weapon of some kind—how else could Jimmy expect to control two men —but the reality was frightening. Jimmy gestured toward the door with his gun and Zach walked forward, the press of the gun barrel to his back as Jimmy fell in behind him tensing his entire body with fear. Surprisingly, he remained calm. He suspected true fear would come with Cameron's arrival.

Jimmy herded him into a small room off an equally small kitchen. It appeared he'd been held in a scantily furnished cottage of some kind. It looked eerily like something his father's followers would have lived in at the commune. The room had a large window through which Zach could see a large body of water a short distance away and little else. He didn't recognize the area, but there didn't seem to be anything—or anyone—else around.

He almost jumped through his skin when he heard a loud knock on the front door. It must be Cameron, and that strange feeling of both dread and happy excitement flooded him once again. Jimmy left him where he was standing with a hissed "don't move" in his ear and walked the few short feet to open the door.

"Oh, Cameron, it's so good to see you again, love. Come in, come in," Jimmy crooned as though the scene playing out was the most normal thing in the world.

The feeling of bugs scuttling all over his skin was back, the hairs on the back of his neck standing tall and straight.

Zach didn't hear any reply from Cameron, but his big body quickly moved past Jimmy, his gaze flicking all around until it landed on Zach. Cameron's eyes softened as they took each other in. The urge to run to him was strong, but Zach fought it, knowing it would only provoke Jimmy. Cameron strode toward him immediately but came to a sudden halt when Jimmy spoke.

"Uh, uh. No, no. You've forgotten everything I ever taught you, Cameron. I know it's been a while, but that's not how you greet me, is it?"

The expressive warmth of Cameron's face shuttered, replaced by an impassive mask. Zach could tell he was going to play his role, put on a show for Jimmy. He turned on his heel and walked back to Jimmy, who held his arms wide, waiting. Cameron stepped into them, and Jimmy kissed him soundly, with his eyes open watching Zach over Cameron's shoulder.

Zach tasted bile in the back of his throat. His fingers itched to wrap around Jimmy's throat and squeeze and squeeze.

When they finally broke apart, Jimmy raised his flushed, smiling face to Zach, his eyes a little glassy with lust. Cameron faced him, too, but his face was pale, and he couldn't quite meet Zach's eyes. He had to know Zach understood what he was doing.

"Let him go, Jimmy. He's just a kid I was helping out. He means nothing. Let him go, and I'll show you how much I missed you." Cameron's voice was strong and calm.

"Don't worry, Cameron, I will be showing you how much I missed you very soon, but I'm afraid I cannot let things go unpunished. You know that."

The gun was still in Jimmy's hand; Cameron must have noticed it, but he didn't seem at all interested. He was inching farther into the room, getting closer to Zach, bringing Jimmy with him.

"Then punish me. It's my fault, not his. I failed again. I forgot."

How easily those words fell from Cameron's mouth with Jimmy around, whether part of an act or not—and Zach hated it. Anger bubbled up to replace the fear, and he wondered which emotion would hold him in better stead for the fight soon approaching. He moved as innocently as possible, trying to get himself between Jimmy and Cameron without either registering what he was doing.

"Do you know he's in love with you? Are you going to tell me that's your fault, Cameron? What did you do to make him fall in love with you?" Jimmy spat the question as though he found it completely unfathomable anybody could fall in love with Cameron. He had no idea of the precious heart he'd once held in his hands and crushed so violently. "How could *you* make him fall in love with you? Tell me the truth, or your punishment will be so much worse. I'll make him suffer before the end," he sneered.

Zach saw the turmoil in Cameron's eyes. Cameron was trying to take the blame to spare Zach, and yet Jimmy knew he'd left him with no self-esteem. How could a man with no self-esteem claim to believe he made someone fall in love with him? Zach understood the mind games—he'd watched his father play them for years, and the longer Cameron was around it, the more wounds were being reopened and the more damage Jimmy was inflicting.

Zach took another step closer; he was practically between them now, but Cameron moved, too, so Jimmy followed as though he was an orbiting moon. Zach tried again, but like some ridiculous slapstick comedy routine, each of his moves prompted a move from Cameron, and of course, a countermove from Jimmy.

"Zach, please. You need to leave," Cameron pleaded and then turned to Jimmy. "He doesn't need to be here, Jimmy. I don't want him here. I made him fall in love with me. I did. It was easy because he had no one. His father never loved him—no one ever had. I didn't even have to be anything special he was so desperate for any kind of affection." He looked frantically at Jimmy.

"There now. Not so hard to admit you aren't anything special." Jimmy's voice was cold and calm. "But you're lying to me again. I saw your photograph in the papers, you know. At his father's indictment. You were behind him, but you were looking at him, and I could tell, Cameron. I could tell from the way you were looking at him he meant something to you. That's when I knew I had to come back. I'm the only man in your life, Cameron, and you forgot that."

Zach was almost between them again; Cameron was glaring at him, his eyes flicking toward the window. Jimmy moved to stand closer behind Zach—too close. He pressed the barrel of the gun to Zach's temple and then slowly dragged it down over his cheek to his lips.

"Open up," Jimmy murmured, and Zach instinctively obeyed, still looking for his moment to fight back.

The gun was cool in his mouth and way too hard. Jimmy pulled it almost out and then slid it back in. Like a sick parody of oral sex. Cameron's face was pale, and he was shaking as Jimmy practically fucked Zach's mouth with the gun. Zach's body trembled violently, bile flooded his throat, and if Jimmy's arm wasn't wrapped around his waist, he doubted he'd still be on his feet.

"He seems a natural, Cameron. Maybe we should—"

"No." Cameron's voice cracked out sharp as a whip.

Jimmy released him and removed the gun. He walked around Zach and turned slowly to face him, never putting his back fully to Cameron. His sneer was firmly in place. "Seems our Cameron really does care about you, Zach, and I can't have that. He's forgotten I don't share him. He'll never forget again," he hissed and began raising the gun—and everything slowed down.

Zach lunged forward and grabbed Jimmy, throwing them both sideways to the ground, hoping the momentum would prevent the gun from coming up any higher. "Cam, run," he screamed.

When they landed, he was kind of half on top of Jimmy so the arms grabbing him from above could not have been Jimmy's. They were Cameron's. His heart sank when he realized he had not run—he should have known better. Cameron would never leave him.

Cameron hoisted him from the ground and dragged him off Jimmy, practically throwing him toward the door.

Zach fought to get his feet under him when he landed and turned to see what was happening behind him. Jimmy and Cameron were on the floor, a few yards away from him, nothing but a tangle of limbs as they struggled. One of Cameron's thick arms pulled back, and Zach heard a satisfying crack as he launched his fist forward, landing his blow somewhere on Jimmy's head. A muted grunt was followed by an angered roar, and Cameron's body buckled upward. He flopped back down and Zach hoped the weight of him might knock the wind out of Jimmy. But he'd seen his father in a maddened rage and knew in those moments their bodies were fueled and strengthened by insanity.

The tangled bodies rolled and slid, limbs blindly lashing out, looking for purchase, hoping to damage. He thought he saw a flash of metal spin away from them across to the other side of the room. The gun. Perhaps he could get to it.

Cameron somehow got to his knees and again pulled back his arm and punched Jimmy. There was no crack this time, but there was still a whoosh of air and a thud, letting Zach know the strike had connected. Cameron stood and backed away on wobbly legs.

Zach took a step toward Cameron, but he flung out his hand and called out "stop."

Zach froze. Jimmy was using the arm of a chair to help himself stand. Blood was flowing from his nose, and his right eye was already swollen so badly it was almost closed over.

"What. The fuck. Do you think you're doing, Cameron?" Jimmy snarled and then spat a mouthful of blood. He took one step toward Cameron, who never backed away.

"You'll never touch me again, you piece of shit, and you sure as hell will never lay one goddamn finger on Zach."

"So you think you've found your backbone? I'll crush it again, Cameron. Annihilate it this time," he screamed.

"No, Jimmy. Not ever again. After today I won't ever see you again or speak your name. I won't ever even think of you again. You'll mean less to me than nothing."

Jimmy's face was a mask of shock as it registered he'd lost control of Cameron. Zach perceived this was when Jimmy would be at his most dangerous. Now there was no reason for him not to kill Cameron. Jimmy threw himself down and back, and Zach knew he was going for the gun.

As Zach moved forward in the foolish hope of stopping him, Cameron turned to him, quickly closing the distance between them. Cameron gripped Zach's upper arm and turned him. His other large hand pushed on the back of his head, bending him over, head down, as he forced him forward running for the door. Zach couldn't see Jimmy or much of anything now, but just as they reached the door, he heard a gunshot followed by shattering glass. The shot was much louder than he expected from Jimmy's little gun. He didn't feel a bullet tear through his flesh, and Cameron never stopped moving, so he had to assume he hadn't been hit either.

As they crashed through the door into the brightness of the midafternoon sun, he waited for a second shot, but it never came. Cameron never slowed down and never let him put his head up until they'd reached a car about two hundred feet to the left of the house. The motor was running, but he couldn't see anyone sitting behind the wheel. Cameron shoved him in the back seat and followed him in, all while keeping his head pressed low.

Minutes later, Ben threw himself in the driver's seat and the car roared away, leaving the little cabin as though they'd never been there.

When Zach tried to turn his head to look back, Cameron wouldn't let him, but he couldn't stop him from seeing the flames in the rearview mirror.

Chapter Twenty-Five

CAMERON

Cameron had Zach pulled so tightly against him, so close, he may as well have been sitting in his lap. Zach was trembling, but Cameron couldn't be sure if that was just because *he* was shaking so badly. He knew Jimmy was dead. He didn't need to see the body. He'd known as soon as he'd heard the gunshot.

Ben and Alec hadn't told him which one of them was going to pull the trigger; apparently, the less he knew, the better. Cam had fought to even get into the cabin. Ben had wanted him and Alec to storm it while Cameron stayed safely out of the way. But it had been Cameron's fight. In the end, they'd told him to get Jimmy in front of the window and keep himself and Zach out of the line of fire if possible. Zach hadn't made it easy, determined as he'd been to put himself between him and Jimmy.

He bent forward and pressed a kiss to the top of Zach's head as he recalled Zach shuffling his body around in the cabin, trying to stand between Cam and danger.

"He's dead...isn't he?" Zach murmured.

"Yeah." It occurred to Cameron, for the first time, Zach may not be okay with what they'd done. Most people wouldn't. There were laws and the justice system for a reason.

"Good. He was crazy, and he wasn't ever going to let you go, Cam."

Cameron flicked his gaze up and caught Ben watching in the rearview mirror, a grim look in his eyes. Alec would be following behind in Jimmy's car.

"Did he hurt you, Zach?" Cameron asked, dreading the answer. He'd imagined Jimmy defiling Zach during the long hours he'd been missing, stealing his virginity in a violent and unwanted manner. Or beating him, torturing him. He'd imagined a million different ways Jimmy could have hurt him.

"No. He was waiting for you. He was going to kill me in front of you. To punish you. He kept telling me... Cameron, you listen to me—" Zach sat up and away from Cameron. He put his hands on both sides of Cameron's face and stared fiercely into his eyes. "There is nothing wrong with you. I know he tried to make you believe you weren't good enough, but you are. God, you so are. You listen to me, you believe *me,* not him, because I do love you—he never did—and you're perfect. Perfect," he finished on a whisper and then pulled Cameron's face toward his and pressed their lips together.

Cameron lost himself in the kiss. It was soft and sweet, a slow exploration of rediscovery. He tasted Zach's captivity on his breath, but it didn't matter because he couldn't get enough of the intimacy. Unbridled passion was wonderful, but there was a lot to be said for this kind of tenderness. With each gentle slide and press of their lips, the tension eased from Cameron's muscles, the ache in his heart subsided, and the burden in his mind lightened until he almost felt weightless enough that he might float away.

Cameron was panting hard by the time Zach pulled back. It was on the tip of his tongue to return the "I love you," but the back seat of a car with his brother able to listen from the front didn't seem the right time or place. Cameron wanted that moment to be perfect.

"Every second you were gone, I kept thinking over and over about what he might be doing to you. Every second," he whispered.

"Oh, Cam." Zach curled his body into him again and laid his head on his chest. Cameron tangled his fingers in Zach's soft hair, anchoring him to his body for the remainder of the trip home. It was a quiet drive. Each man lost to his own thoughts.

Ethan was waiting for them when they returned and took Ben straight into his arms with hushed words flowing between them. Alec would be by some time later in the night when he finished with Jimmy's car. Tomorrow, after they'd all rested, there would be a debriefing to make sure they hadn't missed any loose ends. But for now, he only wanted to get Zach alone, and he was sure Ben was feeling the same about Ethan.

"I'm gonna get Zach settled, and I need some sleep myself. Ben, you know where everything is. I'll see you both in the morning," Cameron said without preamble. He gave his brother a quick hug, nodding when Ben whispered how much he loved him and how glad he was that the nightmare of Jimmy was over. There'd be time to talk more in the morning.

He led Zach by the hand to his bedroom. It wasn't particularly late, but once the adrenaline dried up, his body was leaden with exhaustion and he imagined Zach must have been just as tired.

He flicked on the lamp when he entered the room, never releasing Zach's hand. Then he turned and carefully began removing Zach's clothes while watching for any sign of discomfort or hesitation from Zach. Once he had them both naked, he led Zach into the shower.

It only took a few moments to get the spray of water to a temperature hot enough to burn away the remnants of Jimmy from their skin. Cameron guided Zach under the spray and lathered up his washcloth. He curled his hands around Zach's neck and began washing, circling the cloth all over his solid chest and down his sinewy arms, turning him so he could cleanse his strong back. He sporadically pressed openmouthed kisses to Zach's skin, tasting the clean flesh.

When he was satisfied, he dipped lower to work on the supple muscles of his legs, saving the most intimate areas till last. Zach's hands rested gently on his head, his fingers lightly tracing patterns on his scalp as he worked and then gripped tighter when Cameron carefully washed his cock and balls, lightly fondling them as he went.

"My turn," Zach whispered as Cameron stood.

Cameron had never known an intimacy like those long minutes in the shower with Zach. They were washing away each other's sins, an absolution of sorts. Cameron had never felt so clean of body or soul. That feeling of lightness returned, like a natural high Zach somehow managed to give him.

They dried each other while sharing kisses and eventually fumbled their way to the bed, lying face-to-face, laughing and touching because they *had* to, as much as they wanted to.

"I need you." Zach's words were a mere breath against his ear, but Cameron heard them as loud as a drumbeat. There'd be no denying him this time.

"You can have me, Zach. I'm yours. I've been yours from the start." And that was all it took. Zach suddenly reared up, pushing his hips toward Cameron's groin and deepening their kisses. Cameron opened his mouth, allowing Zach's tongue to tangle with his. Zach's hands were everywhere as they lay side by side, Cameron's leg pressing between Zach's.

Zach cupped Cameron's ass and pulled their groins tightly together, their bare cocks rubbing. Cameron slipped a hand between their bodies and grabbed Zach's shaft, giving it a squeeze. Zach grunted and broke their kiss. He stared at Cameron for a moment and then smiled.

"Trust me?"

"I do," Cameron answered with absolute conviction.

"Roll over, on your tummy." Zach's tone was commanding, sending a little shiver up Cameron's spine. He wasn't into Dominant/submissive sex, especially after years of Jimmy's unwelcome control, but he didn't mind following Zach's enthusiastic commands because he knew they were for *their* pleasure rather than *his* degradation.

As he was rolling over, he saw Zach, out of the corner of his eye, rummaging around in his bedside table and knew exactly what he was looking for. Zach held up the lube and a condom with a triumphant smile before returning his attention to Cameron.

"I've watched how to do this—you know, on the Internet—but you have to promise you'll tell me if I hurt you, or if I'm doing it wrong. Okay?" Zach said as he positioned himself so he was sitting on the back of Cameron's slightly spread thighs.

"Promise."

Cameron buried his face in his folded arms and waited for what he knew was to come. He heard the snick of the lube cap, and moments later, he felt the cool moisture as Zach's finger spread the lube around his hole. Zach played for a while, his finger just rimming his hole, the tip dipping in every now and then, never fully breaching. Zach was silent as he played, but Cameron heard his breath quickening as he seemed to become more and more fascinated with exploring.

Suddenly Zach's finger pressed inside his body, stealing Cameron's breath. He was relaxed enough so it didn't hurt. When Zach found his prostate, he rubbed his finger over it, sending Cameron's hips into an uncontrollable spasm, the pleasure riding him now. Oh, thank god for porn was all he could think as Zach added another finger, crooked them, and nailed that spot over and over.

Cameron wondered if he was going to try to make him come from that alone when suddenly his fingers were gone. Zach was mumbling something Cameron couldn't quite understand, but he recognized the sound of the condom pack ripping open.

"I'm not sure how..."

"Let me help," Cameron murmured and turned over to help Zach roll the condom down his thick erection.

Out of habit, he then moved to rise onto all fours—it was usually how Jimmy had demanded to have him—but Zach eased him back down and encouraged him over onto his back. Cameron closed his eyes, the emotions flooding him becoming almost too much to bear.

"Open your eyes," Zach whispered as he wedged a pillow under Cameron's ass.

Cameron did, and Zach was right there, watching him. How could he not kiss him when he looked so beautiful, so vulnerable? Cameron pulled him closer and slid his lips over Zach's. Nothing in Cameron's life had ever felt as right as Zach in his arms.

The head of Zach's cock nudged at his entrance. Cameron widened his legs, the movement enough to spur Zach on. He pulled away from the kiss and smiled down at Cameron.

"Ready?"

"More than."

"Don't shut your eyes, Cam. Look at me."

Cameron had to admit he was a little surprised at this more dominant side of Zach, but he wasn't going to complain about it. He loved it.

He never looked away from Zach as he slowly pushed his cock inside Cameron's body, concentrating so hard he was chewing on his bottom lip the whole time. The burn snatched Cameron's breath away, but god, it lit his body up with pleasure. He relaxed into it, trusting deep in his bones that Zach wouldn't hurt him.

Zach's eyes were wide and held a wild, almost feral look within them, his breathing quick and heavy. Cameron could see he was fighting for control.

"Oh god," Zach moaned as he bottomed out. Cameron grunted in reply, overwhelmed by the exquisite fullness. For a moment, neither man moved and both held their breath. Then Zach pulled back just a little, testing the waters before pushing back in. He gave a few more tentative thrusts before he seemed to find both his confidence and his rhythm.

Cameron wrapped his legs around Zach's back as he picked up the pace and began really moving inside him. Their skin slapped together with every thrust and the look in Zach's eyes became more and more wild. The sensations and sounds of the experience were so good it was hard to believe Zach had never done this before.

Cameron wiggled a little as Zach's cock slid over his prostate, the pleasure so intense he knew he wouldn't last much longer. He reached between their bodies and curled his hand around his own hard cock, pumping it in time with Zach's thrusts.

"Cam...Cam," Zach chanted as Cameron felt Zach's cock thicken and his body tense. Cameron stroked faster, wanting them to come together. Zach's movements became increasingly erratic as he lost control in the final moments before he shuddered. A stifled shout buried in Cameron's neck announced Zach's orgasm.

Zach's loss of control in the face of his lust for Cameron was enough to tip Cameron over the edge, and he came in long spurts between their bellies, his warm come smearing in his smattering of hair and along the ridges of Zach's taut abs.

Zach collapsed on top of him, completely spent and apparently unable to hold himself up a second longer. Cameron lay still, allowing Zach to lie there and recover.

It only took a few minutes for him to raise his head, a wildly enthusiastic smile covering his beautiful face. "That. Was. Awesome."

Cameron laughed, couldn't have kept it in if he'd wanted to. "That *was* awesome," he replied.

"Yeah? You really enjoyed it? I was okay?"

"Couldn't you tell how much I enjoyed it?" Cameron ran his fingers down the side of Zach's face. "I loved it, Zach. I love you."

Zach moved quickly, a little too fast, causing Cameron to wince. "Ah hell, sorry. But you love me?"

"I do. I should have told you a while ago. I love your sweetness. I love your intelligence. I love how you didn't let your upbringing break you. I love how you grab my fingers to still them when I can't stop fidgeting. I love your scent and how you love chocolate. And I love how you never gave up on me." Cameron smiled. "I love every single thing about you, Zachary Abraham Piper."

"Jesus, Cam, this is big, really big, but I won't hurt you. I won't break your heart. I promise you." Zach looked so earnest—he was taking this very seriously—and it was serious. It was always momentous when someone handed over their heart.

Cameron should be terrified, given his past—but he wasn't. Zach had him and he believed everything Zach just said.

"I know, Zach. I trust you." Cameron couldn't believe the words coming out of his mouth. He never thought he'd be able to say them again—and mean them. "And ditto. I promise I won't hurt you either."

Cameron expected they'd snuggle down and probably fall into an exhausted sleep now, but Zach seemed ready to jump out of his skin. Cameron cleaned them up and did his best to settle them, but Zach talked on and on into the night about anything and everything. And Cameron listened to— and loved—every word.

They made love a second time at some point in the early hours of the morning, and if their first time hadn't cemented just how strong Zach's hold on his heart was, their second time clinched it. They held and petted each other, whispering soft words between them as they brought their bodies to peaks of pleasure previously unknown.

Chapter Twenty-Six

ZACH

Zach woke the next morning, not because he wanted to, but because he had to. At some point during the night, he'd burrowed under Cameron's bigger body, and now he was overheated and having trouble breathing comfortably. He knew he tossed and turned a lot in his sleep, but it didn't seem to be bothering Cameron, who was snoring soundly beside him, or above him depending on how you looked at it.

Doing his best not to wake Cameron, Zach shuffled backward, disentangling limbs as he went. Once he was free of Cameron's arms, legs, and the bedding, he carefully stood and just stared.

Cameron was lying flat on his back, his arms stretched wide, one leg bent and the other straight out. The sheet was tangled around his waist and legs, but his flaccid cock was visible as it lay against his thigh. He was extraordinarily beautiful.

Zach's fingers itched to reach out and twist through the thick expanse of light hair that curled over Cameron's chest and trailed all the way down to the thick patch at his groin. Zach had no chest hair, but he loved pressing his chest to Cameron's so he could feel the hair tickle against his smooth skin.

Just looking at Cameron had his cock twitching. Thinking about what they'd shared last night had him hardening, his hips rolling a little in anticipation of the pleasure Cameron gave him. He'd never be able to go out in public with Cameron again if he couldn't learn to control himself.

Only a growing urgency to pee dragged him away from Cameron, and once that was taken care of, his rumbling tummy lured him to the kitchen. The house was quiet as he moved through. Ben and Ethan were still asleep, or they'd left, although he couldn't imagine they'd have gone without seeing Cameron.

Despite only viewing the man's back, Zach recognized Alec Banner as soon as he walked into the kitchen. The wild ginger hair was a dead giveaway. Alec was leaning against the counter, facing the window.

"How'd you sleep, Zach?"

"How'd you know it was me?"

"Trick of the trade. I could tell you, but then I'd have to kill you," Alec said, without turning around.

Zach had met Alec a handful of times; he liked him but didn't know him very well. Though he suspected the reverse wasn't true. Alec would know him exceptionally well from his interviews.

"How's Cameron?" Alec asked when Zach remained silent.

"Fast asleep."

Alec nodded but still didn't turn to look at him. "Good. He needs it. Never seen a man look as haunted as he was when you were gone. I've seen plenty of people look terrified, but Cameron...looked as if he was ready to flay himself open and spill his guts all over the ground if he believed that'd get you back. And make no mistake, Zach, if he hadn't rescued you, he'd have never gotten over it."

"He loves me," Zach said simply and easily.

"Yes, he does. Finally told you, did he?" Alec turned and faced him at last. There was a half smile hiding the sadness in Alec's eyes.

"You knew?"

"Everyone knew. We all knew after your father's indictment, and I only saw you together for five minutes then. We've all been placing bets for months on when he'd finally fess up."

Zach laughed, even though Cameron would be mortified if he knew about the bets. "I wish you'd have all given him a kick in the ass to hurry him up."

"Mm. The foolishness of men." Alec pulled out one of the stools from the breakfast bar and sat. Zach took the seat opposite. "So I wanted to tell you that my friend in the FBI is still working on trying to trace the movements of the cult. See if we can pinpoint where you were when...well, when your mom disappeared. I'll be honest though, Zach, it's a long shot we'll ever find anything. Even if we find where you were camped, the chances that we'd find a body—sorry." Alec winced.

"It's okay. I know. In my heart, I believe my father killed her. I don't know why or where and probably never will, but I know she's not out there alive somewhere."

"Coffee?" Alec stood.

"Thanks. Black, no sugar."

"Ugh. The tough stuff, hey? Okay." Alec moved around as though he was the one who'd lived here for months rather than the relative stranger he was. "So what are you going to do about your mom's family?"

"I've got to wait to hear from Detective Marshall, but if they want to, I'll do the DNA test, and I'd love to meet them."

"They'll be lucky to have you in their family, Zach." Alec spoke with such a sense of wistfulness that Zach yearned to ask him what was upsetting him so much.

"Are you okay, Alec?"

"Banner's always okay, Zach. He only has two moods— grumpy and happy." Ben scuffed Zach's hair as he walked past, Ethan close on his heels. "You know how I have mine, Banner." Ben leaned against the far bench. Ethan stood beside him, but he remained ramrod straight.

"One for you, Ethan?" Alec asked.

"Please."

"So, I can't help noticing my brother hasn't made it out of bed yet. You must have worn him out last night, Zach." Ben winked, and Zach felt color staining his cheeks.

"Jesus, Ben." Cameron's voice was so close behind him he felt his breath blowing over his ear. His body came up close behind Zach, the heat of it searing him. Zach tipped his head back, and Cameron leaned over him for an awkward, perfect upside-down kiss.

"Oh, so you are up. But I, uh, can't help notice you walking a bit gingerly there, Cam. Anything you'd like to share with the group?"

Oh god, Zach thought he might actually go up in flames. He couldn't believe what he was hearing, and yet there was something so embracing about it—so accepting. He belonged here among this group of men, and what he and Cameron shared was nothing to be ashamed of.

"When the hell are you going to grow up, Ben?" Cameron sighed.

"I'm betting never," Alec quipped.

"Ethan tells me I'm perfect, and he wouldn't change a thing about me, thank you very much." Ben sniffed.

"Well, now, there's always a little room for improvement…" Ethan jumped away as soon as he spoke, narrowly missing the swatting hand Ben launched at him.

"I hate to break this up, but I have to get on the road. I may have a case, so let's get this done, okay?" It looked like Alec had flipped back to grumpy. Zach got the feeling again that something was wrong with him.

Cameron remained where he was with his front pressing against Zach's back, his arms draped over his shoulders. Every now and then his lips pressed into Zach's hair, and he'd swear Cameron was inhaling his scent.

"So," Alec began as he passed around coffees. "I dumped the car as discussed. There'll be nothing in there to link Zach, and Jacey confirmed she can't find anything linking Jimmy to the car. I'm guessing he stole it somewhere. So we're clear there."

"Body's being taken care of—less you know the better—shack was burned down, so there'll be no trace evidence there. Alec, Jacey found nothing on the shack?" Ben asked.

"Nothing linking Jimmy to it."

"Zach, you all right?" Ethan asked.

Zach wasn't sure if it was the fact he was shaking or the color had drained from his face, but something had drawn Ethan's attention. "Yeah," he murmured. He was, on the face of it. But deep down… They'd taken a man's life.

"This isn't on you, Zach," Cameron said. "This was us. Me. My decision."

"Fuck that, Cam. I'd have done it whether you wanted to or not," Ben scoffed.

"Me too," Alec stated. "Look, I was the law—so were you, Ethan—I know how it can work sometimes. Jimmy would have been out in a few years, if he even got jail time.

And he wouldn't have stopped until Zach, and eventually you, Cam, were dead. I'm not saying I want to run around dishing out vigilante justice, but sometimes the law doesn't protect the innocent, so I will."

"It won't be a habit though, will it?" Ethan asked, his dark blue eyes intent on Ben.

"No. No, I promise. I didn't kill Piper, and if I'd have just come across Jimmy in the street minding his business I'd have hauled him to the cops and let them deal with him, but he'd kidnapped Zach and he was going to kill him and then do god knows what to my brother, so yeah, I'm okay with what we did, but no, it won't be what we do going forward."

Ethan nodded and whispered, "Good." Then he drew Ben into his arms and kissed him gently. "Let's go home to the girls?"

"Yeah. Can't believe how much I miss those little pixies. Cam, Zach, you two okay with all of this?"

"Hearing that, I am now. I can't thank you all enough for what you've done for Zach and me. I hated asking you, Ben. If I could have done it by myself, I would have."

"Love you, brother." Ben stepped out of Ethan's arms and into his brother's.

Alec gave a disgusted snort and threw his hands in the air. "That's it. I've had enough of this sappy shit. I'm out of here. Cronins, Ethan, Zach. I'll see you all when I see you. Ben, I'll let you know about the new case."

Zach watched as both Ben and Cameron walked forward as though to hug or at the very least shake Alec's hand, but he deftly dodged them and threw a wave to the room in general over his shoulder. Ben and Cameron glanced at each other and shrugged their shoulders.

"Thank you, Alec," Zach and Cameron called out at the same time, bringing a smile to Zach's face.

"Is Alec all right?" Ethan asked.

"Nope. I don't know what's wrong, but he won't say anything till he's good and ready. I'll call him in a few days and check in." Ben dropped a kiss on Ethan's lips, and rather than his usual longing when he witnessed such things, Zach felt nothing but excitement that he could easily turn and share just such a kiss with the man he loved as well.

"Right. Let's make plans to get home then." Ben clapped his hands. Zach wondered if the events of the last twenty-four hours would really roll so easily off his back. He suspected not.

"I'll go book our flights," Ethan reluctantly moved away from Ben, and Cameron followed him out, leaving him and Ben alone.

They were silent for a while, each watching the other, until Ben finally spoke.

"I'm guessing Cameron told you all about Jimmy?"

"Yeah," he whispered, hating to even think about that man and the vile things he'd done.

"We'll never know everything, Zach, but Cam's going to be okay now, and that's because of you and because Jimmy's gone. So when you start doubting what we did, look at my brother, how happy he is, and know we did the right thing."

"I will. I can't thank you all enough for coming after me. For doing what you did for Cam."

"I'd do anything for him—for family. And that means you too now. You were family even before you and Cam bumped uglies. Cameron was a dead man walking until you came along. He was...cold. You saved him from a life of nothing, Zach."

Bumped uglies? What the hell did that mean? Zach had no idea what Ben was talking about aside from the notion of being part of a family. He'd been raised surrounded by people. People who should have been family and loved him like they were family, but they didn't. He must be the luckiest person on the planet to find it now and perhaps he'd even have his mother's family in his life.

"Two o'clock flight out of Cody, Ben. I called Ryan and told him we'd be there first thing in the morning to get the girls. Thought we'd have tonight to ourselves." Ethan waggled his eyebrows as he walked back into the room, Cameron right beside him.

"Perfect. I was just telling Zach here that he's family, especially now that he's bumped uglies with you, brother." Ben's smile was enormous.

"You did not say that to him?" Cameron palmed his forehead.

"I did. He might as well get to know what his future brother-in-law is like." Ben turned and winked at him as he spoke. Zach laughed, knowing Ben was doing his best to tease the hell out of poor Cameron.

Cameron, meanwhile, seemed to be choking on his own tongue as he coughed and spluttered something about "too soon for marriage" but Zach only laughed louder. Cameron was adorable, and now that he had him, there was nothing Zach wouldn't do to keep him.

"I love you, Ben, but Jesus, you're an asshole." Ethan smiled with nothing but adoration written all over his face. Zach knew then how they'd all known about him and Cameron because when you loved someone—adored them— you wore those feelings for everyone to see.

Chapter Twenty-Seven

CAMERON

"I told you I'm not ticklish."

"You must be, somewhere." Zach's voice was muffled under the sheets. His entire body was buried under there, his head down near Cameron's groin as he unsuccessfully sought out a ticklish spot somewhere on Cameron's body. Cameron had come hard only moments ago, but Zach's lips brushing against his thigh as he spoke had his cock valiantly attempting a revival.

It was a week since Jimmy, a week since Ben and Ethan went home—a week since Zach had first been inside his body, and he'd almost lost count of how many times it had been since then. Zach was an enthusiastic and bossy lover, eager to try every position he could remember from his porn-watching days. Cameron's body ached deliciously from Zach's attention every day, and he gave serious thought to sending Pornhub a personal thank you card.

"I'm not sure I've tried here," Zach mumbled as his long thin fingers played in the crease between his thigh and cock. Cameron jolted, not because it tickled but from the pleasure.

"That's the first place you tried. But if you want to revisit it, I'm okay with that."

Cameron felt, more than heard, Zach laugh under the covers. He loved this. That they could have fun during such intimacy was a revelation. Sex with Jimmy had been pleasant at the start, perfunctory in the middle, and a nightmare by the end of their relationship. It had never been fun and rarely brought him the joy that sex with Zach did.

"Cam?"

"Mm-hmm."

"Maybe next time... I think maybe next time I'd like you to top me."

They'd talked about it a little, Zach making it clear he was open to it, but Cameron wasn't going to push. Zach would come to him when he was ready.

"Yeah?"

"Yeah. Don't think this means I've exhausted all the ways I wanna do it with you or anything... I just think my poor dick and your poor ass might need a break." Zach finished as his smiling face burst from under the covers. He was getting quite the dirty mouth on him and Cameron approved.

Cameron dragged him close and pressed his mouth to his, kissing him through his laughter. "Oh yeah? I've worn you out? Well, I'd love to get inside you, Zach." He hadn't topped since a college boyfriend years ago. Jimmy had never allowed it.

He had much more to say on the matter, but Zach's phone trilled from the bedside table. It rang so rarely they both just stared at each other for a moment.

Zach snapped out of it first and leaned over Cameron's body to answer it.

"Hello... Yes... Oh."

Zach was silent for a while, nodding at whatever the caller was saying as though they could see him. Cameron was content to simply look at him, marveling as he often did that this wonderful man had somehow fallen into his lap.

"Really? Oh my god. Yes, of course...uh huh... Tomorrow nine a.m. See you then. Thank you."

Zach ended the call and tossed the phone to the foot of the bed. He sat up with his legs crossed, staring straight ahead with a wide grin on his face.

"Zach?"

"Cam, oh god. That was Detective Marshall. She went to see the Malcolms, told them all about me, and showed them my photo. They've agreed to the DNA test, but they told her they are confident my mom was their daughter. They said I look just like my uncle, and they wanna meet me tomorrow in Cheyenne. My grandparents, Cam. My grandparents."

Zach bounded out of bed doing some kind of dance around the room. Cameron's heart both ached and bloomed for him. He hoped to god the Malcolms were right.

"That's great. Try not to get too excited till the results come back, but it sounds very promising, Zach."

"Family, Cam. I mean you're my family, and Ben, Ethan, Ryan, Lucas, possibly even Alec, but this is blood family...my mom's family. I know I've got my father and some siblings, but I can't really count them because they don't want me. But maybe these guys do."

Zach jumped on the bed and grabbed Cameron by his shoulders; he pulled him close and kissed him breathless. "We can drive there now. It's not that late and we can be there by two; we'll still get a few hours sleep before we meet them at nine. We can do it, can't we?"

How could he, and why would he, say no in the face of such enthusiasm? This was Zach's family, and he deserved the chance to meet them—Zach's mother deserved for her son to meet her family.

Cameron jumped up, taking Zach with him. "Let's go. Get packed. We're out the door in ten."

The two of them flew around like twin tornados throwing clothes, toiletries, and other necessities into a couple of bags. Zach chattered the whole time, wondering different things about the people he was going to meet tomorrow. It was always "when we meet them," and Cameron wondered if that was such a good idea. He didn't know what the Malcolms were like; for all he knew, they might be raging homophobes, and the last thing he wanted to do was expose Zach to that.

"Maybe you should meet them first, without me." Cameron hedged.

"Why would I do that?" Zach glanced at him quickly and then went back to tossing a shirt in his bag.

"We've talked about how not everyone is so accepting of gay people, Zach. Maybe your grandparents—"

"Then they'll lose their grandson. Look, Cam, I don't remember a great deal about my mom, but I remember she loved me, and Detective Marshall said her parents never stopped looking for her. That tells me they're loving parents too. I don't think it's going to be a problem, and if it is...it's theirs. You and me...we're a package deal."

"Package deal. Okay." Cameron nodded. "I love you, Zach, and I'll be there for you no matter what happens."

"I love you too. Let's get going. We've got family to meet," Zach said with his inexhaustible optimism.

They threw their bags in the back of the Bronco, and Zach locked up while Cameron reversed out. As soon as Zach jumped up into the passenger seat, Cameron popped it into gear and took off.

It was a clear night, so if the weather held, they should make it there in less than six hours. The fastest route took them through Shoshoni, but Cameron dreaded the memories it might bring back. Fortunately, the little cabin had been well off the main thoroughfare so they wouldn't be able to see it—or rather the burned out shell.

Nothing had come back to bite them yet. Nothing from the cabin, Jimmy's car—Jimmy's body. In the back of his mind, Cameron knew he'd always worry there'd be a knock on the door but that was a worry far easier to live with than Jimmy showing up one day and killing him, or worse, Zach.

"What do you think they'll want me to call them?" Zach asked, thankfully breaking into Cameron's reverie.

"Not sure. Maybe Mr. and Mrs. Malcolm to start off with."

"Yeah, but after, when we know for sure, they're my grandparents. What did you call yours?"

Cameron hadn't known either set of grandparents very well. His grandmother on his father's side he hadn't known at all; she'd died before he'd even been born. "Um...my dad's father I called pop, and my mom's parents I called Nana and Poppa when I was little, but I probably would have grown out of that, and it would have just been nan and pop."

"Nan and pop. I like it. I wonder what my cousins call them. I'll probably call them whatever they do. Detective Marshall said it was a big family. If Mom had me so young, there might be some little ones." Zach was practically bouncing in his seat. Cameron was really hoping this went well for him. He hated to imagine the drive home beside a despondent Zach if it all went to shit.

"You really like kids, don't you?"

"I do. I'm still dreaming of working with them someday—maybe as part of Chasing Hope."

"What?" Cameron damn near ran off the road. Zach wanted to work with his brother to find missing kids. That could be dangerous work. Cameron wasn't at all sure how he felt about the idea.

"Don't panic, Cam. I meant as a therapist working with the kids they rescue. They've gotta need help; eventually I might even go in when they're rescuing them, if needed."

"I had no idea you were thinking that way, though I should have guessed."

Zach's hand pressed on his thigh and squeezed. "I've been so lucky. Twice now I've seen what your brother can do, how he can help. I want to be a part of that. Give back."

Cameron smiled. "That sounds like you."

"Maybe we could both help out one day. If you'd be interested..."

Zach turned to look back out the window leaving Cameron to his thoughts. He definitely could be interested in something along those lines. He wasn't at all sure what he had to offer, but there had to be something. For years, Cameron had drifted like flotsam through his life, letting it toss him here and there. That had to change; he needed to take control back. It was time he started thinking about his future—one that included Zach.

Chapter Twenty-Eight

ZACH

It was almost 2:00 a.m. by the time they reached Cheyenne. Zach had been out in the real world for many months now, but sometimes simple things like being able to check into a hotel in the middle of the night still astounded him.

He'd trudged through the hotel beside Cameron, both of them dead on their feet, before they'd fallen into bed. But Zach had only managed a few hours sleep before nerves had woken him.

All the memories he had of his mother, aside from that last day by the creek, were good ones, loving ones. He'd never get her back—he knew that—but maybe he could have the next best thing—her family.

During the quiet times of the drive from Cody, he'd tried to conjure up images of his mother's face. The most vivid one was the image of the photograph Detective Marshall had shown him, but there were others swimming around in his mind. Did his grandmother look like her? Had his mother gotten her eyes from his grandfather? He could hardly wait to meet them.

Beside him, Cameron squirmed, drawing his attention. They rarely slept in clothes, and Cameron didn't like the tangle of blankets, preferring instead to heat or cool the room to a comfortable temperature if necessary. Cameron's body ran so naturally hot that artificial heat was rarely needed, and Zach benefited by having an unfettered view of Cameron's naked body as he slept.

Cameron was on his stomach. His head was facing away from Zach with his legs slightly scissored apart. His arms were curled under his head, stretching the muscles of his back taut. God, he was a masterpiece.

Zach shifted closer and lightly pressed the tip of his nose to the small of Cameron's back. He trailed it up his spine, inhaling his musky scent as he went. When he reached his neck, he turned, ghosting his nose toward Cameron's ear, nuzzling in behind it. Soft hairs tickled at his face, and he sucked at Cameron's earlobe.

Zach's body was pressed along the length of Cameron's, and he felt the tiny shudder signaling that Cameron was waking to his ministrations. Zach let his fingertips gently play all along Cameron's side, occasionally curling around to his stomach before turning back to cup his ass cheek. Cameron's breath quickened, but he remained pliant beneath Zach's touch.

"Do you remember what I asked for earlier?" he whispered into Cameron's ear, setting off another tremor in his lover's big body.

"Yeah."

"I still want it, Cam. Now…please." Zach tugged on Cameron's shoulder, rolling him onto his back. He didn't give him a chance to answer before he kissed his full lips, stealing whatever words he'd been about to utter. Cameron's hands came up to tangle in his hair and hold him close as they always did when they kissed. The way Cam held him made Zach feel as though Cameron was afraid he was going to run away—or be stolen away again. Perhaps one day he'd be able to stop worrying because Zach wasn't going anywhere.

"Roll over," Cameron murmured.

Zach moved onto his back, and Cameron rose up so he was resting on one elbow. With his other hand, he gently pressed his fingertips to the hollow of Zach's throat and then circled patterns all over his smooth chest. Cameron tweaked his nipples, teasing the small buds into hardened peaks before his fingers continued their journey south.

Sometimes they fucked fast and hard, but this was Zach's favorite. When they slowly explored each other's bodies, the hard plains, the dips and valleys, the little spots that made their toes curl and their hips circle, seeking out more.

The tip of Cameron's finger dipped into his belly button and circled around, Zach's stomach quivering at the sensation. Zach was watching Cameron, whose eyes never looked away from where his fingers were. He wanted to see if the pale blue of his eyes was lit from behind with adoration like they often were these days. Zach hoped that light never went out.

"Hey," he whispered, drawing Cameron's gaze. There it was. He smiled. "I love you."

"Love you, too. So much, Zach."

Cameron's thick fingers finally reached his cock, feathering a line from tip to root. His cock jumped against his stomach at the touch, a drop of precome trickling out of his slit to his abs below. Cameron scooped it up with his thumb and smeared it around the head. He curled his fist around the shaft and pumped him a few times. Zach closed his eyes, his head thumping back on the pillow.

After a few strokes, Cameron released him and shuffled around on the bed. Zach split open one eyelid to watch as he fumbled at the bedside table and then maneuvered himself to the end of the bed. Cameron coaxed his legs apart and then settled his shoulders between them. The most intimate parts of his body were literally right before Cameron's eyes.

Cameron looked up at him and Zach did his best not to let his nerves show. The last thing he wanted Cameron to do was slow down—or worse, stop—because he was worried about Zach.

"Relax, Zach. We've done this part before," Cameron encouraged before licking a path up his shaft. Zach's cock hardened impossibly mere seconds before it was engulfed in the warmth of Cameron's mouth. He'd never get used to the sensation of his cock hitting the back of Cameron's throat. His hips bucked and Cameron grabbed at them, not to stop him but to encourage him. He exhaled a moan and relaxed into the pleasure.

Cameron's right hand released his hip, moving lower to play with his balls, rolling them between his fingers. Zach instinctively bent his knees, opening himself for Cameron's exploring fingers.

Cameron sucked him deep a few times and then released him. He reached up and traced Zach's mouth with his finger, gently prying his lips open and slipping two fingers inside. "Suck them, Zach. Get them nice and wet."

Zach pulled hard on Cameron's fingers, rolling his tongue around them as if they were Cameron's cock. He knew what was coming, and he couldn't wait. His heart was beating hard enough to pound right out of his chest. It was only Cameron's eyes fixed on his that kept him grounded.

The thick fingers were pulled from his mouth as Cameron surged up, replacing them with his tongue. Zach kissed him with all the passion and enthusiasm hurtling through his body. He was so wired he thought he might explode if he didn't get some release soon. While Cameron's tongue fucked his mouth, his fingers pressed against his hole. Zach tried to relax when the tip of Cameron's finger dipped inside.

Cameron's mouth caught his gasp from the quick sharp burn, the kiss dulling the ache. His mind was racing at what was happening and what was to come. He had part of Cameron inside, but it wasn't enough. He heard Cameron growling through the kiss and wondered if he was feeling as out of control as Zach was.

While Cameron's tongue wreaked havoc on his mouth, Cameron pushed a second finger into Zach's ass. He squirmed when the fingers moved, searching until Cameron found what he was looking for. Zach grunted and pumped his hips as Cameron massaged his prostate. He couldn't have stayed still if he tried. His hips rolled, his eyelids fluttered, and his fingers tightened in Cameron's hair with every pass over his prostate.

Zach pulled away from Cameron unable to keep up the pretense that he was capable of kissing him back at this point. He was overwhelmed. "Cameron...please."

"Shh. It's okay. Roll over. On your belly," Cameron murmured as he gently pulled his fingers from Zach's body.

Zach complied immediately, more than ready to have Cameron's cock inside him. Cameron grabbed his hips and pulled him up onto all fours. He loved Cameron a little more then. He must have remembered Zach telling him late one night that he was dying for Cameron to fuck him this way.

Zach shuddered when the cool lube dribbled over his hole and Cameron's fingers rubbed all over, dipping just inside. He heard the familiar sound of a condom wrapper, and before he knew it, felt the tip of Cameron's cock resting at his entrance.

Cameron held his hip with one hand and smoothed the other over his back. "Relax, Zach. Remember, I love you," he whispered. The hand on his back disappeared, and Cameron pushed into him, slowly and gently. It hurt, and for a moment, Zach thought he might have to pull away from Cameron, but then suddenly Cameron's cock popped through his ring of muscle and eased all the way in. The initial bite of pain was lessening, leaving a not-altogether-unpleasant burn.

Neither of them moved, and then Cameron's hand returned to his back, rubbing circles into his damp skin. Zach heard Cameron's heavy breaths and knew how hard he was working to restrain his movements. Cameron's body lowered over him and a line of openmouthed kisses was pressed along his spine. There was nothing but pleasure now.

"I'm okay, now," he panted.

Cameron rolled his hips and gave a few tentative thrusts. It was good, so good, but not enough. "More, Cam. Harder"

Cameron gripped his hips tightly, pulling out before shoving back inside. The thrust nearly forced him to his stomach, but his arms held, and he was rewarded with another and another and another. The room was filled with the sound of the heavy slap of flesh and unbridled grunts.

"Fuck, Zach. Oh god, you're so tight. So good," Cameron moaned.

Zach wanted to reply, to say something filthy back to him, but words were lost. All he could offer was a litany of moans and whimpers.

Cameron's body lay over his back, his arms around his chest. Those strong arms hoisted him up until they were kneeling upright. Zach's head flopped back onto Cameron's shoulder. Cameron kept one of his thick arms around Zach's chest and the other went lower, his hand grabbing Zach's cock. Cameron started pumping him in time to his thrusts.

"I'm gonna come, Zach. Come with me. Come with me."

Zach didn't need to be told twice. His orgasm tore through him, ripping pleasure along with it. Thick ropes of come shot out of him, hitting Cameron's hand, the sheets, even the headboard. Zach brought his arms up to circle Cameron's neck behind him, anchoring himself to his body. Cameron growled in his ear, and his body jerked uncontrollably as his own orgasm hit, sending them both to the mattress.

They lay where they fell as they tried to come down from the high they'd just experienced. Zach was on his stomach, his arms above his head, his legs askew. Cameron's body blanketed him completely, one of his hands sliding up and down his side from his armpit to his thigh, over and over. Zach never wanted to move.

"You are so amazing," Cameron whispered in his ear.

Zach laughed. "You know what's amazing?"

"What?" Cameron asked before pressing kisses to his temple, cheek, anywhere he could reach.

"I just came so damn hard, but I can already feel my dick getting ready to go again because of how good your body feels lying all over me." He loved sex. It was messy and fun and something so very special he and Cameron shared.

"This is what I get for falling for a younger man." Cameron nipped his shoulder. "But believe me, if we didn't have to get ready to go meet your family, I'd have you again right now."

Only the thought of meeting his mother's family could have dragged Zach away from Cameron right then.

Chapter Twenty-Nine

ZACH

With every step he took, Zach was reminded of where Cameron had been in his body, so he couldn't wipe the smile from his face, despite where he was headed.

Marco Cortez had called five minutes after Cameron had gently pulled out of Zach to tell them there'd been a change of plan. Arnold Piper had decided to talk, but he was only going to talk to Zach, and it had to be now.

What he wanted to talk about no one knew, nor were they certain how long the offer might last, so Zach and Cameron had been flown here to the state penitentiary immediately. It had been strange to fly in a helicopter piloted by someone other than Cameron.

The Malcolms remained in Cheyenne, and they were going to meet them tonight instead. Zach would much rather be with them right now than walking along a drab gray corridor, Cameron beside him, a guard in front and Marco Cortez behind, on their way to meet with a monster.

The guard led them into a meeting room; it was small, containing only a table and two chairs and nothing else. His father hadn't arrived yet.

"You know the drill." It was more of a statement than a question addressed to Marco, and the guard left as soon as Marco nodded his assent.

Cameron hadn't let go of his hand since they'd passed security, and from the grip, Zach suspected he wasn't going to. He wondered how his father would react to that.

"You okay?" Cameron asked.

Zach nodded. He wasn't really, but this might save everyone a trial, so he was willing to do it.

"Just let him talk, Zach. Maybe you'll be able to get a confession out of him. He's waved his right to a lawyer, so I'm here for you and the other victims. Hopefully we can wrap this up today with a confession." Marco placed his briefcase on the table and ferreted around for his tape recorder. Not only had his father declined a lawyer, but he'd asked for this meeting to be recorded. He'd told everyone who'd had the misfortune of having to listen that he'd placed himself in the hands of god and his will would be done.

The door cracked open and a different guard entered, followed moments later by his father.

Zach hadn't seen Arnold Piper since the indictment. He hadn't spoken directly to him for even longer. The familiar tightening in his stomach returned but he reminded himself he no longer had to be afraid. His father couldn't hurt him anymore, and if Cameron could conquer his monster, then he could definitely stand up to his.

Zach watched his father closely as he sat and his chained wrists and ankles were shackled to the table. Marco stood and began the recording, mentioning times, date, names of people present while the guard worked. Once he was restrained, the guard left with a nod, leaving only the four of them.

"Why's he here?" Piper asked no one in particular but gestured toward Cameron.

"He's here for me," Zach answered.

"The useless little boy needs a man to hold his hand, does he?" His father sneered, his gaze falling to their joined hands. Nobody answered him.

"You called us here to talk, Mr. Piper, so what do you want to talk about?" Marco finally asked.

His father gave Zach another scowl and looked him up and down, sneer firmly in place. "I hear you're going to meet your mother's family."

Of all the things Zach had expected from his father, that hadn't been one of them. Cameron's hand tightened around his own. How had his father known?

"I am."

"Well, I guess they'll be disappointed in you too. Though they didn't raise much of a daughter, so maybe they'll like the pitiful grandson she gave them."

Zach's mouth closed with such an audible snap, he worried about cracking his teeth. If Cameron hadn't been holding his hand so tightly, he no doubt would have flung himself across the table and beat the living hell out of the miserable excuse for a father.

"Can you tell us what happened to Anna, Mr. Piper?"

"God called her home," Piper said, his malicious gaze never leaving Zach's. "You tell your grandparents that god called their daughter home because she failed. She failed and she was as useless as her son is. She couldn't even get that right—giving me a decent son. Instead, she gave birth to you. You're not even a man." It was the smirk as much as the words about his mother that did it. It lit Zach's fuse and blew his temper sky-high despite his promise he wouldn't let his father get to him.

"My mother was a better person than you'll ever be. She was kind and loving and good. You ruined her. You destroyed her. You destroy everyone around you. You arrogant, hateful son of a bitch."

"Your mother was useless. She only gave me one child and what a disappointment that one is. When the lord called me to marry other women, instead of accepting god's command, she said I was disgusting. *I* was disgusting!" Piper thundered. "I was her god on earth to be worshipped and obeyed above all others, and she said *I* was disgusting. She threatened to go to the police and tell them I was going to marry another child, as though the laws here apply to me. How dare she? How dare she! The lord chose my wives." His father was breathing hard, sucking in air as his crazed anger worked through his body. "No, I couldn't have that, Zach, so I sent her to god, and I should have sent you with her that same day, you filthy abomination."

Zach didn't believe his father realized or cared what he'd just admitted.

"She loved me. She. Loved. Me. And you'll never take that away from me." Zach had no idea how he'd gotten into Cameron's arms, but his big body was all around him—it was the only thing holding him up, literally and figuratively.

He heard scuffling all around him as the guards entered the room to take his father away, but Zach wasn't done yet. He pushed his way out of Cameron's arms, not going too far before he gripped Cameron's hand and turned to face his father.

"You killed her. Didn't you? That day at the stream. You killed my mother?"

"I sent her back to god. She was defective."

"You are the one who is defective. You are the one who judges everyone and you are the one who will burn in hell." Zach finished. He was done with his father and knew the man held no more power over him. He stepped back, allowing Cameron to wrap his arms around him from behind and press a gentle kiss into his hair.

He saw it register with his father at last. "You disgusting pervert. I should have killed you too. I should have bashed your skull in the same as I did with your mother. Let me go—"

His father ranted all the way down the corridor, but not a word of it bothered him. He'd beaten his father. He would walk out of here and not think of him again.

"Did we get him?" Zach turned to Marco.

Marco didn't really need to answer; his grin said it all, but he answered anyway. "You got him, Zach. What he said was... It was enough."

"Good." Zach sagged into Cameron, drained from the confrontation.

"I'm proud of you," Cameron said, speaking for the first time since Piper had entered the room.

"Why do you think he did that?" Zach couldn't understand why he'd been called to speak to him. If he hadn't, they would never have known for sure about his mother."

"It's hard to say. Somehow he found out about your grandparents, and I guess he just couldn't stand the thought of you being happy."

"Let's go. Can we go? I've got family to meet." Zach felt surprisingly light. The man had confessed to killing his mother, but on some level, Zach had always known. Maybe now her family—and his mother—could be at peace and his nightmares would stop.

They were quiet on the flight back to Cheyenne, all three of them. Marco furiously made notes the entire way, hopefully plotting his case against his father. Zach sat contentedly beside Cameron, their hands entwined.

"Should we tell the Malcolms?" Zach suddenly asked. He didn't really want to ruin his first meeting with his family, but how could they keep something like that from them?

"I think honesty is best. They know where you went this morning, so they're bound to ask how it went," Cameron answered. "I can tell them if you want. Unless... Is there a protocol, Marco?"

"Huh? Oh no. No reason they can't be told. I'm going to call Detective Marshall, see if maybe she can meet us with the Malcolms. Help ease the way if you like."

His poor grandparents. Twenty-five years of hope and it was all about to be blown to pieces, but at least now they'd know.

Marco had a car waiting for them at the helipad, and they were shuttled to the Spring Hill Suites. The original plan had been to meet his grandparents in a restaurant, but once again, his father had changed their plans. How could they sit in a restaurant and tell his grandparents that their daughter was dead?

Once they arrived at the hotel, Zach's stomach knotted with nerves. He wasn't at all sure he could do this. The warmth of Cameron beside him, his callused fingers slipping into his hand, helped him believe he was going to be okay.

As soon as they entered the conference room with Marco leading the way, Zach saw Detective Marshall sitting with an elderly couple. The first thing he noticed about them was the tears sliding down their cheeks, so he suspected the detective had already shared the news with them. The three stood as Zach, Cameron, and Marco approached.

Lee Malcolm was close to Zach's height and had a similar build. His hair was gray, and he'd lost a considerable amount from the top. His hazel eyes watched Zach from behind the thick lenses of his dark-rimmed glasses and the pain of a missing—now dead—child was etched into the deep lines of his face. He carried himself with a dignity Zach immediately admired.

Abigail Malcolm, Zach could tell, was using her husband to keep herself on her feet. She was beautiful, of average height, with gorgeous silver hair piled high on her head. She might normally be a strong elegant-looking lady, but right now, she looked frail. Her green eyes could not contain her tears as they spilled unhindered down her cheek. Zach couldn't stop himself from going to her and gently enfolding her in his arms.

Eventually, the tears stopped, and she pulled back to look at him. She cupped his cheek with her hand and stared at him for long minutes. "So handsome. You look exactly like your uncle Wade, but your eyes...your eyes are all your mother's." She smiled sadly and then turned to her husband. "Meet your grandson, Lee."

Zach turned and faced his grandfather. He knew they were still going to wait for the DNA results to make it official, but these people were his family—he knew it.

"Sir."

"That's Pop, Zach. It's good to meet you, son." The older man was doing his best to choke back his tears. Zach understood the whirlwind they were feeling right now.

"Pop and...Nana?" he hedged, turning to his grandmother.

"Yes, Zach. Yes, please. Nana. And who else have we here?" Abigail asked, shifting to look at Cameron and Marco who were standing a little behind them.

Zach knew Cameron was worried how their relationship was going to be received by his family, but Zach wasn't. His mother had been a good person; these were good people. He wasn't worried at all.

"This is Marco Cortez. He's the prosecutor working to put my father away, where he belongs." His grandparents shook Marco's hand, both of them offering encouragement to him to make sure Arnold Piper was put away for good. They were remarkably calm, all things considered, and Zach wondered if they were still in shock.

"And this is Cameron Cronin. He's the man who has been there for me every day since I escaped my father. He's the man I love. He is my boyfriend." As confident as he'd been, Zach still held his breath as he waited for his grandparents' reaction.

They moved forward together. His grandfather shook Cameron's hand. "Good to meet you, son." He clapped Cameron on the shoulder.

His grandmother did her best to drag Cameron down for a hug, kissing him on the cheek. A flush crept up Cameron's cheeks as he accepted her embrace, gently returning it. "We can't thank you enough for being there for our boy."

"It's been my honor, ma'am. You should be very proud of him. He's a remarkable young man."

Abigail turned and looked Zach over, smiling, and then looked to her husband. "What do you say we take our two remarkable young men out for dinner, Lee?"

Marco Cortez and Detective Marshall begged off when Lee also offered for them to go to dinner. They both left after giving assurances that they'd do everything they could to make sure Arnold Piper was convicted and their daughter's remains found.

The restaurant in the hotel was still quiet at this early hour. They chose a booth toward the back that would afford them as much privacy as possible. General chitchat and discussion of the menu took place while they situated themselves and their orders were taken. Zach sat between his grandparents with Cameron across from him.

As soon as the waiter moved away, his grandmother took his hand and held his gaze. Her eyes were a similar green to his, but the shape was slightly different. "Now, we've got a lot to talk about, the four of us. So much has happened, so much sadness, but tonight I want this to be a happy reunion. We've got our grandson back, and that's something to celebrate. So for tonight, I want to hear all about you, Zach, all the good stuff: what you enjoy doing, what you like to eat, your favorite things in the world. I want to get to know my grandson. And I want to hear all about your young man too," she added, throwing a warm smile across to Cameron. "Do you think we can do that?"

Zach knew he'd be able to talk about Cameron all night. He could gush for hours about how wonderful Cameron was. As hard as this must be for his grandmother, he was thankful that she was choosing for the night to go this way. This was a happy reunion. Though the confirmation of his mother's death was sitting like a heavy weight on their shoulders, these wonderful people were his, and just for tonight, he'd put all the horror to the side and enjoy getting to know his family.

Zach glanced across at Cameron. He was smiling at Zach, and Zach could almost feel the relief rolling off him. Cameron had been worried about Zach's sexuality being accepted by his family, but they hadn't even blinked. Cameron gave him a small nod—all the encouragement he needed.

"Okay," Zach said. "What do you want to know?"

Chapter Thirty

CAMERON

"We've just walked in the door. Yeah…uh huh, it was a good trip." Zach looked over at him and smiled, rolling his eyes a little as he spoke into the phone.

They'd promised to call Abigail and Lee as soon as they'd arrived safely home from Cheyenne, but Abigail had called before they'd even gotten the chance. Zach's grandparents were awesome. They were everything a loving family should be, and from the sound of it, his extended family would be the same when they eventually met.

Their dinner had lasted long into the night. Nobody wanted to break it up, least of all Zach, who demanded to hear all about his cousins—and there were plenty of them. Cameron left them close to midnight to give them the opportunity to get to know each other without him around, not that he didn't feel welcome, but they were family. Zach got back to their room sometime around three this morning and so slept most of the drive home.

Cameron leaned against the kitchen cabinet and watched as Zach talked to his grandmother. Zach was radiant. He was practically glowing with happiness, taking Cameron's breath away.

"Yep, I promise. We'll get back to you with dates. Okay, talk to you later." Zach clicked off his phone and laughed. There were few things better than watching Zach laugh, so

Cameron sat back and enjoyed it. He'd find out what had amused him soon enough.

"I can't believe Nana, Cam. She is just...she's perfect. She calculated how long it should take us to drive home, and when we hadn't called within five minutes, she called us. She's so sweet." Zach walked over to him and Cameron opened his arms, happily enfolding him into a hug.

"They both seemed like wonderful people." He agreed. Zach's grandmother was a retired veterinarian and his grandfather a retired journalist, though he still wrote some freelance articles for his local newspaper to keep his mind active. They'd raised five children including Zach's mother, who had been the middle child. Zach was now part of an extended family of thirty-seven and Abigail Malcolm was determined he meet them all as soon as humanly possible.

"Mm, they are. I think you left before Nana said she still works casually at the local animal shelter. They're having a fundraiser in a few weeks, and all the family is going to be there. So Nana is hoping we'll be free to attend..."

Cameron palmed Zach's cheek and tipped his head back. He pressed his lips to Zach's, savoring the soft warmth and the hint of coffee from their last stop on the road. "I'll make sure I'm free. Sounds great."

"I can't believe this. All of this. Can it be real?"

Cameron laughed. "It's real. It's all real, Zach."

"It's over, isn't it? I mean I know it's not *over* over, but my father's in jail, and he won't be going anywhere, and Jimmy... He's gone. And you and me have finally worked things out."

"There'll always be ups and downs; that's how life goes, but yeah, I think the worst is over, Zach. You've been through a lot the last few weeks and now with hearing about your mother... Are you doing okay?"

Zach pressed a kiss to his lips and Cameron melted into it. This was the kind of shared intimacy that can only be had in a loving relationship. Cameron had never had it before, not even in the early days with Jimmy. He loved every second of it. He left his hand cupping Zach's cheek after they broke the kiss.

"I'm good. I *knew* about Mom. All the nightmares, the way my father was... I knew. I'm glad my grandparents won't have to wonder anymore what happened to her." Zach reached over and tucked a loose wisp of his hair behind his ear, leaving his fingers there to gently play in the strands. "I wish you could have met her. My memories aren't very clear, but you know how you just have a feeling about someone...? That's how it is with my mom. I know she was a good person, and she loved me. And oddly, that helped me all those years I was alone."

Cameron rubbed his thumb across Zach's cheek. The green of his eyes was luminescent as he looked at him with a depth of emotion Cameron hadn't experienced before.

"She was the only person to ever love me...until you," Zach whispered.

Cameron pulled him tighter against his body, enjoying the hard planes pressing against his own. He tilted Zach's head back and tasted his lips, licking the seam to encourage Zach to open to him. As soon as he did, Cameron plunged his tongue inside, loving every second of their shared kiss. He'd never get enough of this, not ever.

Zach was restless in his arms, his body in constant motion, his hands everywhere. Cameron understood the lack of control; he felt the same way whenever he had Zach within reach. It was a battle to keep his body from coming too soon. He'd never reacted as powerfully to anyone as he did with Zach. Even the little whimpers that escaped him sent shivers of lust up his spine.

"Cam, I need you."

Cameron heard the desire in Zach's voice. He took his hand and led him into their bedroom. He didn't even try to kid himself Zach would ever return to the guest room that was his for months. Zach belonged in his bed every night.

As soon as they entered the room, Zach reached for the hem of his shirt and began pulling it over his head. Cameron batted his hands away. "That's my job," he growled. Undressing Zach was definitely one of his most favorite things to do.

He finished tugging the shirt over Zach's head, dropping it behind him. He raised Zach's arms and put them around his neck and then he wrapped his arms around the back of Zach's thighs and lifted him. He took two steps forward and carefully tossed him onto the bed, Zach giggling as he flew through the air.

He followed him down and then he went to work on the buttons of Zach's pants. His eager fingers making short work of them and the zipper. Then he was easily sliding the chinos down Zach's legs. He tore the shoes from his feet and then wrestled the pants the rest of the way off.

When Zach lay gloriously naked on the bed, Cameron fell on him like a starving man. He kissed and nipped at every inch of skin he could reach. He was determined to touch it all. He swirled his tongue around Zach's quivering belly button. Zach's fingers tightened in his hair and pulled him back up to his lips.

"How do you want me?" he whispered into Zach's ear. The way their bodies were writhing against each other, Cameron knew no matter how Zach wanted him this wasn't going to last long.

"I can't think—I just want—" Zach cut himself off by plastering his lips once again to Cameron's, stealing his breath.

"Naked. You're not naked," Zach gasped when they broke apart. Cameron leaped from the bed and quickly divested himself of his clothes. He was sure he looked quite comical as he tripped and struggled to get the cloth from his body. But he saw nothing but burning desire in Zach's eyes.

He fell back onto Zach, covering his body. God, the feel of his lover's naked body against his own was something he'd never get used to, and he didn't want to. Both he and Zach had gone through the ringer to get to each other, and Cameron didn't ever want to take Zach for granted. He wanted to feel that spark of lust and love every single time their bodies touched.

From beneath him, Zach rolled so they were both on their sides, their legs naturally entwining while their hands gripped and explored. Cameron was completely overwhelmed with Zach: his taste, scent, the feel of his warm, smooth skin.

"Roll over...keep going," Zach instructed until Cameron was on his other side facing away from Zach.

One of Zach's arms slid under him so he was able to rest his head on it and the other came over his body, tracing the ridges of his abs until he finally gripped Cameron's cock. Zach pressed openmouthed kisses behind his ear, down his neck and over his shoulders.

"I can't..." Cameron breathed. Zach was driving him fucking crazy, and all he wanted was to feel him inside. "Please."

Zach pushed at his top leg, rolling him a little farther onto his tummy and opening him up. He sensed Zach moving around behind him, and then a cool trickle of lube ran down his crack, Zach's fingers spreading the liquid around his hole. Zach wasted no time preparing him, and his heavy breathing told Cameron he was just as on edge.

Finally, the tip of Zach's cock pushed at his entrance. Zach shuffled even closer so Cameron doubted even a sheet of paper could have slipped between their bodies.

"I love you," Zach murmured into his ear. "I can't imagine loving anyone as much or as fiercely as I love you. I'd do anything for you, Cam."

Cameron wished he was able to find the words to tell Zach the feeling was entirely mutual, but all managed was a few frantic moans as their bodies joined. Zach stilled behind him as they both fought to steady themselves. Zach's hand rubbed over his hip, soothing the building passion though he knew as soon as Zach moved the tempest would rage.

"You're so beautiful, Cam. So tight and perfect and—" Zach rolled his hips, triggering an indecent moan before he continued. "And you feel so good."

Zach kept his movements slow and languorous. Cameron squirmed as his body was lulled into a pleasing rhythm. Cameron had enjoyed every second of the many ways they'd made love, but the sensuous way Zach slowly rolled in and out of his body, grinding his pelvis on Cameron's ass was one of his favorites.

Cameron groaned, long and torturous, when Zach's cock slid over his prostate. Zach gripped Cameron's hip tightly and began thrusting hard. There was nothing better than this. The slap of skin, the feel of Zach's cock moving inside him, Zach's breath on his neck. It was perfect.

Zach's movements faltered, and Cameron was suddenly manhandled onto his back, then Zach was pushing back into him, but this time with their eyes locked on each other. Beads of sweat trickled down Zach's face as he pistoned in and out. Cameron reached for his cock, but Zach slapped his hand away and grabbed it himself, working it to the same rhythm as his thrusts.

Neither man looked away as they came within moments of each other. Cameron clung to Zach as desperately as Zach held on to him. There could be no greater pleasure in this world.

Eventually Zach carefully pulled out and collapsed beside him. Cameron scooped him into his arms, careless of the need to clean up. He couldn't let go of the intimacy yet.

"How did I get so lucky?" he whispered against Zach's ear.

"It's not luck. We earned this happiness, both of us."

Cameron jolted as the truth of Zach's words hit him. Zach had been telling him for weeks—months even—how wonderful he was and he deserved good things. After what Jimmy had put him through, Cameron didn't think he'd ever believe him—but he did.

"You've given me back my confidence. Did you understand what you've done for me? I've felt so...worthless for such a long time, but we belong together, Zach. There's nothing surer than that. And you've helped me believe it."

Zach pushed up on his elbow and peered down. With his other hand, he trailed his fingers through the hair on Cameron's chest. "We do belong together and we've both worked hard to deal with our past. We deserve this—us. We've got so much to look forward to, and I can't wait to spend every second I can with you."

It was almost a vow; one Cameron was happy to return. Zach snuggled back into his arms, and Cameron held him as tightly as he dared.

Life was no picnic—Cameron knew that, but he had the right person at his side now, and that was going to make all the difference.

Epilogue

FIVE MONTHS LATER

Zach was used to being surrounded by a large group of people. After all, he'd grown up in his father's religious cult. The difference was back then he'd been a pariah—ignored and despised by everyone around him. Today, the people around him all cared about him—loved him. They were family, whether by blood or because they'd chosen each other as family.

It had been a long day, but a happy one. Zach was tired and content just to sit back in the shadows and watch. He laughed as his sixty-four-year-old grandmother attempted to chase after a crowd of children who were all under seven years old. The group included several of his cousins and Ben and Ethan's now four-year-old twin girls, Maya and Riley. Some of the older children were watching and doing their best not to smile and look like they might want to join in. They'd clearly decided they were too cool for it, but they weren't fooling anyone. Ben, of course, was right in the thick of it, egging the little ones on, scooping them up and twirling them around.

Zach's heart ached a little as he watched Ryan just off to the side a little with his and Lucas's little boy. They'd adopted the two-year-old three months ago, and he was clearly the love of their lives. He was also profoundly deaf, and while they were wonderful with him, they were also having some struggles, especially when it came to encouraging him to interact with other children. Maya and Riley had become terrific friends with little Charlie but getting him to play with the other children here today was proving difficult.

Not too far away, Lucas, Ethan, his grandfather, and two of his uncles stood together talking. Zach noticed how Lucas's gaze returned to Ryan and Charlie over and over. He also noticed how Lucas's body tensed when one of Zach's aunts and her youngest daughter wandered over to join Ryan and Charlie. Zach smiled when little Amy pulled out a couple of toy trucks and handed one to Charlie. They both sat where they'd stood and began playing. The relief on Ryan's face was almost palpable as he spoke to Zach's aunt, his gaze never leaving his son as he laughed with Amy and they crashed their trucks into each other.

Marco Cortez was holding court with a couple of Zach's older cousins who'd been particularly interested in his father's trial. Life without the possibility of parole. That's why they were celebrating today. His father had been sentenced, and he'd never be getting out—could never hurt anyone again. The confession Zach had gotten out of him had gone a long way to speeding things up and securing both his conviction and the appropriate sentence.

Zach had felt so many emotions when the sentence had been handed down but chief among them had been relief. It was over. He never had to think about that man again. Never had to worry somehow he might get out and do this all over again.

Zach looked around for Cameron. His lover and best friend. The man who had been at his side every step of the way since he'd escaped from his father. They'd both been seeing Dr. Warren ever since the disaster with Jimmy.

Cameron was amazing, but he still needed some help breaking free of the shit Jimmy had heaped on him.

There were big changes coming up, and they, too, were part of today's celebrations. Zach was going to college, and Cameron was moving with him—and they had another big surprise for their family. How his life had changed in the last fourteen months was nothing short of a miracle.

He spotted Cameron talking to Alec Banner. Both men wore a serious expression, and Zach hoped everything was all right. They hadn't seen much of Alec since the incident with Jimmy. He knew he'd been working a lot with Ben and Ethan, and together they'd rescued many children. Zach was holding tight to the dream of one day joining them.

Cameron turned to watch him as he made his way over, his eyes softening when his gaze connected with Zach's. If it was possible, Cameron was even more beautiful now than when they'd first met.

As he approached, he caught wisps of their conversation. Alec looked exhausted. Zach knew there'd been a case a few months ago that had come close to costing Alec his life, and he knew it wasn't over yet.

"At least I know Asher's safe. He won't let Ben tell me where he is, but I know he's safe. That helps." Alec's voice broke a little, and Zach heard the pain behind it.

Cameron's gaze flicked to him briefly before returning to Alec. "I'm so sorry about what happened. You must know it wasn't your fault."

"I fucked up, Cameron. I fucked it all up. I deserve what I'm getting." Alec turned to face Zach, and all Zach could see in his handsome face was fear and misery.

"Hey, Alec. Good to see you."

"You too, Zach. I'm glad to hear about your father's sentence." Alec cast his gaze around the yard, looking more lost than Zach had ever seen him. "Anyway, I should let you two get back to your guests."

"You let us know if there's anything we can do, Alec. Anything at all." Cameron offered.

"Thank you. I...ah, guess I should get going."

"Stay, Alec. Please stay," Zach urged. "You're family and you should be here today. Cameron and I have a lot to be grateful to you for."

Alec gave him a weak smile and nodded. Zach had no idea who Asher was and what had happened, but he knew Alec was hurting and Zach hated seeing it.

"Get yourself a drink and join us, Alec," Cameron added. "Zach and I have some more good news to share, and we want all of our family here to celebrate."

"Mm, intriguing. Of course, I'll stick around for a while. Thank you both for including me."

"Always," Cameron replied and then took Zach's hand and led him away.

"Is he all right?" Zach quietly asked.

"Not really. I'll tell you about it later but for now... Are you ready for this?"

"More than ready," Zach answered. "You know Nana is going to go crazy when she hears this. Are you ready for that?"

Cameron suddenly stopped and pulled Zach flush against him. "Don't you know I'd go through anything—any kind of crazy or whatever—to have you, Zach? Anything to make you my husband?"

Zach didn't know when or where; there were no specific plans, and no one else knew, but in the quiet stillness after they'd made love last night, Cameron had whispered in his ear to ask Zach to be his husband. It was so unbelievably amazing that Zach had thought it all a dream when he woke up this morning—until Cameron began talking about how to announce the news to their family.

Zach couldn't get a response out before Cameron's lips were pressed to his in an urgent kiss. This kiss was kindling to the fire within him that burned for Cameron as it always did. Some days it felt like they could never get enough of each other.

"Okay," Zach whispered a little breathlessly when the kiss ended. "Let's go and tell our family the news."

About the Author

Karrie lives in Australia's sunshine state with her husband and two sons, though she hates the sun with a passion. She dreams of one day living in the wettest and coldest habitable place she can find. She's been writing stories in her head for years but has finally managed to pull the words out of her head and share them with others. She spends her days trying to type her stories on the computer without disturbing her beloved cat, Lu, curled up on the keyboard. She probably reads far too much.

Email: author@karrieroman.com

Twitter: @karrie_roman

Website: www.karrieroman.com

Other books by this author

Saved
Advent Adventure (Coming November 2018)
Shipped
New Year's Shippin' Eve (Coming November 2018)
Sentinel

Coming Soon from Karrie Roman

Valor

Until You, Book Four

PROLOGUE

Jesus Christ, he couldn't get out of that happy fucking home quickly enough. The fact that he'd put a bullet between the eyes of an abusive monster less than twenty-four hours ago wasn't what had Alec Banner's heart aching, his breath stuttering, and his legs itching to run. No, he'd had little trouble doing that.

What had him fleeing from the company of a man he considered his best friend and three other men who'd become very important to him had been all the fucking love wafting around the room—infecting everyone but him, apparently.

Alec had been friends with Ben Cronin for well over a decade. Though they'd lost contact for a few years, they'd reconnected close to a year ago. These days he spent plenty of time with Ben. They'd been working together for several months now, locating missing and abducted children. It was hard work, but very rewarding. Alec didn't regret leaving the FBI to join Ben's company, at all.

It wasn't Ben he was fleeing, though. Nor was it Ben's partner. Ethan was a fucking dreamboat, but Ben was the lucky asshole who'd snagged his heart. Alec had no problem admitting he had a tiny crush on Ethan. Would it ever cause trouble between him and Ben? Fuck no, because no matter what, there was no way Alec would ever do anything about it. Alec Banner had a lot of faults, but disloyalty wasn't one of them. He'd pine away for Ethan like a miserable bastard until he—hopefully—found a dreamboat of his own to love.

No, despite his messy feelings, the reason Alec was fleeing Ben's brother's house before he completely fucking lost it was because he couldn't stand to see how happy the two couples were. He'd watched Ben and Ethan for months and despite the fact they'd been going through a really rough time, they'd been going through it together. Alec had seen firsthand what it should be like to have a real partner. Someone to love, to care about. Someone who'd have your back, no matter what.

And now he was expected to fucking sit back and watch how happy Ben's brother, Cameron, and his lover, Zach, were? He couldn't fucking do it. Selfish maybe, but he was nearly forty years old, and he'd had one boyfriend who'd lasted six months and a nine-month relationship with a woman that had been explosive but ultimately fizzled out because she wouldn't walk down the aisle with him. It had hurt like hell at the time, but looking back on it now, years later, he was so glad Heather had rejected him. He was pretty sure he'd be a divorced father of three by now if she hadn't.

And now, here was Zach who was twenty-fucking-two and had found the love of his life in Cameron, and try as he might, Alec couldn't shake the jealousy. He wanted that, he wanted what those men had.

There was only one thing Alec knew of that helped when your life went to shit and that was work. He never turned to the bottle or eating his feelings when he was down, like some people did. Alec's choice of pick-me-up was to stick his head down and his ass up and get stuck into as much work as possible.

He pulled out his phone and thumbed through his contacts. Ryan Lowe was near the top of his list. Ryan was the brains and bank behind Chasing Hope, the company he worked for locating missing kids. He'd told Alec earlier that he may have a job for him, and as he hit the dial button, he hoped to god he did. Alec desperately needed something to keep him busy.

"Alec, how'd it go?" Ryan answered without preamble.

Alec knew Ryan would have heard from Ben or Ethan that they'd rescued Zach from Cameron's crazy ex, but he wasn't exactly sure if they'd have told him just how far they'd gone, so he offered only a concise answer. "Good. All done. What else have you got for me?"

"Well, I'm sure we've got a case, but I'm just waiting to hear back. I've already got Jacey putting a file together for you. Little boy, four, was taken this morning from his local park. The family is affluent and well-known in their community, and the mother is certain there'll be a ransom demand. She wants the cops called, but she's getting pushback from her husband and the in-laws. I think you should head out to them ASAP, see what you think, and be ready to go."

Alec heard his phone beep as Ryan spoke and knew it'd be the file from Jacey. She was an absolute genius with technology, and he expected she'd have provided him with information, not just about the immediate family, but the extended one including friends, staff, and coworkers. Knowing Jacey, he'd even get information about the people the parents went to kindergarten with. She'd have dug up whatever dirt there was to find in a short amount of time, and no doubt she'd already be getting back among the filth to find even more.

"Got it. Where am I headed?"

"Del Mar. Get a flight to San Diego. I'll get a hotel booked for you and text the details."

"On my way."

"Hey...you okay, Alec?"

Ryan was a sweetheart, tender and caring and far too innocent for this line of work. And yet he'd dragged himself into the misery of missing kids because he wanted to help—and was now in a position where he could. He was one of the good guys, but Alec worried how it would all affect him. Alec had been dealing with scum for years; he knew the horror stories and he'd hardened his heart to them, but Ryan? Alec worried about him.

"Tired, that's all. I'm fine, Ryan, but thanks for caring."

They exchanged niceties about Ryan and his partner, Lucas. Alec repeated several more times that he was, in fact, all right despite the events of the past twenty-four hours when Ryan asked again before hanging up.

Alec made his way to the airport and settled in to wait for his flight. Getting in and out of Cody, Wyoming, wasn't always easy. He didn't mind curling up on one of the uncomfortable chairs common to most airports while he waited, though. He pulled out his tablet and opened the file Jacey had sent him.

The Winsome family of Del Mar wasn't just affluent, they were filthy fucking rich. The patriarch was one Edmund Winsome who was a founding partner of one of the biggest law firms in Southern California. Matriarch Phyllis Winsome had brought her family's considerable wealth to the marriage, and together, they had built a formidable empire for their two sons. From the images Jacey sent, they were an austere-looking couple who screamed wealth from every perfectly coiffed hair on their heads.

Oldest son—and father of the missing boy—Kane Winsome worked for his father's company. He hadn't quite made partner yet, but from what Alec read, he was well on his way. Alec found the photo Jacey had sent and studied the image of Kane Winsome. He was a younger version of his father. Light brown hair was cut to within an inch of its life and was gelled into what was probably the latest style; steel gray eyes glared at the lens, and thin lips pursed to show their impatience with whoever had taken the photo. Alec tried not to judge a book by its cover, but if he had to then the title would probably be *Pride and Prejudice*. A more modern day Fitzwilliam Darcy he couldn't imagine finding.

Kane's wife, Madeline, came from a wealthy family herself, though not on the scale of the Winsome's wealth. She worked as a florist and could not look more opposite to her husband if she tried. She had a mane of flowing, dark, almost-black hair that perfectly matched her dark skin. Her eyes were a deep brown but were lit up by what Alec suspected was her natural *joie de vivre*. It was hard to tell from a photo, but she looked petite. Alec had no doubt she would probably be a lioness, though, when it came to her loved ones. While her husband glared and pouted at the camera, Madeline Winsome laughed and flirted with it.

He scrolled to another image, this one of Kane and Madeline together, each holding hands with a toddling child he assumed to be the missing Jack. The photo must be at least a year old, given that Jack was now four. The family looked—happy. Gone was Kane's stern face, replaced with a beaming smile, his gaze fixed on his son. Madeline looked just the same as the solo photo as she, too, stared at her son. The little boy was adorable. His smile matched his parents as he seemed to be frozen in an attempt to take an ungainly step. The photo captured more than just a simple image of family—it portrayed love, pure and simple.

Alec would read the file more thoroughly on the plane and probably over the days to come, but for now, he just wanted to get a feel for this family. He couldn't even begin to imagine the hell they must be going through right now.

Movement around him alerted him that his flight was boarding. Alec took his place in line, greeting the staff politely as always. He was a firm believer in catching more flies with honey than vinegar and a pleasant exchange with airline staff had him either sitting in an exit row or with an extra meal more times than he cared to remember.

He made his way to his seat, delighted to see it was an almost empty flight. With luck, the two seats beside him would remain vacant, so he might be able to get a couple of hours sleep. He settled in and took another look at the files while he waited for takeoff.

Next in the file was the second son, Kane's brother. Alec skimmed his bio and knew instantly that Asher Winsome was the black sheep of the family. He, too, had studied law just like his father and brother, but Asher's most recent job was listed as marine photographer, location—varied. Interesting.

Alec scrolled to the attached photograph and felt his eyes pop like some kind of cartoon characters. Jesus Christ, he'd never seen anyone more gorgeous. Asher Winsome was drop-dead stunning. The photo wasn't even a good quality one, so he could only imagine how devastating the man would be in real life. His hair was a few shades darker than his brother's, and he wore it long. His gray eyes were lighter than Kane's. Alec couldn't wait to see them in person to find out if they were as silver as they looked. His smile was crooked and shy; his entire demeanor seemed coy. Alec was insanely jealous of whoever had taken the photo and coaxed that look out of the man.

He knew he sat there staring too long when the flight attendant had to tap his arm to get him to prepare for takeoff. He shut down his tablet and got his seat belt fastened. He leaned his head against the fuselage, letting his eyes drift shut. Glimmering gray eyes and a crooked smile followed him into sleep.